Stolen Love
Before/After

Stolen Love
Before/After

Loyd Hill

Copyright © 2015 by Loyd Hill.

Library of Congress Control Number:		2015909042
ISBN:	Hardcover	978-1-5035-7632-2
	Softcover	978-1-5035-7631-5
	eBook	978-1-5035-7630-8

All rights reserved. No part of this book may be reproduced or transmitted in any form or by any means, electronic or mechanical, including photocopying, recording, or by any information storage and retrieval system, without permission in writing from the copyright owner.

This is a work of fiction. Names, characters, places and incidents either are the product of the author's imagination or are used fictitiously, and any resemblance to any actual persons, living or dead, events, or locales is entirely coincidental.

Any people depicted in stock imagery provided by Thinkstock are models, and such images are being used for illustrative purposes only.
Certain stock imagery © Thinkstock.

Print information available on the last page.

Rev. date: 06/15/2015

To order additional copies of this book, contact:
Xlibris
1-888-795-4274
www.Xlibris.com
Orders@Xlibris.com

Dedication

I wish to dedicate this novel to the multitude of couples that I have observed as they exhibited true love for one another, especially in marriage and relationship toward their families. To me, it is so obvious in the warmth they show in a look, a touch, a show of affection, tenderness, attraction, delights of attention to each other and support in their daily lives. Of course, I am not privy to their very personal life they share like passion and sex, a bundle of love, which I feel had been a true bonding in their marriage as well as other shared activities. Finally, true love can make life with each other truly beautiful.

I also wish to dedicate this novel to the people in management, who are currently striving to serve their employees and customers in a way that always create value to all concerned. Employees who provide the best value in their service to their management and customers are also dedicated here.

I wish to dedicate this novel to my son, who, as I described the love and life of the main characters, Alvin and Marilyn. Son, Larry exclaimed, "Alvin married well."
This gave me the ending of the novel with his comment.

Finally, I wish to dedicate the novel to a certain associate paster in my church. She had spoken on God's forgiveness of sinners. This gave me the title for this book. Alvin's life before meeting the heavenly Marilyn had been a BEFORE that he could not take pride in.
His new life with Marilyn, the family and the successes of their life was the blissful AFTER.

Stolen Love
Before/After
Loyd E. Hill

CHAPTER 1

IT WAS 0900 Honolulu, Hawaii time. The fog was just lifting. I had gone through the routine of boarding the Aircraft Carrier, which was transporting me back to the states for discharge from the United States Navy. I had enlisted four years ago, right out of High School. I had only been a few months shy of 18 at the time, a tall kid of 74 inches, 165 pounds, and still very unsure of myself.

Now, as I boarded the Carrier, the Chief Petty Officer on duty greeted me. As I saluted the chief he said, "name?"

I said, "Alvin Knight, Sir," and quickly gave him my serial number and handed him my orders.

After the chief carefully examined my orders, he said, "welcome aboard, Knight," and told me where I could store my gear.

I followed his instructions and after securing everything, I decided to go topside.

I remember it, as if it were yesterday. It was a beautiful late-spring morning as we eased out of Pearl Harbor. I was headed back to San Diego, California, to receive my discharge papers from the US Navy.

I was glad to be going back to San Diego, where I had completed my basic training, nearly four years ago; there, we were interviewed to determine our aptitude or qualifications and educational status, in order to determine how best to utilize our skills. Then, we would be assigned to schooling, which trained us effectively. We were placed into units and assign-ed to quarters (housing). In the days that followed (nearly three months), we took a physical examination, shots were administered, our heads were shaved and we learned to drill by marching in cadence and any drills that the Chief Petty Officer decided to put us through. The chief was tough and was very much disliked by most of us. We thought he pushed us too far and beyond endurance. He said that, "he was going to make men out of us," and washed out a lot of good men, who just could not take it, and were terminated. At that time, we thought he was a shit-head. Later we realized that he was just doing his job; he was trying to prepare us for what we were going to face in our tour of duty and in life changing-threats of battle, which we may encounter during the rest of our careers in the Navy.

I am sure that he was correct and most of us grew up to be men during our short time there, in basic training.

I recall that many of we sailors were asked by the chief to, "go ashore with him and have a few beers," after graduation from basic training. Many of the sailors had felt abused by his driving force during training and refused to go ashore with him, but some of us, including me, were glad to go.

My schooling had been in Disbursing and Supply Distribution and I remember many of those good looking WAVES, they were lady sailors and we took our training together. I recall a few dates with some of them as we went ashore on leave in San Diego, down town and the beaches. There were no romances that I can recall, just passing the time.

I was pleased to learn that I was being assigned to the Submarine Base at Pearl Harbor (near Honolulu, Hawaii). My orders were to San Francisco in order to fly to the Island of Oahu and proceed to the Submarine base.

When arriving, I realized that I was in paradise and loved the wonderful weather; sunny and 85 degrees. Back home, it was January, 1953 and the temperature was probably in the 30's.

Arriving at the Submarine Base and reporting to the duty officer, I was assigned to quarters and the department, where I would be working, and was told of my assigned duties and when to report.

I was excited about the view we had of Pearl Harbor, which was struck by waves of Japanese warplanes, causing the United States to declare war on the Japanese, and enter World War II back in 1941.

The only sign of that attack was a flag over the spot where the Battleship, Arizona, had gone down with many of it's crew still entombed. It was said that oil from the ship often rose to the surface to this day.

CHAPTER 2

YES, BOOT CAMP had been pretty tough, but that had been four years ago. And now, I was leaving my naval experiences behind. Now I was standing on the upper deck of the carrier, near the port bow, as we eased along, slowly on our way past Honolulu. I was leaving a lot of my experiences behind, but not my memories. I was deep in thought, but noticed the small skiffs that the locals used to brave the wake from our bow. The natives were there to dive for coins, which they hoped that we would toss out to them.

A young, trim, native boy dived as I threw the fifty cent piece as far as I could toward him to retrieve. As the coin hit the greenish-blue water, which was slightly disturbed by our wake, he came up with it and smiled a broad, youthful smile in anticipation that others would follow my lead.

Other sailors were most generous and tossed coins. Some tossed leas that they had worn aboard the carrier.

I was wearing my white-dress sailors outfit, with my white-sailors hat tossed to the back of my head. As we eased past and left the divers and and their skiffs behind, I noticed the beautiful, totally-white ocean liner, Lurline, in her dock there in downtown Honolulu. I wondered what group of fun lovers she had brought for the fun on the island, and especially Wakiki Beach. In the distance I could hear the faint playing of the local and popular Aloha Oe; I recalled that I had enjoyed that song so many times, while here in Hawaii. And I remembered that, according to custom, Hawaii was calling you to return someday.

As I stood in silence, my thoughts went back to the many people who had influenced my life, while I had stayed on the Island of Oahu, Hawaii.

I remembered Loraine!

By the time I met her, I was already a 3rd Class Petty Officer (still an enlisted man). I was standing watch there in the lobby of the Sub Base Theater on a Thursday night. It was February, with a slight chill in the air.

Darkness was descending and the crowd was the usual-- a few officers and their wives, kids, base sailors and submariners from subs, moored along our docks for refitting and resupplying. Some of the sailors had brought dates.

Loraine walked in and lit up the place, a small boy was hanging onto her tight fitting skirt. A light-blue sweater enclosed proud, pouting breasts.

How could I not notice her right away?

She was one of the most beautiful women that I had ever seen; an emerald-green eyed, flaming red head, tall and trim. As I glanced her way, those emerald-green eyes flashed my way and met mine. I could not help smiling, and she radiated a smile my way. I must now admit that I could not help falling in love with her, right away.

After the movie, a popular Fred Astaire dance musical, I continued my watch until everyone was out of the building. Then, I went back to the barracks to lie on my bunk to read, but I could not concentrate on the mystery I had been reading. All I could think about was those emerald-green eyes that had smiled at me with an immediate recognition of--you are someone special, "I want to know you better." I knew that I wanted to know her better.

Who is she? What could she have seen in me that caused this fiery recognition? I had always been told that I was attractive, a nice guy, and somewhat good looking. But why me? And why me at this time? I have never had this kind of reaction from an attractive female before. Was this some game that she had to be playing? And had she played this game some time before? It was obvious to me that she had to be in her mid to late twenties. Who cares, I thought she was the most ravishing woman that I had ever had the pleasure to see. She carried herself with such dignity, and it was obvious that she was a true lady of quality.

I tried to put her out of my thoughts and dug deeper into the true gangster mystery, that I had been trying to get through for too many days.

It was about this Chicago crime spree of Al Capone. Al seemed to be a figure that the public was pulling for, even though they knew that he was a heartless thug, who would get his just due in the long run.

Finally, I realized that I had a big day ahead of me tomorrow and gathered up my shower equipment and headed to the Head (Navy slang for the bath and shower room), showered, brushed my teeth and got ready for bed. My bunk assignment was the one on the top. Tom, from Indiana, was on the bottom and was already sound asleep. I read a few pages and slept.

CHAPTER 3

IN HIGH SCHOOL I had been a star baseball pitcher and was highly recruited to go to college on a baseball scholarship. Instead I chose to join the Navy. The Sub Pac baseball team was glad that I was available to pitch in Oahu, Hawaii, Military League. True, I had never been a winner with the ladies, but I had been a constant winner in baseball as a pitcher. The newspapers back home had called me "fireball," which may have been a slight exaggeration. I was fast and accurate, but my best pitch was the curve ball that had a sharp drop, as it arrived at the plate. A loss was something that I seldom had to endure.

Today, we played a baseball game against the Air Force at Hickam Field. We won, and I was the winning pitcher, having gone eight innings. We beat the Air Force by four runs, and 6-2 was the final score. We were now leading the league. The Marine Base is our biggest rival and they are now in 2nd place, a half-game behind us.

As for my work at the Submarine Base at Pearl Harbor, I was working in the Supply Department with a fairly dull job, but an important one in the war effort. We supplied all of the pay, clothing, spare parts, repairs and refitting for the Submarines, which came and went on new tours. Our men of the Silent Service, Com Sub Pac were fighting in the Pacific realm during the Korean War and our job was to provide for all of their needs to fight for us, and our country.

I recall that the submarine force, operating out of Pearl Harbor, during World War ll, had destroyed an overwhelming majority of the Japanese shipping and much of the Japanese fighting fleet. The Submarine Force was putting their life on the line every time they engaged in any type of action, which they encountered and we, at the Sub Base, were proud to provide value in every opportunity of service to them.

But, it was not all work and no play. I personally had an old jalopy that I had purchased for a song. It was a 1938 Ford with white-wall tires and a rumble seat. I often secured a pass and drove into Honolulu and down to Waikiki Beach and took a great swim, lay on the beautiful white sands, just listening to the surf and music from local open bars of the hotels.

I often got a group of guys from my company, especially on Sunday, and we would drive past Honolulu, the Peach Bowl and out over the Pali Pass. By that time we would have consumed a six-pack of Bud or Miller Life.

We would stop at the overlooks and look down at the immense greenness, way, way down into the valley below. The beautiful sight was breath taking.

We would continue around the northern part of the island and pausing at most of the beautiful beaches.

We made numerous trips like this around the northern and eastern coast of Oahu, stopping along the way to take in all of the beauty of the scenery.

When we passed Sandy Beach, where high-crashing waves came roaring in, then becoming white crested, before diving into the white sand with force. Then it would quickly retreat into the ocean to reform and come again. It was all so beautiful and exciting. We knew that we would be coming back many times in the future. As we continued around the island, we knew that the Blow Hole and Diamond Head lay just beyond, before reaching Waikiki Beach. Of course, Waikiki Beach is always another story.

I recall many trips like this, normally on Sunday, when pass in hand, and we were off duty, we sought another adventure. Yes, we were a fun loving group with nothing much in common, except our duty stations and several of the guys were from the Sub Pac baseball team.

As I mentioned, Sandy Beach was one of our most popular beach stops.

We were there one afternoon, just lounging on the beach and observing a group of local boys, with Hawaiian features, as they paddled around in the surf, on mini-surfboards.

The beach was crowded that day to observe the large waves. One of our fool sailors had dived into a wave and suddenly found himself too far out into the waves, that were crashing around him. He became frightened and realized that he was in trouble and could not get back to safety on his own, he was fully exhausted from fighting the undertow. He managed to yell for help and six or eight of the natives, who we had been watching, paddled their way out and were able to bring the sailor back in safely. Even the natives were totally exhausted and some required help, themselves.

The poor sailor told us later, that he had resigned himself to a watery grave as his life flashed before him, as he anticipated death. We were glad to get him back to the base, lucky guy. If the locals had not been there, you would have read about him back in the stateside newspapers; sailor lost at sea, off Oahu, Hawaii.

Sandy beach and other beaches had, at times, been closed off to military personnel, because of earlier episodes of close calls due to high wave activity. The undertow was really treacherous as the waves come into the beach. Our guy had confided to us, after the episode at Sandy Beach, he said, "he had just jumped into a wave and came up more than fifty yards out to sea." He said, "he had been considered a good swimmer, but he was no match for the conditions there on Sandy Beach, that day."

From that day foreword, we did return many times to Sandy Beach, but mostly, sat on the beach to get some sun and look at the girls. We very carefully entered the ocean when the waves were much smaller than they were that day, of the episode of our friend's nearly demise.

CHAPTER 4

THE WEEK DRAGGED by and Thursday finally came. Again, I had security watch at the theater. It was a fairly sparse crowd and I was off duty, but stayed to watch a dull musical.

No, the red headed goddess did not show up. Disappointed, I went back to the barrack and talked a buddy into going down to the canteen to get a shake at the fountain. Mine was strawberry and Jim preferred chocolate.

Later, lying in my bunk, I tried to remember every little thing about Loraine, how she looked, carried herself, and most of all, her smile. Well, I said to myself, maybe she will show up next week.

Any way, I was dying to see her again. I suddenly realized that I had it bad and realized that I needed Loraine too much for my own good.

I realized that there were other adventures waiting for me that did not involve my craving for this obviously married woman, who must be at least eight or nine years older than myself. Maybe I should expand my lifestyle by meeting other women closer to my age, which at that time was nineteen.

On Saturday, with pass in hand, I drove down to Wakiki Beach.

After changing into swimwear and doning my sunglasses, I hit the beach with just a little swagger. I was a little proud of my physique as I chose a good spot to observe the surging waves and passing girls.

After laying out a large beach towel, that I had brought with me, I sat there enjoying the warm breeze and listening to the Hawaiian music, that always came from the patio bars of the Royal Hawaiian Hotel.

Very relaxed by the atmosphere of this beautiful setting, I made a few, occasional, ventures into the quite surf.

I am not a loner, but I often went to Wakiki by myself and sat on the sand to soak up the healing sun. Of course, watches and duty often broke up the group of guys, that I chose to surround myself with, on long drives around the island. Besides, some of our guys were not very particular, drank too much beer and went after the first piece of ass, that they saw.

That was not my style. I have always thought, to this day that the quality and the adventure was what I sought after, and I am sure that this has saved me much grief to this day, in my life.

Loraine, now that was a mystery and adventure, I thought.

I remembered that, back in High School days, I had a few light romances, but back in those days it was not unusual for a guy to get through high school without getting laid. Yes, I was still a virgin when I graduated from high school. This author believes that that would be laughable in present day society of far looser morals. Girls of today are often the aggressors, who initiate sexual encounters, after the high availability of birth control and condoms to avert venereal and social diseases.

Even tho I was still a virgin after high school, I must admit that I had tried to have sex on several occasions, all I got was, "I am not that kind of girl, but let's still be friends." And we were.

Luckily, I was too involved in baseball, being an All-Star Pitcher.

Winning came easily. We won the County and State Championship, my sophomore year and County Championship my senior year. My summers were filled with semi-pro baseball in the region, and I excelled there. It was said that, "I had a great future in baseball."

I had a blazing fastball, followed by a wicked curveball. These had given me many strikeouts during high school and semi-pro ball games. My curveball had a nasty drop as it reached the plate and had become my strike-out preference pitch.

I am not a loner. Now that I am here in Hawaii, I love touring the Island with the guys. Perhaps one reason that I often traveled alone, was remembering one night back in high school when a group of us seniors managed to get a fifth of whiskey and some beer. Some in the group decided that we wanted to take over a dance in a nearby town.

My group started the fight, although I was not totally committed.

My only desire was to get all of us to hell out of there, alive.

We avoided serious injury, but came back with cuts, bruises and some black eyes.

I never went out with that group again. That was just not my style.

Yes, I have always desired a woman. However, quality has always been my desire. I sought an attractive girl, who was intelligent, a clever conversationalist, with all around friendly personality. I must admit that my early life had made a deep impression on me.

I remember to this day an experience, that was formative; I was only six or seven and my brother was fourteen. Dad was working and mother had taken my sisters to a movie. It was Saturday and brother told me that "he was bringing two neighborhood girls to our house to have a good time."

"We are going to play post office," he said. The girls came and they were ten and thirteen. After some cookies for all of us, brother had sex with the thirteen year old in one room and brought her into my room. He told me that, "she was going to deliver the mail."

She was sort of heavy, and not very pretty, looked as if she was from a poor family. She obviously thought I knew what to do. We laid down and I tried to insert my little penis, and "I asked her if it was in?"

She smiled and said, "no, it is on my leg."

This ended my early sex life and left a lasting impression on my ego.

CHAPTER 5

LATER WE MOVED to a farm in another city, and in an area where father and mother had grown up. By this time, I was thirteen and had a lot of cousins living nearby. Most of them were a few years older than I was.

They taught me how to masturbate. They called it "jerking off." I found that I liked the feeling very much, and did it frequently when I was alone by myself.

Later, when I was fourteen or fifteen, I was working in a store and was in the stock room with a very pretty girl sorting products that we had received. I guess I had been sort of staring at her while we worked, and she looked at me rather coyly and said, "I'll bet you would like to kiss me."

I looked down at her sweet, heaving breasts and quickly said, "you bet", and timidly, I tried to kiss her.

She said, "we had better get back to work."

I do not recall if I ever got that kiss, but I do know, that is as far as I ever got with her.

Back in Hawaii, Thursday came and I had security at the theater.

Loraine came in with her small son, flashed a big smile at me and they went into the theater and took their seats. I thought to myself, her smile had a meaning that she wanted to know me better. I had to struggle to suppress a quick erection. By this time, I was nearly twenty years old, six foot-three, and some called me handsome. I had matured a nice mustache and had gained a lot of confidence in myself.

After the movie, she stopped by on the way out and asked my name.

"Alvin Knight," I said proudly, and spoke to the little boy. He was very shy, and just continued to clutch her skirt; looking a little sleepy. I then, asked, "who she was?"

She said, "Loraine Mosley."

I thought that her name was musical and she was playing my emotions. I could hear the crescendo crashing down on me from all directions. I asked her, "if she came to the movies, often?"

"About every Thursday," she replied.

Unsure of what to say next, I asked her, "how she liked the movie?"

"Good," she said. Her eyes sparkled and I could see she was questioning me in her thoughts, as if to say, when are you going to realize that I want you to want me enough to muster up the strength to ask, when can we get an opportunity to get together?"

Wow! Magic sprang through my body, but I could only muster a mumble of, "hope to see you next Thursday."

"I will be here," she said.

And, as she walked toward the street, knowingly, she turned her head and caught me staring after her.

I was dying to find out more about her and could not wait for next Thursday to come again.

Supply duties carried me through and Wednesday, we beat our baseball rivals, the Marines, by a score of three to two. As usual, I was the winning pitcher and contributed two hits to the cause. I had always been a good hitter; never had the long-ball home runs, but would single and double the opposition, while having a very high percentage of being on base.

But, I was thinking about Thursday.

I had early duty watch on Thursday, and when Loraine came into the theater, I was ready to go off watch, and told her so.

She said that, "she had been looking forward to seeing me." Maybe you can stay over and sit with Timmy and me.

I told her that, I did not have any prior plans, and that sounds good to me.

"Please save a seat for me."

"She agreed," and with a knowing smile, that seemed to say, "well, now, I believe we are getting somewhere!"

Later, as we sat through the movie, her hand was suddenly placed on mine. Electricity suddenly sprang through my body! Bells went off in my head, and, later I did not remember anything about the movie on the screen.

The movie was over, and as we walked out, Loraine asked me. "Will you walk me to my car?"

"Sure," I managed to say, as I took her extended arm, as we walked several blocks to her automobile, parked down by a large supply warehouse.

She was driving a fifty three or fifty four black Buick.

Loraine set Timmy in the back seat and he was immediately asleep.

Loraine asked me, "if I would like to sit a moment and talk?" Reluctantly, I agreed, but knowing the watch schedule in that area, I knew that they would be passing by this spot in about thirty minutes.

CHAPTER 6

WE SAT THERE and talked, mostly about her. Loraine was twenty seven and Timmy was three. Husband, Bob was several years older than Loraine. He currently was at sea and had not been home for three months and was not expected to return to Pearl Harbor for at least two more months. He was commanding a Destroyer in the Western Pacific.

We just sat there, electricity pulsating in the air, both quite nervous. and not knowing quite what to do, and where this was going.

We both enjoyed our closeness and the quite ness of that place, as Timmy slept, quietly in the back seat. Suddenly I realized the truth, security could come by any moment and discover our hideaway. I was an enlisted man; her husband was an officer, a Commander. The thought of serving time in Leavenworth Prison suddenly brought me to my senses.

I touched her luscious lips with my finger tip and slowly drew it across to the other side seemingly, with a promise that more would come, later. I told her that, "I hoped to see her again, soon."

I watched as she drove away, then went back to the barracks.

I undressed and knew that I had to take a shower, since I had creamed in my shorts. Later, I drifted off to sleep in contentment of what had occurred.

I thought of nothing but Loraine, all day Friday, but I was beginning to realize that I was in over my head. This woman was so perfect, so real, so beautiful and obviously more experienced than I was. Suddenly I realized that I had to have time to think.

Remember I was still only twenty years old!

At twenty I could have fallen madly in love with this beautiful red-headed woman. However, I asked myself, where could it go but to disaster, especially for me. Leavenworth, Kansas was the place that they sent service enlisted men, who defiled officer's wives.

And I was getting closer and closer to the probability that Leavenworth was going to be my destination. I had to realize that Loraine had far less to lose than me. She could always claim that I kept coming on to her and raped her.

She had tried to fight me off, but I overpowered her. I began to wonder, was this just a game for her? Had she played this game before? If it was not me, would there be someone else?

The questions in my mind kept coming to me. But it was too late. I was completely under her spell. Loraine was playing me like a yoyo, up and down, up and down.

I fully knew what the stakes were, but I could not wait to see her again.

I was intoxicated by her, and I was hell bent to have her, and it appeared that she felt the same way about me, at least for the moment.

Maybe I need to get away for a little while, at least to think about what the future should be.

CHAPTER 7

LATE SATURDAY AFTERNOON, Steve, a guy from my barracks, and I decided to drive to Wakiki Beach to have dinner and have a few drinks.

Of course, actually we were hoping to find some female companionship, and decided on a bar and night club situated across from the Moana and Royal Hawaiian Hotels, where a lot of tourists from the states frequented, when they arrived in Hawaii.

We parked in a public parking area and walked a short distance to the bar. We slipped into the leather padded booth and noted the crowd and decor of the restaurant were quite impressive. We were in class!

We had worn our civilian cloths, jeans, Hawaiian shirts and loafers.

The waitress, an oriental, came over, sized us up and asked what we were having. I am sure she thought that we were typical tourists, and I am sure that we did not want to do anything to dispel that image. Steve ordered a burger and a Miller Highlife. I ordered a burger and a vodka and tonic.

I lit up a Marlboro, which was popular for macho men at that time, and set back observing the crowd. At the smoke filled bar sat two sailors and two army guys, I thought to myself, as they drank their beers, this could possibly lead to an explosive combination, as it frequently had been in less quality bars.

A native guy was strumming on his guitar, singing a Hawaiian song. Later, he took a break and Steve and I fed some quarters into the juke box, to play some of our favorite songs. We were not into jitterbug and played the smooth music of the day.

There were couples in the bar, who began dancing on the small, recessed dance floor. I observed that they loved dancing to the smooth songs, where they could cling close to each other. I noticed that they returned to their booths when the hot jitterbug songs were being played.

Most of the people in the bar and restaurant were tourists, in their civilian clothes. Some still had the leas hanging around their necks, having received them as they landed on Hawaii.

Finally, what we had been looking for came bouncing through the door. Two brunets, obviously tourists, fresh from the states, had arrived. I checked out the classy outfits which they were wearing;

leas still around their necks, high heels which made their legs look even more shapely. They chose a booth, opposite from where we were sitting. I wondered if it was by chance, or if they were looking for some action, as we were.

They ordered fruity drinks, that were popular in Hawaii at that time, and Waldorf Salads. I thought maybe it was my imagination, but they seemed to turn our way several times, as if they were checking us out, as we had already checked them out.

After they had finished their meal, I slipped over and asked the tallest girl, "if she would like to dance?"

She looked directly into my eyes and said, "sure, I would like that," and slid into my arms. She danced beautifully and followed my every lead. I had become a very good dancer, since I had been taking dance lessons from the local Author Murray Dance Studio, and felt very comfortable, especially in smooth dances. As I said, she followed my leads smoothly and fit comfortably into my arms as we glided, lightly, over the dance floor. We shared many more dances.

I asked her, "to tell me about herself?"

"Her name was Anne," she said. "She was from the state of Washington, where she lived with her parents. She and Melissa, her friend, had recently graduated from Washington State University. She explained that both she and Melissa had been given, as a graduation gift, this trip to this island paradise. They had flown in on American Airlines earlier in the week, and had a full week at a beach house, several blocks behind this restaurant, where we were dancing."

I just volunteered that, "my name is Alvin and my friend is Steve."

By this time, Steve had gotten up the nerve to ask Melissa if she would like to dance. Steve was a country boy from the mid-west and was not too sure of himself on the dance floor, but he seemed to be doing alright, because the girls soon suggested we join them at their table.

We talked and they told us about their home and life back in Washington and their trip over to this island. Later, about 2230, they suggested that "we go to their beach-house and have some peanuts and wine by the pool."

Steve and I nodded to each other, and said in unison, "sounds great, sounds like fun." Steve and I paid the restaurant tab and joined the girls in the brief walk to their place. I must admit that I was quite impressed by their beach-house; very Hawaiian, fenced in hedges with a small pool.

They put on some groovy music and we danced for a while.

The red wine was served and we sat by the pool. The girls asked, "if we would like to go in for a swim?"

We explained that, "we would like to, but, unfortunately, had not brought our swim suits," however, we did not want to keep them from their swim. The girls retreated inside to change into their swim-wear, and Steve and I sat by the pool enjoying some very good, red wine.

The girls soon returned and swam while we sat and got an eyeful of their well tanned, curvaceous bodies.

When they finished their swim, Anne was still in her swim-wear, which left very little to the imagination. She had put on some soft music, and we were dancing very close to the point of embracing.

Suddenly our lips met. Her sweet, sweet, lips seemed to want more.

Anne and I, had lost touch with time, but I am sure it was about 2400, midnight. We had forgotten about Steve and Melissa.

Suddenly, Melissa let out a yell! "No, I am not going to do this, leave me alone!" "Get the hell out! Now!"

Steve sort of staggered out and Anne ran toward the screen door to see what in the world the trouble was. Melissa came to the door and belted out that, "the son-of-a-bitch tried to rape me!" As Steve came by Anne, he attempted to grope her and tried to lay her down. I ran to him, laid a quick right to his chin. His head flew back and the fight went out of him.

CHAPTER 8

SUDDENLY, I REALIZED the severity of our position. I quickly told Anne, "how sorry I was, that this had happened and insisted that I had not known this side of him." Melissa had gone for the telephone. Obviously she was attempting to call the Honolulu Police Department. I told Steve that "we must get the hell out of there." I pulled him to the fence and we jumped hedge rows and ran to the car.

We were gone into the night, back to Pearl Harbor.

All the way back to the Sub Base I told him, "what a miserable, low down piece of shit he was, and how close we both came to going to jail, and that we were lucky that we got out before the Honolulu cops came."

Maybe, I hoped that Anne was able to calm Melissa down before the cops got there. Anyway, we never heard what had happened or if the cops were looking for us. At least, I hope Anne and Melissa enjoyed the rest of their vacation in Hawaii. No telling what their adventures were there in Hawaii, after we had fled and left them that night.

That was the last time that I went off base with Steve. We still were housed in the same barrack and worked closely together, but I had lost all respect for him. By this time, I had learned that you do not blatantly use force on a woman, having said that, I was a lover, not a fighter. I knew that class always shows through.

Still, I could not help but remember the way that Anne had clung to me and lingered on our kisses.

Work took up most of my time, and I became involved with my responsibilities of supplying work clothes and uniforms at the base; ordering, replacing and disbursing supplies, which were purchased by the sailors, non-commissioned officers and the sailors from the submarines, that refitted along our docks.

This effort filled my days except for Sub-Pac baseball games and practice, where this pitcher normally excelled in winning games. We won many and lost a few.

Next time we played Hickam Field, the Airforce team. We were wiped out by the score of 6-1 and dropped out of first place. I was sorry that I was not called on to be the starting pitcher. The week dragged by, but Thursday finally came and I was back on watch at the theater.

CHAPTER 9

LORAINE WALKED IN and was alone. She had not brought Timmy.

As usual, she looked so beautiful in her green-velvet dress. Her hair was radiant in its red sheen, and as usual, her emerald eyes gleamed, and I am sure that every eye in the theater turned to admire this lovely creature.

I could not miss that special glance my way, as she made her way by me to her seat. I was still on duty when she exited from the musical.

Loraine paused by me on the way out and asked, "if I could get a pass to leave the base?"

I assured her, "that would not be a problem."

Then, she whispered that, "Timmy was with friends," and slipped me a note with directions to her home. She whispered that we would be alone, and not to worry. "Be there in 30 minutes," she said, and was gone.

Holly crap, I said to myself, this was the moment that I had been waiting for these many months of admiring and desiring this beautiful seductress. I immediately went to the duty officer and requested a pass to leave the base. Encountering no problem, I left happily and went to my quarters and donned civilian clothes and headed for my car.

I was so excited, as I cleared the security gate, that I drove in a daze to the address that Loraine had given me. Wow! This was what I had been waiting for and I could not back out now.

I found 1021 Wendover Way Drive and observed that Loraine lived on a street, which was typically built for military personnel. Her house was a freestanding house in an area that contained many individual houses and duplexes. I suspect that the duplexes were built for Junior Officers, and non-commissioned officers and their families.

I parked down the street about a block, so as to keep from drawing attention to myself and went back to her door, where Loraine had been waiting, patiently. I entered quickly, feeling a little uncertain, but she soon put me to rest by throwing herself into my waiting arms and offered those wonderful lips in a lingering kiss, that I can feel to this day. I recall that I did not want to let her go, and continued to draw her close, gazing into those beautiful emerald-green eyes.

Finally she did break free and told me, "how wonderful it was to have me all to herself, and asked, if I was hungry?"

Dinner had been a long time ago and, I said, "yes, I was a little hungry."

She quickly prepared a sandwich and a glass of milk for me and sat watching me as I devoured the sandwich and milk. We talked and then, later, "she offered me a glass of red wine."

"Sure," I said, and "asked her to join me on the sofa with a glass of her own."

We continued to look and touch one another, both in a need for more, closer contact.

Soon, she led me into the bedroom and "asked me to make myself comfortable, while she donned some more appropriate attire from the bathroom." When she returned, Loraine had put on a very blue night gown that revealed the sweetest set of breasts, that I had ever seen, not too big, but very firm. I thought that they were a C cup with just a few cute freckles.

Remember, she was a redhead, and they do have some freckles.

She came into my arms and offered to help me take off some of my clothing. I let her help, as she removed my clothing down to my shorts.

Loraine quickly took those off and I stood proudly before her. My bronze body was now available to her and I was proud to share it with her, as I was in great physical shape. I proceeded to take off her gown and we were soon one.

I could not tell Loraine, but she was only the second woman that I had been with in bed.

The first had been after graduating from Boot Camp at San Diego Naval Training Center. A group of us guys had decided to celebrate our graduation by going to Tijuana, Mexico, just across the border from San Diego, California. We guys had been to a bar there in Tijuana, drinking

Tequila, and when we came out of the bar, a kid, about ten years old, was standing on the curb by a lineup of Taxi cabs. The kid asked us, "do you want to fucka my sister?" "She is French," he added.

I went along with the guys. We were all a little foggy from drinks consumed.

We boarded a cab and drove into the countryside. When we arrived there, we saw a lot of small rooms with a girl in each one. I was sent in to Maria.

Maria was not French!

She asked, "for ten dollars and told me what she was going to do for me."

I must admit that I was ready to run, but, hey, I was half drunk and did not want to tell the guys that I had chickened out. It was over quickly and she had earned her ten dollars. As for me, I thought it was not such a big deal.

I guess the cheapness of the experience had gotten to me.

Thank goodness that she had washed up at a water basin before we had sex, but she had smelled bad.

Fortunately, I was not too drunk and had put on a condom prior to the sex. However, I found out the next week that she had given me the pesky crabs, and I was miserable. The Naval Clinic was able to take care of the situation. The powder that the doctor prescribed took care of the pests.

I sure was glad that I had worn a condom and got no serious disease.

But, that had been a long time ago, and I had almost forgotten about that incident in Tijuana, Mexico.

CHAPTER 10

AS I HELD Loraine in my arms, everything else was blacked out of my thoughts. She could not get enough of my kisses. They were lingering almost until we could not breath. Then we just slurped and had slow pecks of the cheeks, then the ears, and down to her elegant throat with nibbles, then back to those wonderful lips. I was not the only aggressor. Loraine was just as wild as I was. She continued to offer her body to me in any way that I desired. At times it was just a nibble and other times it was a slurp of wanting to devour and give as well as receive wild pleasure, in so many ways. Loraine seemed to go wild about my body. It was easy to see that she was a very sexual person, and had not had the opportunity of having a passionate man for some time, and could not get enough of me and my wild desire. I lightly touched her pouting breasts, which were inflated with lust. Lightly caressing each in turn with light fingers that circled each one and followed with light licks of each, with my tongue.

I moved down to the most beautiful belly button one could ever possibly imagine and showed my pleasure there. I could tell that she was lunging against my maleness and wanted more than my kisses and fondling. I wanted just one more passionate kiss and then entered her pulsating vagina, first softly and then with deep probes, which she took with great emotion.

We were both pretty far along and quickly she gasped with pleasure and we both came together, and lay totally exhausted. It was at this time that she seemed to appreciate my tenderness and we just lay there touching and loving each other.

She suggested that, "we have another glass of wine and talk."

This was a real woman. How lucky could I be, I thought.

As we sipped our wine, I asked about her husband. His name was Bob. He had studied hard to build his status in the Navy and had risen to the rank of Commander and was now commanding a Destroyer at sea, and had been gone at least three months, patrolling in the Pacific, near Korea, and would not return for another month, at least.

I sensed that she was not interested in talking anymore when she led me back to bed and touched my male object. We spent the next two hours enjoying each others bodies and the several orgasms, that we were able to enjoy together. This was so perfect, I thought.
Loraine had no odor at all. She only gave off a sweet fragrance.
I had been completely surprised by her lack of an odor. After all, I had been around women, who, when aroused, let off a slightly pungent odor.
Not Loraine, I thought after we parted and I returned to the base.
Perhaps I was too conscious of feminine odor. When I was thirteen years old, back in my hometown, I recalled Anita Armond, who lived down the hill, beside the creek. Anita went to the same church, where I attended group parties and functions. Anita was fourteen and going on fifteen and I realized that she, at times, had a very pungent odor. So much to the extent that I did not want to be around her. Anita lived with her father, Raymond, in that unassuming yellow house with a dark roof. I wondered whether Anita had a mother living with the family. I do not ever recall ever seeing her, or if she was living. Any way, I never asked. I wondered why her father did not seek professional help for her. It was such a shame that he let her go through this embarrassment that Anita must have felt.
Raymond was well regarded in the church and was a Deacon.
Anita was a pretty girl. I wonder what ever became of her. I really felt sorry for her, knowing that she had to be self conscious. She had to know that she had a problem; she just did not know what to do about it.

About this time I began playing baseball, first as an outfielder in pickup games, and in church leagues. Many of the players on our team were related to each other. I recall that four brothers of stairstep ages were playing in the same games and had their respective positions.

Here, I was at age fourteen playing with these brothers, a first baseman, a pitcher, a catcher and a second baseman, all much older than myself.

Not too many hitters were getting the hits to the outfield, but I caught a lot that got into left field. We played like this for several years.

One of the players on our team was a sophomore in high school, and I was a freshman. The sophomore played center field on our team and, also, was playing center field on the high school team.

His name was Andy, and said to me that, "he had been noticing that I had a very good arm and would make a good pitcher." We began working together between games and I honed my pitching technique with him as we practiced. Later, I got to pitch in a few games in our church league, that summer. When I became a sophomore in high school, I tried out for our high school team as a pitcher and became an immediate success. My throws were fast and accurate and they said, "I was destined to be a star." This was also chronicled in the local newspapers, on the sports pages, which wrote up the news results of our games.

Our coach, Al Kiser, had become a very successful coach and had accumulated a big-winning record. He worked with me to develop a style of delivery that was comfortable to me and provided me a senior catcher, Barry, who was also headed for stardom in college and, later, coaching in college.

This was Barry's third season as a catcher, and he taught me a lot. I recall that he said to me, "I will make my signals clear and put the catchers mitt where I want you to throw your pitches to me. If they miss, that is fine, but if they hit it, our guys will chase it down for an out." And they did. At least six of our players went on to play professional baseball, as I did.

Winning became easy, I won ten games in my sophomore year and set a strikeout record for our school. I recall that during one game we won thirteen to zero and I recorded eighteen strikeouts and gave up only one hit, a single.

In addition to my fastball, by this time, I had acquired a curveball that disappeared, seemingly, as it approached the strike zone and dropped out of reach of the hitter, as he swung weakly at the ball.

CHAPTER 11

AFTER THAT NIGHT at Loraine's, I managed to get through the week; my job and a baseball game kept me busy. We beat the Army at Sedgefield Barracks. All this managed to keep me from thinking a lot about Loraine. I realized that I was intoxicated by her beauty and the way that she looked at me and the quite way she had moaned when we came together, that night at her home.

Thursday night came and I was on duty. Not surprisingly to me, Loraine came in with Timmy holding her well manicured hand. Not surprising to me, I received the usual smile as she entered the theater.

Later, after she was exiting the theater, she said, "lets talk outside."

Since the theater had cleared and I became off duty, I followed her to her Buick. On the way, she told me about a dance coming up Saturday at the Chiefs Club. "Would you like to go?" she asked.

I replied with, "you know that I am not a Chief Petty Officer."

Loraine assured me, "that would not be a problem," and added, it will be OK! And reminded me that, "I should dress in civilian clothes."

"No problem," I said. "I will wear my Tuxedo outfit."

I had purchased a white dinner jacket, appropriate shirt with stud insert buttons and black pants with a tuxedo stripe down the sides, earlier, at a good price. I had worn it before, and I was very pleased with the way it made me feel and look.

Saturday night came and I met Loraine at the Chiefs Club. As she drove up and exited the Buick, I gasped at her beauty. Her red hair, tossed above a green-velvet evening gown, diamond necklace clinging to her elegant neck, small black handbag and red high-heel shoes, which enhanced those beautiful legs.

Wanting to compliment her, I had worn my white dinner jacket, well studded shirt and tux pants. I told Loraine that, "I was glad that she had reminded me to wear civilian clothes so I could complement her ravishing appearance."

The Chiefs Club was a lot more elegant than I had anticipated; it contained a large bandbox and recessed dance floor, able to accommodate at least twenty dancing couples at a time. The well padded, black leather booths surrounded the dance floor. The lights were low and the naval band was playing softly. They had left nothing undone in furbishing the club with a beautiful bar, with surrounding stools. The well stocked bar was manned by a professional bartender, who was kept very busy.

Dinner was provided by a well stocked buffet of everything that one might choose. We quickly enjoyed dinner and waited patiently for the band to begin the dance. Finally, the band came to full action and the dance floor filled up quickly.

The crowd was what I had expected, and more. Many of the Chiefs had brought their wives; others had brought WAVES from the surrounding units. In my observation, the chief's wives were rather plain and did not stand out, at least to me. I am sure that I was well influenced by this beautiful creature that I was honored to be with.

Loraine stood out in the crowd and as we took the dance floor to dance, to music by the Naval Band, I was very proud of her, but I could not help but wonder if any of those attending, knew Loraine's husband, and wondered what my relationship with Loraine really was, and may have correctly guessed.

Anyway, we danced for several hours and finally, the smoke from the cigarette smokers and overall clamor of the place, got to us and we agreed to split. Fortunately I had secured a pass prior to coming and told Loraine that, "I was hers for the evening."

Loraine said that, "she had a plan," and we left the club, got into her Buick and she drove, silently into the night.

She just drove, under a full moon, along the countryside.

It became fully aware to me that she was looking for a place to park, where we could be alone. We were passing a field of sugar cane that stood row after row, that seemed to go on for miles.

Finally she selected a narrow road that led into the field and slowly drove until she found a secluded spot to her liking, and parked, killed the engine, and reached out for me to take her into my loving arms.

I could see the gleam in her eyes and knew what she wanted to happen. We embraced and our kisses drove us to quickly devour each other, and furiously made love to each other as if there were no more tomorrows. The little sobs and a quite gasp exited her throat as she came, and I exploded in waves of light. Not wanting to ever let go of each other, we continued our embrace. Everything was so quite and very peaceful as we relaxed, and may even have napped for a brief time.

Finally I suggested that, "we should go." Loraine drove back to a spot near the Sub Base Security Entrance and parked. Quickly we embraced with a lingering kiss that promised so much more, later.

Soon, we parted, Loraine to her home and I went back to the barrack.

I tried to fall asleep, but could only lay there and think of the beautiful, Loraine.

CHAPTER 12

THE WEEK WENT by uneventful and Thursday came and went. I had no duty at the theater and was not sure if Loraine had come to the movie, or not. I was missing Loraine and I did not want to wait until Thursday to possibly see her about a plan that I had in mind. So I called her on Friday, but she did not answer the phone. Desperate, I called again later, and that lovely voice answered. I told her that, "I was missing her and wondered if she had come to the theater last night."

She said that "she was still thinking about that beautiful night we shared, after attending the Chief's club and our secluded visit to the sugarcane field." Everything had been so very special to her, and she was missing me too, but had not attended the theater.

I told her that I, also, had not attended the theater and hoped to see her next Thursday. But, I wanted to share a plan that I was thinking about for next Friday evening Loraine assured me, "she planned to be there next Thursday and she hoped to see me there."

I confirmed that, "yes, I would be on duty there." And continued, my plan for next Friday, if you will agree, is for a special night at the beach.

"I will get a pass and meet you down at Wakiki. You could park your car and we would drive on down to Sandy Beach and have a nice swim and walk on the beach in the moonlight."

Loraine said, "that sounds so romantic, let's do it." She added that, we should remember to bring our swim suits and a couple of large blankets.

We agreed on a place to meet on Friday, and we were all set.

Finally, Thursday came and I was again standing watch at the theater.

One of the better movies had been advertised and the house was filling.

Loraine came in with Timmy and took her usual seat, near the aisle and right front area.

As the theater emptied she stopped by and confirmed the location where she was going to meet me tomorrow, around dark for our trip down to Sandy Beach. We agreed on our meeting at 1800. She said, "she was so excited and would bring a food basket of sandwiches and red wine."

On Friday I secured my pass to leave the base and proceeded to Wakiki and met Loraine in the public parking lot, where she was parked.

We loaded the food basket and several large blankets into my car and we headed out over Diamond Head and the Blow Hole, on to Sandy Beach, arriving just before sundown, so we could be sure that we were alone, and had our very own island paradise to ourselves.

The parking lot was just off the main highway and just above the beach. We walked down the path to the beach with our food basket and blankets. As we had agreed, we pulled off our clothes down to the swim suits, as we had planned, spread out our blankets and had our dinner right there by the blankets. She had brought towels to dry off from the surf.

Loraine had thought of everything and brought out glasses for our wine, a very good brand, I noted, sandwiches and various fruit slices and grapes. I have told you before that this was a lady of true quality and I was wild about her. I told her so during our tasty and filling dinner in our secluded hideaway.

After dinner we just walked on the beach, proudly, and may have been a little playful as we enjoyed each other. The sand glistened in the moonlight as we left our marks in the sand and listened to the surging waves, as they crashed against the shore. Testing the water, we stayed close to the shore in the safety of not endangering ourselves. We mostly frolicked there up to our waists and enjoyed the feeling of excitement that was driving us on to what we both knew would soon happen to us, there on those blankets, that we had laid out. We knew that we would need only one for our comfort, but we laid one on the top of the other for greater support against the sand.

Since we had been there, every thing that we had done, the kisses, the fondling, touching, glances and whispers had to rival that famous movie of Burt Lancaster and Deborah Kerr in that beautiful, sensual beach scene, which I have now seen, quite a few times. When I saw the movie, I knew that our emotions were just as high as those portrayed by those movie stars.

Realizing that we were alone in our romantic world, we lay together on the blanket and devoured each other. It had begun with light touching and tracing the lips, mouth, the throat and now hardening breasts. Our kisses were so intoxicating and seemed to last a lifetime. I now began to fondle those marvelous, pouting breasts; first the area where they formed and moved to her large nipples and finally, I put my lips to her breasts and sipped, so lightly, showing my great pleasure of their breathtaking beauty.

By this time, we had torn each others swim suit off, and Loraine's moaning seemed uncontrollable and then I began plunging faster and faster and deeper and deeper as she gasped with so much pleasure as she exploded and clung to me as if she never wanted to let me go. I then exploded, also, with pleasure and we lay there, just clinging to each other for what seemed to be hours.

Later, as we drove back toward Wakiki Beach and her parked Buick, Loraine told me about her life with her husband, Bob and her previous life. "She was from Saint Louis, had met Bob, a career Naval Officer. Their stations had moved around quite a bit and had been stationed in Los Alamos for a period, during and after World War11."

"Bob was very possessive and at times, had hurt her to the point of abuse."

"Do you love Bob?" I asked.
"No! Not any more." "Of course I did in the very beginning. Bob is married to the Navy and his duties as a weapons expert.We no longer have anything in common except Timmy," she continued.

By this time we were passing the Moana Hotel and I asked, "if she would like to have dinner and dance there on the next Saturday Night?"

She said, "that would be wonderful, and would meet me there in the parking lot next Saturday at 1800."

We did not want to leave each other, the moment was so very much electrical. All we could do was to cling to one another and sip each others lips, mouth and tongue.

CHAPTER 13

MY LIFE STAYED busy, and Saturday night I had duty at the Officers Club on the Sub Base. A Christmas Party was scheduled and my duty was limited to making sure the officers and guests were not interrupted.

I really just monitored the office and routed a few phone calls.

As I anticipated, Loraine did not come for this party. Naturally I checked the ladies out as they were arriving, for the party. None of the ladies, I decided, could hold a candle to Loraine, but, of course I was prejudiced. Many of the ladies were quite attractive and their officer, escorts looked extremely smart, in their dress uniforms.

I was a little envious that I could not be a part of it all as the food smelled so good and the drinking glasses clinked, as the eggnog and champaign flowed freely.

After dinner, the officers and their guests danced to music of the day, provided by the Naval Base Band. I really got into the music, since it was just my style. The dance floor was very close to my work station and the music was performed in the Glenn Miller style. My favorite song was 'Moonlight Serenade', and still is my favorite, to this day.

The dance ended with 'Good Night Ladies' and I suppose there was time taken for that last drink and possibly a kiss as the officers and guests exited in a very festive manner, to their very own destination.

I anticipated what was going to happen when they reached home!

I was on extended duty and after everyone left, and the cleaning crew had done their thing and left, I checked out the kitchen. I had never been in such a splendid kitchen environment. I was sure that these facilities would rival most fine hotels.

The freezers, refrigerators and ranges were made from the finest stainless steel, and were spotless. I was a little hungry and curiously opened the freezer. Happily, I found a tray of left over sandwiches and helped myself to a couple of them. Delicious, I thought, as I consumed them, quickly. Next I noted that there was plenty of eggnog left and I had to enjoy a glass of that delicious nectar. Who would know, and to this day, I really do not feel that I was violating my duty or responsibilities entrusted to me.

The following Wednesday, we beat the Naval Base Team, two to one, and gained back the league lead. I was the starting and winning pitcher, and now enjoy a record of seven wins and one loss for the season. Saturday, as planned, Loraine was in the lobby waiting, and we walked into dinner.

We chose a table close to the stage, where the band would perform, and just off the dance floor. As we waited for dinner, we observed a photographer, provided by the club, as she approached couples or groups at their tables.

For a small price, she gladly took a photo of the moment that could be long enjoyed by those who accepted her offer, to record the moment. As she came to our table, "I asked Loraine if she would like a photo of the occasion"? She accepted and, later as we were able to view it, we were very pleased by her work. To this day I do not know what became of the photo, but I wish that I had a copy.

After a wonderful dinner, the band struck up and we danced for several hours. As usual, Loraine was the most beautiful woman and dancer on the floor. And, as usual, all eyes turned to us as we danced around the plush, crowded, floor in these beautiful surroundings.

I recall dancing close to the stage as the vocalist was singing a slow love song. She appeared to be an island girl with mixed white parentage.

I noted that she was very attractive, and I observed her smile of recognition and somewhat amusement, as we glided by.

Of course, Loraine looked stunning in red velvet, and I was in my white dinner jacket and tux pants. The vocalist seemed to be running the statistics---beautiful woman of obvious culture, about twenty eight, and her guy, sharp in a white dinner jacket, could not be over twenty.

She was thinking that there had to be a story there somewhere; just one of the many times that seemed to amuse her as she sang and we danced.

I could see that she was intrigued by Loraine and me.

Later, after 'Moonlight Serenade' and 'Good Night Ladies' were played, we slipped outside, and not wanting the night to end, we kissed a lingering kiss and continued to cling to each other. Finally, Loraine got into her car and sped home. I returned to the Sub Base and dreamed of this beautiful seductress.

CHAPTER 14

I KEPT THINKING ABOUT the picture and knew that Loraine had it.
Things were going too fast!!
At some point in time, her husband Bob was bound to see our photo and put the pieces together. How far am I from going toward being in jail, at Leavenworth. I could almost hear the clang of the cell door and smell the stench of that awful place.

Loraine's husband sailed into Pearl Harbor and I had not seen her at the theater in several weeks. I suspected that she was feeling my sudden apprehension that my position was of considerable concern for me.

Finally, she and Timmy came to the theater. We spoke after the movie as I walked her to her car. I asked her how the time with Bob went for her and Timmy.

She said that, "he was very happy to have been home, as usual, but, mostly he had been devoted to the retrofitting of his ship and the outfitting of the supplies and ammunition for the new voyage." This had taken most of his time. She added that, "this was OK by her and she was almost glad that he had returned to sea, but wished him well."

I felt like a louse, but knew that I finally had to get something off my chest about our relationship. "I told her that I had been giving a lot of consideration, as to the possibility of our on-going relationship, and the knowledge of what would happen to us, if we were caught in our relationship."

"This could possibly destroy her future and send me to Leavenworth, for our actions."

"I told her how much I cared for her," and added, "we need to cool off for a while. I need you too much," I whispered.

Loraine drew back in shock. But I think she understood where I was coming from, still we kissed a lingering kiss and I held her tight.

Then she started to enter the Buick, turned and looked at me once more and was gone, for the last time I saw her!

The baseball season was over and we had won the championship.

I became interested in tennis and soon started spending a lot of time down at Fort Derussy, sort of a recreation center with lighted tennis courts available for all military, families and guests. They also had bunks available to use in case you needed to stay overnight before returning to base, in the next morning.

I had dropped out of the theater watch pool and was avoiding any relationships there. Also, this gave me a little more break time and pass opportunity. This enabled me the opportunity to meet girls near my own age, I thought. And yes, I did start meeting girls.

I met Sherry, a tall virginal looking girl who lived with her family on a hill, overlooking the Punch Bowl. The Punch Bowl was one of the largest Military Cemetery in the Pacific Zone. I believe it was started during World War II and was still growing.

We enjoyed playing tennis and she told me about her family. "She had a younger brother and sister, mother was a homemaker and Dad, David, was a Lt. Commander, a career Naval Officer, who had a desk job at the Naval Base here in Pearl Harbor."

One day we were playing tennis and Sherry invited me to attend church with the family. She told me that "we would be going to Christ Episcopal." We went the next Sunday and I enjoyed the service.

As we exited the church, Sherry and her mother invited me to their home for dinner. I accepted the offer and enjoyed a wonderful home cooked meal. During the dinner, Sherry's father, obviously the 'Gatekeeper' for his special daughter, was very courteous but not overly impressed by me. I suspected that he was looking for someone from the Naval Academy for his little girl.

We had a few other dates, played tennis, but I could tell that we were not going anywhere. She was not a keeper for me.

I realized that, at this point, I was not looking for anything serious in my romantic life, but I continued tennis and trips to Wakiki.

One Saturday night, I decided to attend a dance at the Enlisted Mens Club. After a meal and a few beers, I had a few dances with singles who had attended without dates. I met Marie Antonez, who had come as a single. She asked me, "if I came often to the club?"

And I admitted that this was my first time being here before tonight.
As a thought, I decided that this club had very few values that the Chief's Club had. I ordered a beer and asked Marie what kind of beer did she want, and she ordered a beer that was native to the Central America area. She later told me that, "her mother was from Puerto Rico and her father had been Filipino." I thought, sounds like hot blood to me, and it did turn out to be. After a few dances, she "invited me to take her to her home in Honolulu." Marie lived with several small children in a rather plain area of town. She asked me, "if I could stay awhile?"

I told her, "that I had an overnight pass, and could stay awhile."

After the children went to bed, Marie led me to her bedroom. She was somewhat attractive and appeared to be in her late twenties. I could not help but notice her enormous breasts, that I quickly got lost into. Hot blood was right, I could tell that she was not too much into foreplay. She had to have it, and practically tore my clothes off. We practiced exciting sex that night and several passes later. It was OK, but I felt that," how can I do this after the wonderful quality sex that Loraine and I had enjoyed?"

Marie did bring a new element of sex to me. She just loved to go down on me. Not bad, but sometimes she got so excited that it almost hurt, rather than being pleasurable.

We went dancing several more times, but, one night we had taken our bottles of beer out to the car to sip and talk quietly. Suddenly she shocked me by saying, "are you going to marry me?"

I said, "hey, this is going too fast, I like you a lot, but I have not thought that far into the future."

She took the bottle of beer, reached over and cracked the top on the door handle. I saw the jagged edges sparkle. She held the bottle up in front of my face and said, "then take me home."

"And I mean now!"

I could see fire in her eyes. We pulled out, geared up and sped to her house. She got out without saying a word. I knew that there was nothing that I wanted to say. I never saw Marie after that night!

CHAPTER 15

MARIE HAD BEEN a convenience, an experience. I could not have ever considered her in my future life. Remember, I was twenty and going on twenty one.

I knew that there was more out there and I was looking forward to finding it.

After my experience with Marie, I was glad to stay on base for awhile. I joined the Sub Base Bowling League. We competed every Monday and Wednesday nights with other teams on the base. Me, I was never anything special, but managed to carry a 179 average for all games, when I competed. Bowling did keep me busy during that time and I did not have to think about Loraine, all of the moments.

Base life was not entirely uneventful. To pass the time in the barracks, we had a number of game type things that broke out when we were all off duty, especially at night. We had poker players that seemed to be able to send a lot of money home. It was usually the same guys that always won and the same dumb guys that often lost their whole pay. The game normally started out with a nickle ante and dime raises. Bob, from Indianapolis and Nick from New Jersey, got it going and the suckers piled in to lose a good amount of their monthly pay.

Naturally, new recruits were always welcome to opt in and play.

Shooting craps on dice was, also, a popular game. Harry, from Atlanta, I believe, got the crap beat out of himself, one night. It seems that some of the regulars caught him with loaded dice. He had used them one time too many, when the ante was raised. We had all wondered how Harry had been able to come out on top so often. Well, now we knew, and it cost him dearly. The beating was followed by suspension from any following games, where money was being bet on the outcome.

Me, I liked to play Pinochle or Monopoly. If you do not know how these games are played, you are very young, you may want to look them up.

I know that we passed a lot of fun time, and it was mostly played for free. We had a lot of fellowship in participating in those games.

Finally, I was feeling a little more free to spend more time soaking up the sun and fun of Wakiki Beach. I was still into providing value in my job of helping the war effort, by providing and supplying the best equipment and uniforms that fit properly, and provided comfort, style and safety to our forces fighting the war in the Asian Area of operations. Everything had to be perfect, especially for our submariners, who tied up at our docks for rest and recovery, refitting and gathering supplies and ammunition for their next assignment in the war zones. I was not responsible for providing ammunition, but warm blankets, heavy clothing, to provide warmth, life jackets to provide safety, paint supplies and oil products to maintain maintenance for the next voyage.

Nevertheless, I was no longer being called upon to provide watch duty at the theater and had not been going to the movie. I thought this best, especially since I did not want to rekindle my former relationship with Loraine. Hey, I was still having a hard time getting over her, but how could I keep taking the chance of ruining the rest of my life. If we were found out and Bob saw fit to bring charges, my life could be finished.

CHAPTER 16

ON A TRIP to Wakiki Beach, I met Roger and his wife. Roger was a First Class Petty Office, from the Naval Base. I had met them down on the beach.

Sue, his wife, was with Roger. They sat next to me on the beach and went into the surf to cool off. They invited me to share some beer, that they had brought in a cooler.

Before we parted, they invited me to their house for dinner and drinks on the next Sunday afternoon. I accepted their invitation and received direction to their home and agreed to be there at 1700, next Sunday afternoon.

Roger and Sue lived in a duplex on the edge of town. Their apartment was rather plain and smelled heavily of smoke. The radio was playing a sad country song, where someone had done someone wrong. The singer was lamenting that the girl had gone away and left him with a terrible yearning to have her back, even tho she had said that she was through with him and their relationship.

Sue asked me "if I would like to have a beer and indicated that there were several brands in the refrigerator, and to select my preference." Entering the scarred old fridge, I noticed a lot of Budweiser and, instead, selected a Miller High Life.

Soon, as Roger and I talked in the living room, Sue, "called for us to come to the dinning room." Dinner was ready and we pilled into the spaghetti and meatballs and a marvelous salad. After dinner, we enjoyed just sitting in the living room and sipping on a very good glass of red wine.

Later we sat watching TV and a sitcom of that day, I observed the rabbit ears on top of the TV, and noted the foil covering the rabbit ears.

In those days it was said that the foil helped in receiving better reception.

Finally Roger got around to talking about what they had planned for the evening. "They were swingers," he said. "I was welcome to have sex with Sue," only he added, he only wanted to watch as Sue and I enjoyed the moment.

Suddenly, I had heard enough and my stomach churned at the thought, and said, "I really have enjoyed your hospitality, good food, and good company." I continued, "I have never done anything like that. I really do appreciate the offer, but I would not be comfortable in that type of relationship."

I told Sue, "it has nothing to do with you. You are a very attractive person." It is just me, "I am not into that type of relationship." Again, I thanked them for their hospitality, and told them that, "I would see them around, and at the beach."

Feeling a little creepy and dirty from the offer, I left and don't recall ever seeing them again.

I returned to the base and continued my duties of supplying our forces with the best service that I could render with the available, and needed supplies. I really appreciated the service of so many of our fighting service men, who were giving their all in the far flung duties, they performed for our country, all over the Pacific realm. I did feel a little guilt, that I was not with them in their dangerous duties as they protected us from harm. Still, I had their back, by providing the best products available, to serve them in their duties.

Still, I did not hesitate going to Wakiki Beach when presented with a pass. Next time I went ashore, I met Bonnie. She was a big-eyed brunette from the states. Bonnie worked as a civilian secretary in one of the local naval offices. I would describe her as wholesome, maybe a little overweight, but still had a nice figure.

I had met her on the beach, and we talked a lot about her home in Texas and her job here in Hawaii. Later, we shared a few weekend lunches and a few dinners. We just became good friends, who just enjoyed being around each other.

Funny, I thought, but I really don't recall thinking about her in a sexual manner.

I guess I was still thinking about the perfection of Loraine.

No! I had not forgotten Loraine!

After that, I went through a series of insignificant relationships.
You know what I mean; a few dates at the beach, playing tennis at the club at Derussy and some dances; where just dancing was the purpose of just enjoying the atmosphere and passing the time.
Guess that I was still looking for another substitute for Loraine.
I realized that that was just not going to happen.
Thank goodness, I was no longer thinking about that horrible place, Leavenworth. That was a blessing of no longer feeling the possibility that had hung over me like an early morning fog over a lake, for almost a year. Possibly, that fear had hung over me since that first secluded meeting with Loraine, as we sat in her parked Buick, there at the Sub Base, as Timmy slept in the back seat. Thank goodness that we were not discovered by a passing guard on duty, who would have had to file a report.

CHAPTER 17

HOTEL STREET WAS where the service guys went to get a quick piece of ass, or entertainment provided by the Arcades housed there.

We had taken the bus into town and wound up on Hotel Street. It was filled with Arcades that dispensed anything that a guy on the town, wanted. Blaring speakers inviting you to come on in and see what they had for you to enjoy or buy.

I remember Rosemary Clooney singing, 'Come On To My House,' which was still popular at that time.

I had come with Joe and Al, who were guys from our barracks.

I remember a previous trip to the Arcades there on Hotel Street, when we stepped into a tattoo shop. Al was going to get another tattoo.

He already had one on his left shoulder, that said, "Betty," and was enclosed in a big, red heart. Betty must have been a long-lost love, since he had never spoken of a Betty, before in any of our talks, together, and there had been many opportunities that he avoided ever mentioning a Betty.

We had had a few beers prior to entering the tattoo shop, and the guys were trying to get me to let the tattoo artist work wonders on me. I asked, "what if I don't like it and want it removed?"

"Not so easy," they said.

"Forget it then," I said. I could not help but imagine some awful infection that might result from the application or removal of the unwanted tattoo. Anyway, that was just not my style. After all, that was still a time when you did not have to violate your body with a tattoo or group of tattoos to signify that, you should be considered a real 'strong man.'

After Al got his tattoo, we continued on down Hotel Street and found a great Chinese Restaurant.

We were seated by a very attractive Chinese hostess. I noticed that she was very tall, unlike most Chinese women. I asked her what her name was, and she replied, "Sai Ling, and that our waitress would come to take our orders, soon."

Later the waitress did come to take our order and suggested several of their specials for the evening. I ordered Chicken Chow Mein, with a side order of egg drop soup and a Budweiser beer. Joe and Al placed their order and we all enjoyed our meal.

After we had enjoyed our meal, the waitress brought our checks and provided each of us a Chinese Fortune Cookie. I quickly opened my cookie and read something very intriguing. It said that, "you are going to have an exciting adventure." I liked the thought of that. They had agreed that they wanted to go up the street to the Whore House, that they had visited at another time, when I was not out with them.

They wanted me to go. I replied that, "you know that is just not my style." I warned them that I had heard of a lot of sailors being beaten up at that place by other army and marines, and to be careful to not get involved in something that they could not get out of, safely.

After the guys left, I sat quietly and sipped on some coffee that I had ordered. I could not take my eyes off of Sai Ling, the tall hostess at her station. She was wearing a long-flowery dress, which came down to the tops of her shoes. Her long-black, flowing hair stood out and intrigued me.

She must have caught my gaze and shyly lowered her eyes. I could tell that I had struck a nerve and a questioning thought. Me, I had found Sai Ling and I wanted to meet her. Again, I caught her eye and motioned for her to come over. It was late and almost closing time. I asked her, "if I could see her, sometime.?"

I was mighty surprised when she replied, "I will be getting off in five minutes," "we can catch the limousine that I have waiting, I will show you my home," she added.

The Limousine was waiting, nice, but not too elaborate. I opened the door for her and we entered. We drove north toward Wakiki, and on the way, I noted that this was a neighborhood of stylish, upscale homes, surrounded by lagoons and waterways, that appeared to provide passage by canoes and small boats.

Sai Ling's house was very oriental; it rose on all sides to center at the top in true oriental fashion; the rooms had high ceilings and a lot of glass for open viewing; ornate curtains could be drawn for privacy; there was a small pool for swimming, surrounded by the usual fish pools, covered by lily pads and exotic oriental plants, mostly new to me.

I said to myself, this is not the usual restaurant hostess. She probably owns the restaurant. We sat for a while in what appeared to be the living room and talked. Sai Ling suggested that, "I might like some green tea," and left to prepare it in the kitchen. After returning and pouring, we sat for a while, drinking the green tea and talked with oriental music playing softly in the background. I tried to get her to reveal her background to me, but she seemed to not want to reveal herself at all. Finally, she said, "you better go, since it is late and we both need our rest."

We had been sitting close to a large opening to her bedroom, and I noted a large round bed that was visible from where we sat.

I had had a strong sense about her. She had a sweet smell about her, that was obviously not perfume. It was just an aroma that her lithe body generated. I ushered her to the bedroom and asked, "could we just lay here so that I can hold you for a minute?"

"Just a moment, and then you must go." Sai Ling replied.

I held her closely and inhaled her aroma. It was almost overpowering, but very alluring.

After several long kisses that seemed to want much more, she said, "now you must go." "The Limousine is still waiting and he will take you anywhere that you want to go."

Once outside I found the Limousine waiting, as Sai Ling had said. Strange situation, I thought. Maybe he was her protection, or perhaps a relative, or a body guard.

I asked him to drop me off at the YMCA in downtown Honolulu.

And, I spent the night there. I knew that early in the morning, I could return to the Sub Base by bus.

Strange experience! Was her aroma generated from an oriental drug that she was taking, I thought.

I never found out. Strangely, I never went back there. Things just did not look and have the right feel for me. The thought of possible drug involvement by her, was not something that I could stomach in my life.

Drugs had not attained the prominence and notoriety that we hear so much about these days. But, they were probably more wide spread among the orientals, there in Honolulu.

CHAPTER 18

BY THIS TIME, I was managing several warehouses and a paint house.
My supplies contained clothing, including heavy leather jackets, preferred by submariners, spare parts and oxygen containers for supplying the Sub Fleet of Com Sub Pac.

Work and the responsibility, kept me on the base for greater amounts of time. Shore leave was not as available as it had formerly been for me.
On one trip to Honolulu, I met a very pretty Japanese girl who knew where we could get a room. It had been quick, not memorable sex. She had given me a small photo of her in a tight swim suit, showing her cute figure. She had not awakened when I left the next morning.
Again, at the beach, I met an attractive local white girl, who was studying at The University Of Hawaii. After a light dinner, we had a few drinks and drove to a spot overlooking the bright lights of Honolulu.
We sat and talked and I could tell that she wanted sex. It was a good thing that we talked some more, because, as I was getting ready to lay the seat back, she bragged that, "she had been with the entire University Of Hawaii Basketball Team, the night before."

Well, that was not for me! I put all of my cloths back on and asked her where I needed to take her.

Thank you, Lord. You seem to save me whether I deserve it or not!

By this time I was beginning to recognize trash before I got too involved with it.

The thought came back to me from my early years and all the way into my teenage years. My mother had always said to me, just as I was leaving to go anywhere, "now be good."

I had not really known what she meant by always saying that.

But, I remembered that it kept me out of a lot of trouble, that many young people find themselves emmeshed into, especially, today.

I suppose my mother's early warnings had been one of the reasons that I had been so aware of the impending disaster that was likely to happen to me, if I had continued my relationship with Loraine.

CHAPTER 19

BINGO!! THIS TIME I got lucky at the beach at Wakiki. Marilyn looked just like Marilyn Monroe. She had beautiful, blond, short hair, that covered a very expressive mouth that ended in a cute pout.

She had a small son and daughter and introduced them to me, as Matthew and Jennifer. Husband, David, she said, was a Navy pilot and was doing duty on an aircraft carrier in the Western Pacific.

Marilyn let me know right away that, "she liked me-- would even see me on a light date, conversation and just hanging out, maybe at the beach, and maybe dinner at her house from time to time."

Then she dropped the bomb as she said, "I love my husband, but I do get lonely, and I think that David would understand." Then she continued, "I am not looking for cheap sex with you or anyone else."

"O.K," I said, "this is just for laughs."

I did see her several times at the beach and we always talked. She was from the Great Lakes Area, with wealthy parents. Father, Alan Fitzgerald was in the construction business and the war had given him the opportunity to develope contracts for building numerous military locations in the north and southeastern, United States.

Marilyn and David had met in college and were married in his senior year. Upon graduation, David entered the Navy and went immediately to Flight Training. So, I played by her rules, you remember, "there would not be any cheap sex." And when she realized that was the case, she invited me to her home for dinner on a Saturday night. She gave me directions and the address and set the time for 1800.

Work in my supply warehouses kept me quite busy during the week and I was looking forward to seeing her home, and what I was sure would be a delicious meal.

On Saturday, I arrived on time--1800, and I noted that she lived in a very nice section of town, the house was very spacious and looked well built. All of the homes in the area seemed to fit nicely into this beautiful development outside Honolulu.

Marilyn received me and invited me in for tea, while she finished up what, turned out to surpass my early expectations. We dined on a meal of Chicken Tetrazzini, new potatoes, and a marvelous salad and island fruits and desert of vanilla ice cream, topped with hot chocolate.

"I had to congratulate Marilyn for preparing the wonderful meal and insisted that she was a marvelous cook." I offered to help clean up the dishes.

She graciously accepted my offer, and said that, "she could get the children started with their games in the game room."

After I finished the dishes and retiring to the living room, she soon joined me there and said that, "she had already told me a lot about she and her family, and now she wanted to hear more about this mysterious young sailor and specifically about my life back in the states prior to joining the Navy."

I told her, "I was from a small town in North Carolina, and about some of my friends from high school. I had just a few light romances, but nothing serious."

She asked, "if there was a special girl back home waiting for me?"

"I assured her that was not the case. I had been entirely too busy as a star baseball pitcher, to form any serious relationships."

She, then, "wanted to know a little about my childhood and family life."

I explained that, "we, father, mother and my two sisters lived on a small farm, which we did not farm, but an uncle did the farming as we shared the returns from the crops. My uncle and his family lived very close by and I spent a lot of time after school with a cousin, who was about my age, liked to play games such as checkers, card games and a lot of swimming in a creek, which flowed by their house."

"Each Spring, we dammed it up and had a lot of friends in to enjoy the swimming, with us. We also played a lot of Monopoly with any friends who came."

I told her, "about the little town near our farm, our family and life on a small farm. I liked and enjoying parties and activities we experienced, at a small-startup Presbyterian Church, that had been a positive experience in the way I saw myself and those around me."

"My pastor, at that small church, took a personal interest in me. And, I can still hear him asking me, Alvin, how is your constitution?"

By asking me about my constitution, he meant that I should always have a positive attitude and treat others as I would like to always be treated, myself. Naturally, he wanted me to have christian ethics, but, he let me know that he could be a friend with whom I could confide.

Baseball was introduced to me on the church playground and I began spending a lot of time there, especially on Saturday, and when spring brought out the good weather, playing on this church league team was a building block that would eventually make me a star pitcher in high school and in the surrounding counties with many wins and few defeats. Later, I played semi-professional baseball in a league that encompassed at least three counties in the area.

"After I joined the Navy and became stationed at the Submarine Base at Pearl Harbor, I went out for the Sub Pac Baseball Team, and, over a three-year period, helped Sub Pac to win the military league championship for two years running." "Winning was easy for me, and, as a pitcher, I won over ten games each year and added many key hits to our cause."

Marilyn told me that, "she had not had the opportunity to become a baseball fan, but she certainly would have loved to see my games and would have been thrilled to witness my pitching performances."

I told her that, "the baseball season was now over for this year."

I added that, "I had just received information that my term of duty was nearing completion and I would soon be shipped back to San Diego and getting out of the Navy. I would return home to North Carolina and, hopefully, enter college at a small university and prepare myself for later business opportunities."

I was still curious about her life growing up, prior to her marriage. So, I asked her about growing up in the Great Lakes area.

She said that, "life had been easy for her as she grew up." "She was a good student in high school and college, where she met David, and they were married in his senior year."

She continued by describing "her life as being a daddy's girl."

It seems that her father had made great progress in construction and became quite successful in the construction business. This fascinated her and she always thought she would like to follow his lead in her later life.

"As for romance, David had been her love life in college and her marriage had resulted in these two wonderful children, Jennifer and then, Matthew." She was proud that they were well rounded children.

This reminded her that it was time to get the children to bed time and excused herself for about ten minutes.

This brought us up to this date in our strange relationship of respect for each other---not really a romance, but we both knew that the feeling was there, but the respect for her marriage and husband was too strong for anything else in our relationship.

We had made our pact for 'just laughs,' as we had agreed upon from the beginning. The difference in our ages---I was only twenty one and I assumed that she was twenty four or twenty five years old.

This clean relationship had brought a 'cleaning experience', after my many experiences here in Hawaii, up to this time.

I continued to play by her rules. We continued to talk about our past and present lives and the things that we enjoyed. It was agreed that nothing else was going to happen, even though it had to be obvious to each other;

there was a strong feeling that we both shared, and realized that it could not be allowed to happen, at least at this time.

Again, I reminded her that I would soon be completing my tour of duty in the Navy. "I would be returning to my home in North Carolina and starting a new life as a student in college, where I would continue to play baseball and hopefully find suitable employment that would allow me to do all of those things that I wanted to do with the rest of my life."

Marilyn had other hopes and plans for me. She encouraged me to go to Los Angles and Hollywood. She said, "why don't you go to acting school?"

And she added, "you possibly don't realize it, but you do have the good looks that it takes for that profession."

I told her that, "she was being too complimentary, but I appreciated her kind interest in my future." "Time will tell," I added.

I thought that my dark black hair, being well tanned and a great looking mustache, that was well groomed, must be why she suggested Hollywood.

It was getting late and I needed to get back to the base, so, "I told her that I must leave soon, but hoped to see her again before I sailed back to the states and San Diego, for completion of my discharge papers."

Marilyn, again, asked me, "to give her my home address in North Carolina," and came into my arms for a lingering hug and retreated back, appearing almost afraid of what she had done. She quickly regained her composure and said, "Alvin Knight, I hope to see you again!"

I was curious as to why she had asked for my home address, but I gladly gave it to her and we soon parted. I knew that she was the best thing that had ever happened to me. She had shown me, at my tender years of twenty one, what a real woman was, and I knew I had to set my goals high in finding a woman with her strong qualities, and devotion to her marriage.

A few days later, I received my orders to secure my work stations, and report aboard the Aircraft Carrier, located in the harbor on Wednesday, and return to San Diego as soon as possible to receive my discharge papers.

As a courtesy to Marilyn, I did call her and, "told her that I had received my orders to return to the mainland, and would not be able to see her prior to my departure." I did thank her, "for that wonderful dinner and told her that, I respected her very much and wished her much happiness and hoped that David would return home safely, soon."

CHAPTER 20

THE ISLAND OF Oahu disappeared into the distance. I said to myself that, I don't know what my future will bring, but I know that I have already lived a lifetime of experience for a small town, farm boy, now only twenty one years old.

The Aircraft Carrier was huge and a new experience for me. After an uneventful trip to San Diego, California, where I had received my Boot Sailor Training, so long ago, at a very tender age, I now was entering a new stage in my life. There had been the 'BEFORE' in my life and I was now looking forward to the 'AFTER,' that I hoped to bring success and happiness in my future. I continued to mull over those two words as I knew that I had done many things in my youth, up to this point, that I could not possibly be proud of. Certainly, I have told you about many of these in my story, so far.

Now I was headed east to what was to be the 'AFTER', as I boarded a big Grey Hound bus, along with a lot of other travelers to unknown destinations. I knew that for me, I was headed to my home in the Rowan County, of North Carolina.

After a four day ride, we passed the rolling hills of Iredell County and passed through rolling farmland, we entered Rowan County.

"I am home," I said.

But I was a long way from the Hollywood that Marilyn had predicted for me.

Reality had to take over and I had saved very little for my future.

My father and mother assured me that they were delighted to have me home. I was welcome to stay at home in my old bedroom, since my two sisters had married and had a life of their own.

Of course we all knew that I would be seeking employment in order to provide income for myself and contribute to the family expenses, since I realized that dad was drawing a small pension in addition to Social Security.

The only thing that I could put on my Resume was that I had been providing products, which were vital to the war effort, and to the personnel, who were supporting that effort, far away from their homes.

I got my Resume out in a two county area and hoped that I would not have to resort to collecting unemployment compensation.
In those days it was still looked on as charity and a man had to be working if he was worth anything in the community. My pride kept me following up any prospective business that would provide a satisfactory income and offer benefits in an environment that I could take pride in my efforts.

Suddenly, this was the real world. I had formerly been secure in the Navy, where most decisions were made for me by the service.
Soon, I received an offer from a supply firm near town and was glad to except it. Other offers had been from the textile plants that were all over our state, at that time. Those offers were low paying and the working conditions were not too satisfactory.
So, I settled into the supply firm and worked diligently, hoping to make enough savings that could enable me to go on to college. In those days, a college education was a prerequisite to entering any supervisory or management position in the field that I was into at this time.
I personally knew that I was management material, but there seemed to be no possibility of that in this firm, where I was currently working so hard to prove myself. With this in mind, I started looking at other possibilities. When talking to a slick talking Medical Insurance Manager, he told me about the opportunities in the Medical Insurance field. He spoke of the huge commissions that an insurance agent could make in that field and promised to provide leads that I could follow up and visit. "The commissions would pile up quickly," he promised. He did say that there was no guaranteed salary, and I would have to drive my own vehicle and pay my own expenses. He made the commission

sound so high that I finally took the exam to get an insurance sales license and quit my job at the supply firm.

The Personnel Manager at the supply firm said he was sorry to see me go, and that I had been doing a good job and did have a future in this company. He said he had seen a lot of potential in me, but could not promise that any management position would be opening soon. There were too many college graduates that were still in line for those jobs.

I said to myself that, maybe the Medical Insurance would get me on the right track to better financial security. So license in hand, I set out to prove that I would make a great salesman in that field.

CHAPTER 21

THE OFFICE THAT I would be working out of was located in the Wallace Building in downtown Salisbury, North Carolina. Upon reporting for work, the office manager introduced me to a man, who would be my Supervisor. His name was John, and John was going to train me to be their best salesman in the office. I decided that he was right and was determined to make that happen, in the near future. John sat with me over a period of one week and went over the products thoroughly and the applications that I would be filling out after visiting and selling the prospect, and collecting the first months premium.

The manager began supplying the names and addresses of prospects, as he had first promised, when recruiting me as an agent. My Supervisor, John, had provided me with a sound sales presentation and had been letting me practice as if he was the prospect and I was giving that same presentation to a person that I visited to make a sale. Finally, I had it down pat and was ready to go into the field. John would accompany me for the first week, and if I appeared to be loosing the sale, he would enter into the presentation and make a good close, securing the sale and I would ask the health qualifying questions and complete the applications and get the first month premium. Quickly, I became quite proficient in making the sale and soon the management in the office and, in the Home Office of the company, realized that I had a great future with the company and had great Supervisory potential.

The commissions were coming in and I was enjoying my work and my clients seemed to appreciate the products that I was protecting them with and, often offered the names of friends in the neighborhood who they would recommend me to see if they might need the protection that we offered. Often, family members of my present policy holders called for me to visit them and see if my products were right for them.

I was finally making good money and thought that my future was on the right track.

There in the Wallace Building one day, when I had a little leisure time, I decided to see what other offices were there in the Wallace Building. Perhaps I could do a little prospecting and pass out a few of my business cards that could advertise me and my company. I was up on the sixth floor and passing by another insurance company office. The door was open and I noticed a very cute girl, who was the receptionist or secretary. I thought to myself that it had been some time since I had thought about a woman in a romantic way, so I decided to meet this lady.

I had not met anyone that interested me since I had left Hawaii, now over a year ago. So I went in and presented my card and asked, the lady what type of business they represented.

She answered that, "we are in the business of life insurance, and she added, we are one of the largest life insurance companies in the country," she proudly exclaimed.

Well, I could not top that and "told her that my company was in the business of offering cancer protection to individuals and families."

And, added that, "I had only been with the company for eight months." I mentioned that there was a part of our applications that referred to 'Basil Metabolism' and asked if she would explain what that referred to.

She said, Basil Metabolism refers to the condition of a person's body conditions and it's functions.

By the way, she added, "my name is Michele."

During this time, I had become aware of this petite secretary's nice rounded breasts, which were visible in her tight-fitting sweater.

I decided that I wanted to know her better and and said, "Michele, what is your last name"?

She replied, "Robinson," but, "what is your name?"

"Alvin Knight," I replied, with a little uplifted pride in my name.

I then told her that, "I had served a tour in the US Navy in Hawaii and had been home a little over a year and was now trying to make a future for myself, hopefully in the Insurance Business."

I added, "my office is on this floor." 'I know that this is a little presumptuous, but, could we do lunch together, sometime?"

She seemed to size me up, "maybe tomorrow," she said.

"Great." I exclaimed, "we can go over to Blackwelders BBQ, on West Innes Street. I will pick you up at 12:00 noon, and we will go to lunch."

"O.K," she said, smilingly.

Something in my mind told me that--you may consider this is what you have been looking for. I had never considered the possibility of marriage in any of my relationships, before. And God knows, there had been many others in my life.

I never thought of Michele Robinson as just another piece of tail.

We met at noon and drove to Blackwelders BBQ and parked on the curb. A sharp looking guy--the college type (probably Catawba College) curb waiter, took our order.

Michele ordered a burger, "explaining that it was their usual special, and a coke."

As for me, I ordered a burger and a bottle of Cheerwine, which I remembered fondly, before I left for the Navy. "Bring us an order of french-fries to share," I added.

This was our routine for a few times.

Finally, Michele invited me to visit her home and family, out on Patterson Road, just west of Salisbury and off Mooresville Road.

Patterson Road was mostly large tracts of farmland, I noted, as I drove out on Saturday night. Most of the families had been on the land for two hundred years, where their ancestors had settled when Rowan County was just becoming a destination.

The soil appeared rich and I had noted a heavy concentration of farm products in various growth stages all around, as I proceeded on my search for Michele's home. Most of the tracts were huge and extended into the distance from the road as I passed by.

Most of the homes were deep, two story homes that housed large families to run the large farms. They had grown up there and handled all of the chores required of a working farm.

Later, the children would inherit their own portion of the land and continue farming their own inheritance.

The Robinson family home had been built in the late 1940's, or early 1950's. The home was comfortable, but not elaborate, just large enough to accommodate Thomas and Margaret, Michele and Jamie, who was fifteen at the time. Michele was twenty one.

Thomas ran the farm during the day and then cleaned up to travel to Kannapolis to the textile plant, some thirteen miles away, on the 2nd shift. Obviously, he had to be a good man to do all of that.

Margaret sold Avon products in and around the area. She often held product parties in client homes, where her clients promoted her products, and orders were taken. It was said that she was a top agent.

Margaret was a very pretty woman and I wondered how much Michele would look like her mother in the twenty years that follow.

Michele was smart and had attended and received an Associates Degree in Secretarial Science from the local business college, having graduated with honors.

Jamie would be a sophomore at China Grove High School, this year.

When I arrived at the Robinson Family home, Michele introduced me to the family. Thomas, I could tell was reserving his opinion of me, but Margaret seemed to like me immediately, maybe that was because I liked her immediately and shared my warm feeling for her. I thought she was strikingly beautiful, especially for a woman in her mid forties, I was guessing. As for Michele, she looked very much like her mother must have looked about twenty five years before.

This family, I thought did not seem to fit the others that I had passed.

The family was smaller and the house and farm did not appear as large as those I had observed as I had approached the Robinson home.

I enjoyed the visit to Michele and her family very much and was treated to a wonderful meal and a very good reception by the family and, later a very pleasant and private time for Michele and myself to get to know each other much better. I felt that she was a very nice girl, smart and a good conversationalist.

Later, I graciously thanked the family for the wonderful meal and their kind reception.

I realize that it was very early in our relationship, but I think that both of us, Michele and me, had thoughts of a possible, eventual marriage.

We even had sent little hints to each other how we felt about each other and our friends and acquaintances had been hinting that we were right for each other.

But that was not to be!!

CHAPTER 22

THEN ON MONDAY, the letter came from Marilyn. I was shocked.

I thought she was still in Hawaii.

You remember! She was the Marilyn Monroe look alike that I had shared my last date, or what ever it was. I remembered that wonderful meal that she had prepared and shared the last night before I was told to prepare for my returning to San Diego for my discharge from the Navy, via an Aircraft Carrier, anchored in Pearl Harbor.

The letter was postmarked from Pensacola, Florida.

Surprised, I had opened it and found that it was from Marilyn.

Marilyn began, "maybe by now you have heard about David's death. He was on a mission, flying over the Florida Keys and off Florida, when he crashed at sea. I thought you might have heard on the TV or read about it in the newspapers." "You had given me your address back home in North Carolina, when you left Hawaii. I don't know if you are still there in North Carolina or if you took my advice and went to Hollywood to enter acting school as I had suggested."

> "I know that this is being quite presumptuous, but I would like to see you, are you interested?" "I just don't know where to turn!"
>
> Love,
> Marilyn

I read and reread the letter. After my affair with Loraine had seemed to almost destroy me with fear of the possibility of being caught and sent to Leavenworth Prison. My innocent experience with Marilyn had made me realize what a sordid thing Loraine and my affair must have been. Marilyn and her innocence had made me see what a real woman, Marilyn really was. She did not ever want to hurt David, as I am sure that Loraine eventually must have done to Bob, her husband, if and when, she was finally found out.

Suddenly, after all of these years I had forgotten about Loraine, but had not forgotten about Marilyn and her sweet innocence that night before I left Hawaii to return home.

I put the letter away for a few days, knowing that I had to think about which road I should take at this point---should I ignore the letter and see what direction, life would take with Michele? Should I at least write a letter telling her that I had returned home and found a very sweet girl that I could possibly marry and begin life anew? In the letter, I could tell Marilyn how sorry I was that David had had an accident and perished. Then, I could have said that I was sorry that this terrible loss had happened to her and her marriage, and how crushing it must be to Jennifer and Matthew, her children.

The easy choice for me would have been to go ahead and plan for my wedding to Michele. But, did I really love her enough, or was it just convenient to spend the rest of my life with Michele, just because it was expected by friends at home?

By Wednesday, I had found Marilyn's phone number and made the call. It seemed just like magic when she answered the phone.

I said, "Marilyn, this is Alvin Knight."

"Alvin," she screamed, "I was afraid that you would reply to my letter, and more afraid that you would not. Where are you?"
I told her that, "I was still in North Carolina, and was so very sorry to have heard the terrible news of David's death." And I continued, "how are the children?"
Marilyn told me, "they were heartbroken, but that she had told them that life goes on and that we would have to make a lot of new decisions, and, most of all, things would work out for the best."

She continued, "We have each other, and their father would have wanted us to be strong in our family unit, and carry on, as best we could."

Marilyn asked me, "what was going on in your life, since you returned home to North Carolina?"

I told her that, "I had a great job, that had been paying me very well, in the Medical Insurance field, and had bought a nice car, a Ford Fairlaine 500, and had money in the bank."

"Is there a woman in your life?" she asked.

I had to admit that, "yes, I had been seeing a nice girl and she was hinting marriage, but I am not sure that I really love her well enough to go that far, but I really did not want to hurt her, however I do not want to make a commitment, that would end up being wrong for both of us." "By the way, I can imagine what you have gone through, but, do you have a man in your life?"

"Alvin Knight, after the magic that I felt just being with you for those few short moments there in Hawaii, I must confess that I have thought of none other, even though I did love David very much for our life together."

I told Marilyn that, "I needed about several weeks to work things out, but, could I visit you there in Pensacola?"

Marilyn said that, "she had hoped for just that, but had been afraid that I would not be interested."

I told her that, "I had loved her from the first day that I had met her." "And, even more at this moment!"

"My darling, Alvin, you cannot imagine how glad I am to hear you say that." "But, are you sure that you are not just feeling sorry for me?"

"Marilyn, I have watched your goodness and strength for so long and I will be there. Let's see, this is Wednesday, I can make all arrangements and be there on Saturday, the next two weeks, in the early evening." "Is that O.K? Now give me your address and directions to Pensacola. You have my address. Please followup with a brief letter including your address and directions from I-10."

Marilyn said that, "she was really sorry that I had to leave the job that I loved and was doing so well."

I told her that, "I had discovered that I was a very good salesman, especially in the Medical Insurance field, and that my skills would be transferrable to Florida, or anywhere we might decide to make our home."

I reminded her that in Hawaii we agreed that we were together--'Just For Laughs.' "Now, we can make a good life together. We have waited too long, already!"

Marilyn said that, "she no longer had any doubts that we would work everything out and would soon be blissfully together." And she repeated my comment that, "we had waited too long, already. Hurry to me, my darling," she whispered.

Going to Pensacola to be with Marilyn was now my mission, and all that I could think about, but, in reality, I had so many things that I had to accomplish in the next two weeks. My present employer had to be dealt with in a very professional manner, and I approached the company to determine if a transfer to Florida would be a possibility.

I was told that, "I had been an outstanding employee and my loss to the firm would be severely felt. They had future plans in supervision that would now have to be revisited." Then, they said that, "the company did not operate in the State of Florida, but asked if I could work at least one week of notice before leaving the company?"

I assured them that, "this would not be a problem, and I would follow any method they required of me to carry out in preparation for leaving this job, that I have been well trained and loved very much."

They set the conditions and assured me that, "they would be delighted to write a letter of recommendation to any potential employer, that I might reveal to them." And they also, "would give me names of companies in the field, who would be likely to give me the opportunity to apply for an interview."

Finally, they said that, "I would be successful in any thing that I had been trained to do in my present employment."

I was assured that, "my qualifications for sales and sales management were going to make me successful with any company in the Medical Insurance field." "They had sent me through extensive training, which should enable me to move right into a new insurance firm in the State of Florida, but, of course, licensing in that state would be required."

This, I had already anticipated. I felt secure in my experience in my present company, and appreciated, that they were willing to support my move.

They were truly interested in helping me interview with a strong letter of recommendation to companies, I choose to present Resumes to firms in my field in Pensacola, or possibly in the Orlando area, which was a hotbed for the Medical Insurance field in Florida. Marilyn and I would have to talk about whether she wanted to stay in Pensacola, or if she would be OK about a move to a city, which could offer me the best opportunity to provide a better opportunity for my new family. "My new family," I thought.

"Yes, my new family of Marilyn, Jennifer and Matthew." I had to take into consideration Marilyn, and whether she had any strong ties to Pensacola, or possibly she may relish the thought of making a new start in another area, possibly, not even in Florida. I am sure that we needed a little time together to talk about the location for our future life, together.

Marriage was a strong possibility, but I imagined that we needed a little time to make sure that this was going to be right for Marilyn, the children and myself.

Back to Michele, she was a wonderful, sweet girl, and I did not want to hurt her too much with my leaving. Naturally, I could not tell her about Marilyn.

That would be too hurtful. This was the toughest thing that I had to do. I decided to ask her to meet me at a popular restaurant, that we had been to on many occasions. This was the way that I chose to close out our present relationship. After a wonderful dinner we sat and talked. "I told her that there was something I had to tell her, and began by telling her that she was a wonderful girl, and I cared very much for her." Then I lied a little bit by telling her that, "I had a wonderful opportunity for a great move to a new job in Florida and was currently serving a weeks notice to my present company."

I would be in Florida with this new opportunity as soon as I had fulfilled my requirement obligations to my current firm.

I told Michele that, "our relationship had been very special and that I had to break off our relationship." And I continued, "it has nothing to do about you, you are very special. And I wished her a wonderful future. I will remember you, always, but I need to go in another direction that does not involve you."

I took her into my arms and hugged her tightly, holding her for a minute and whispered again that, "it had nothing to do with her, it was me."

Then I walked away, after wishing her a wonderful life!

CHAPTER 23

GOING TO PENSACOLA, Florida to visit Marilyn was going to take a lot of preparation. My present job, now, was to successfully serve the company to my best ability in letting my present clients feel secure that the company would provide the best possible replacement in order to serve these good clients, that I had served so well. I knew that they would be expecting the same quality service that I had been providing for so long. I was not worried about my future.

My qualifications for sales and sales management were assured with the extensive training I had received with my present employer and should enable me to move right into a new medical insurance firm in Florida. I knew that I would have to apply for a license there for Medical Sales or, possibly, Sales Management in that state. I felt secure my experience in my present company would serve me well. They had already agreed to provide what would be an excellent reference, which would assure my acceptance into a very strong relationship with a company, where I could fit in well, with their organization, in or around Orlando or Pensacola, Florida.

I knew that Orlando was a hotbed for the Medical Insurance and Maitland is close by and having a strong reputation in Medical Insurance, as well.

Marilyn's feeling about whether she wanted to stay in the Pensacola area would have to be one consideration and the children, Jennifer and Matthew, would certainly play into the situation. My feeling is that they all might be glad to move to another location, since David was flying out of that area when he had his tragic accident. Cutting tyes with this place may be a southing, to help them forget the past.

The children had to be a stong consideration. Would they accept me into the family? I would have to be assured that they would. If they would accept me, I would certainly accept them and do everything in my power to make myself lovable to them.

As for Marilyn and me, marriage was a strong possibility. I imagine that we will need a little time to make sure that we are doing the right thing. I know that I am serious about this for us, but we need to feel the energy between us.

It had been tough in having to deal with the leaving of the nice Michele, having to be able to explain this sudden change in our relationship and my desire to resign my present job and move to Florida had necessitated that little lie, to avoid hurting her too much. Michele was a very sweet girl and we had had a lot of good times together. Thank God that we had not been sexually involved.

As for my company, I had informed them about my impending move to Florida, knowing that they would make an attempt to keep me here with an offer of increased compensation of commissions, or promotion to Sales Manager.

This would be tempting, but the thought of Marilyn and me was a greater choice for me. So, I thanked them for the confidence in my ability, but that I had already made up my mind and would be leaving for Florida in a little over a week. I was glad to give a week notice, which they accepted. I had agreed to work with them to help fill my position, and promised to work with them in training a replacement which they accepted. I promised to write a letter announcing my resignation to all of my clients, I had brought into the company, and assure them that the company would find a replacement that would serve them as well as I had tried to do for them. In the letter, I would state that I had enjoyed serving them, as well as all of my clients. They had meant so much to me and had been a pleasure to serve. I wished them well in their future.

My present employer had agreed to writing a very positive letter of recommendation to any potential employer, that I might interview with. They assured me that they would be honored to do that and, if I desired, they would supply me with a group of companies in Florida that were in my field of experience.

Their offer included names, locations, contacts, phone numbers and the products provided by those companies.

I gladly accepted their offer and told them how much I had enjoyed working with the firm, and thanked them for giving me the opportunity to have served them and my wonderful clients.

Finally, the extremely hard part had been dealing with Michele.
Not to hurt her any more than I possibly had to. You will recall, my inviting her to that popular restaurant where we had dinner many times before.
After dinner and a glass of wine, I had told her that little lie I had begun by saying "what wonderful times we have had together."
"She was a sweet girl, and that, I now had to go in a new direction, and did not want to hurt her in in any way. This was something that I had to do and would remember her always. Thank you for being a part of my life," I had said to her.

The next week was so involved with my duties in serving my week notice with the firm. It involved writing my letter of resignation from the company. As promised, "I informed my present clients that I had received an offer from a company in Florida, that I could not turn down, and would be leaving my present company with regrets, since they had provided me with wonderful training and experience, which they made available for me." I continued that, "I was positive that the company would provide an experienced agent, who would provide the same good service that I had provided them. I wished them well and thanked them for allowing me to serve them and wished them continued success in the future."
I was completely satisfied with the companies response to my request, and their response in every way to help me make the transition, from me as an employee to the status of my resignation.
Having met with the officers and management groups, I had honored their requests and they had honored mine. They were fully aware of my letter to my clients and had authorized their distribution. I assured them that, "I tried to make the experience a win--win situation for the company as well as myself, saying that I will always remember and appreciate them for being a strong part of what I felt would be a successful career for me."
I continued that, "the company had always been fair to me and that I did consider the company a class act."

CHAPTER 24

I HAD CHECKED OUT of my apartment, serviced and gassed up my Fairlane 500 Ford, and was on my way to my new life. The trip down I-85, to I-77, to Columbia, South Carolina, to I-26, to I-95 through Georgia and to I-10 in Florida, and on to Pensacola. Marilyn had provided detail information of the route to her home in the outskirts. Prior to leaving North Carolina, I had made several stops to purchase gifts for Jennifer and Matthew. I added several cases of that wonderful soft drink, that Salisbury is proud to be the home of, Cheerwine. I feared that I would not be able to find them in Florida. The drinks were for the children and I would tell them about Cheerwine's beginning in the early 1900's. After arriving in Florida, I purchased a dozen long-stemmed roses for Marilyn, the woman that I loved.

Wow! What a reception I received when I drove up to Marilyn's home and rang the door bell. Marilyn opened the door and let out a yell.

"Alvin Knight!" she shouted, and did not shake my extended hand. She flew into my arms and gave me the feeling that she would never let me go.

Then, the children came running to me and I picked them both up and hugged each one at the same time, while telling them that, "I had a present for them in my new red Fairlane 500 Ford, automobile, with a white dome."

They squealed with excitement when I told them that, "I would give them a ride in it, later." We went to the car and I took out their gifts (games and puzzles).

They wanted to go back into the house and start playing with them, immediately.

Marilyn seemed thrilled when I pulled out the fresh, long-stemmed roses and presented them to her. She wanted to display them in a nice container and went into the house. When the children came into the living room, and saw the roses, they both grinned at their mother. It was getting late, and I asked if they had had dinner yet, and they both said in unison, said "No."

So I asked the children, "which restaurant they wanted to go to."
In unison they said, "McDonald's."
I looked at Marilyn and she tilted her pretty head and said, "OK!"

Everyone seemed to enjoy their meal and soon we started back to Marilyn's home. As we arrived, I opened the trunk and told the children that, "I had a treat for them." After we got settled in, I "told them about the treat, Cheerwine is not a wine, it is a soft drink, with a wonderful cherry taste." Marilyn, by this time, had gone to the refrigerator and brought in a tray, where she had placed plenty of ice in each glass. I opened the bottle tops and poured one for each of us, while telling them that, "these drinks of Cheerwine were bottled in my home town of Salisbury, North Carolina."

I went on to say that, "the Cheerwine Bottling Company was started by a family that I know, and it has been in operation there for over fifty years."

This did not seem to impress the children, but Marilyn was certainly very impressed as she was enjoying Cheerwine for the first time. The children did seem to like the taste very much. I told them that, "as far as I knew the Cheerwine was not marketed and available, this far south, but I expected it would be available in years to come."

Soon the children were playing in the play room and Marilyn said that, "she really appreciated the long-stemmed red roses."

"I replied that the beautiful Marilyn deserved anything that I could have ever brought her." Then, I remembered the two bottles of her very favorite red wine and hurried to the car and brought them in and suggested that we toast our being together again.

She just remarked that, "I was so sweet," and took a bottle to the kitchen and returned with fine wine glasses, filled to an appropriate level.

After sipping the wine, Marilyn seemed to want to play with her treat, me! She was acting as if she had all of the prize that she could have hoped for, and just wanted to look at me and be held by me.

I ask my readers, "how could I not love this beautiful creature that seemed to adore me so much?" I began by telling Marilyn that, "she had not changed in the several years, since I first met her there on that beach in Hawaii, and soon sailed home to the mainland."

Marilyn's comment almost made me blush, when she said that, "I had grown better looking since she had suggested that my career should be in Hollywood and I should take acting classes when I returned to the states."

She continued that, "she had remembered that I had an adorable mustache and was delighted that I still had it."

We talked about Honolulu, Hawaii and Wakiki, and the times that we had shared there, I felt that I needed to ask her about David and noticed that her eyes teared a little. "She told me about how life had been after David's death, on a training mission in his Navy plane, when it crashed at sea. She had never been told just how it happened. The Navy had been very thoughtful, just that it was an accident off the Florida Keys. They had been very kind and had helped arrange the funeral service." She seemed to not want to talk about it any further and changed the subject.

She now, "wanted to hear about my life after returning from Hawaii to my home in North Carolina."

I told her that, "my father and mother were well, living there on the farm and enjoying semi-retirement."

She asked, "if there had been a girl in my life?"

I told her, "about my dates with Michel," but assured her by saying, "Marilyn you are the only woman in my life, and I like it that way."

"As for my job, I had become highly qualified as a salesman in the Medical Insurance field and was prepared for a position as sales manager in that area." I told her that, "the company that I resigned from, before coming here, had written a wonderful letter of recommendation, and I planned to begin interviewing for a position in Orlando and Maitland, and perhaps here in Pensacola, if nothing looked promising in Central Florida." By this time it was getting late and she brought the children in to say goodnight and I hugged each one and, told them that it was so good to see them again.

After the children were in bed and we took the last sip of the wine, it became obvious that she wanted to cuddle and be held. She even hinted that, "she wanted more."

I reminded Marilyn that she had told me in Hawaii, on the night I left her, 'this was just for laughs.'

She just giggled and told me frankly and shamelessly that, "she had been sorry that she had previously made that statement, and ever since had been looking forward to see what she had missed out on."

I exclaimed that, "her loyalty to David had made a tremendous impression on me, and made a better man of me." From that point, I told her, "I respected her and the children too much for that to happen this soon, and told her that I now hoped to make her my wife and did not want to cheapen our love at this time."

Marilyn smiled and exclaimed, "wow, the boy that I knew in Hawaii has grown to be quite a strong man, and I love you even more for that." "Thank you for putting me in my place!"

I told her that, "I would need to find a place that I could stay for the present time, and would be going to Orlando on Monday to start my interviewing for suitable employment."

She suggested that, "the Holiday Inn had a good reputation." "You should know that I have an extra bedroom, but for now, the Holiday Inn sounds like a good idea."

"Alvin Knight," she added, "I warn you, I will do everything to make you want me as much as I want you!"

This was music to my ears, so I said, "Marilyn, we are both worth waiting for." "When I have secured a position that I feel I can support this, my family, I will ask for your hand in marriage." Then we will have a life of bliss that we can have for a lifetime. Please respect me for this!

After checking in for two nights. I settled down to review my plans for seeking employment, which I could build upon and provide a good future and income, that could support my new family, in comfort. My resume was solid and the recommendation from my previous employer should give me the opportunity to pick the right employer. My immediate plan was to go to Orlando, secure lodging for the days and pick the best offer, then come home to Pensacola and the Holiday Inn.

I called Marilyn on Sunday morning to ask if she had any plans for the day.

"Please come for lunch, and after a good Florida lunch, then later, we can set down, just get to know one another again and be frank about what we expect of each other in our hopes and plans for the future, hopefully together."

"I told her that my purpose for being there was to set in motion the things that would lead to eternal bliss for our family." There was one thing that I needed to ask of her in planning my employment strategy and location, "are you obligated to stay here in Pensacola? Or, where would you prefer if you had the choice?"

Marilyn answer was what I wanted to hear. She said, "Alvin, where ever you go, I will follow you. I just want to be with you, forever. The children are in school here, and may delay our departure until the summer break, which is coming up soon."

I told Marilyn, "that the children were very much on my mind and their education was a major consideration. I assured her that delaying any move was the thing to do, and would not be a problem."

Arriving about 1:00PM for lunch, gave us a good time to eat and get down to discussions, that were important to me, and I was sure that Marilyn would feel the same way.

When the subject came up, I told her that, "my income, after I got out of the Navy had progressed rapidly, and I had a nice bank account, primarily because I had been thrifty, and had saved most of what I earned. Even tho I was on a commission that depended on a good sales record in my chosen Field of Medical Insurance, I was good in finding needs for insurance and treated my clients with respect and always considered their needs, first and always tried to create value in everything, I tried to do." "It was always the customer first, then company policy and finally, I considered my commissions as well earned. All the while, I was studying to be a sales manager, where I could derive a base income and, also profit from the sales of my agents as they progressed in their production. Training was a very important action designed to train agents what the rules for conduct were, knowledge of the products offered and the customer needs in product and services."

"I told her that I was good in my chosen field and had requested and received a wonderful recommendation from my former employer, who was very sorry to have to receive my resignation."

Marilyn then spoke of, her economic condition and life, first with David and after his death. "David had been a good Navy pilot and had risen to Lieutenant. His salary was not great, as it could have been, if he had been in the civilian market. I am sure that you felt the same way when you were living the life of a sailor. I worked to make income enough for the lifestyle that we enjoyed. His death did provide some insurance but that did not last very long. The good news was that I was a daddy's girl and he had set up an account in my name with a very good investment company. The growth has become very successful and I have never touched the principal, but have often received interest and dividends that supplemented his salary from the Navy. I have held several jobs, both as Secretarial and Administrative Assistant positions. I may be able to assist in some ways in your job search, if you so desire."

"Where ever you decide to settle down will be fine with me and we could sell this house and allow you to keep us comfortable, while you follow our dream and your career takes off."

"That sounds wonderful and gives me great comfort. Tomorrow, I will leave for Orlando and take three or four days there. I do have a favor of you that I would like to ask. In my job search, I will need a location and telephone number for potential employers to leave word as to appointments and questions, that they may want response to. Would this create a problem?"

"Alvin, in my young career, I have had several jobs as a secretary, and Administrative Assistant training, and was a darn good one, too. I will be just delighted to stay here, take care of the children and, when called on, to serve as your Administrative Assistant here at home, while you are away impressing all of those big firms that they must have you in their future growth plans."

CHAPTER 25

MARILYN AND I had spent a wonderful day together, just getting to know more about each other. "I told her that I would be leaving early in the morning for Orlando and would be gone for at least four days."

"I reminded her that I was going to give her address and telephone number, so that I could have a source to receive any communication and phone calls from the firms, that I called on in Orlando and in Maitland."

She reminded me that, "she was now my Administrative Assistant and would give her very best assistance to my search for our future."

On Monday, I took my copies of my resume and cover letter, along with the letter of recommendation that my former employer had so graciously prepared for me, and set out for Orlando. I was not just looking for a job, I was looking for a career. I checked into a nice hotel and, with my information, that I had selected and packaged in a nice portfolio for each stop, the previous night, I determined my first stop, and felt well prepared for the days interviews.

The first interview went very well and I could tell that they knew that I had researched the company and was prepared. I knew the contact person, address, telephone number, economic status of the firm, a list of their Board of Directors, products offered by the company and how, and where they marketed their products.

I always made good eye contact with the interviewer, listened intently to their line of questioning and answered completely their requests for information, When I felt the need to ask questions that were pertinent to the review, I did so in a comfortable and appreciative manner. I did not hesitate to tell them that I was being interviewed by a number of companies in this region and was not expecting an immediate offer from this company, nor was I even prepared to make a commitment at this time.

I then, thanked the interviewer for his time spent with me and left for the next interview that I had previously scheduled.

I had three more stops planned to interview today, and set out for the next one, a slightly smaller company, which was not high on my list, since the reviews I had made on them indicated that it was almost a courtesy call, at least at this time. Anyway, I made sure that I was not closing any doors of possible opportunities, at this time. So the interview went fairly well. Thanking the interviewer, I stoped for lunch, prior to visiting the third company on my well planned day. After a good lunch, I got down to business with number three. Number three was much like the first company and was another good possibility. I repeated the planned process of providing the full portfolio, answering questions that were asked and showed my interest of being considered, yet not prepared to make any commitment, at this time.

Again they appeared interested and I thanked them for allowing me the opportunity to present my qualifications.

I was getting a little tired, but prepared well to close out my last interview for this day. I put my best foot forward and gave them my full attention and showed great interest in their company, as I had planned, and wanted to always present myself well in a business interview. I was somewhat surprised when the interviewer offered to take me to dinner at a nearby restaurant. "I thanked him for the offer, but I had to very graciously decline his offer because of a previous commitment." I had told a little lie. I had no prior commitment, but I did not wish to show any obligation at this time.

The truth was that I wanted to have a light, but quick dinner so that I could get back to the hotel and get my typewriter working in recording my observations of each company, which I had visited today.

They would include the name of the interviewer, company and address.

After recording this information, I was ready to send out a 'Thank You Letter' to each company that I had interviewed with, during the day.

Before I retired for the night, I set up plans to interview at another three promising companies on Tuesday -- locations and routing. Finally,

I decided to call Marilyn to tell her how much I missed her and the children and gave her a brief review of how I thought the day had gone.

Naturally, as you have begun to expect, our talk was a little bit mushy. It contained all of those sweet nothings that two people, who are very much in love, say and do for the one they love. Of course, we have just now gotten together in a very meaningful way. But if you want your happiness to be complete and have a life of pure bliss, you might consider doing this to the one you love on a daily basis. Neither of you should ever get tired of letting your love show through in every opportunity you get.

Well, that is enough for the love lesson for the day from this author. Put it to good use and you will never be disappointed, I promise!

True to my plan, on Wednesday I went to Maitland, Florida, only a few miles north of Orlando. There were a number of companies there, who specialized in the area, which I was greatly familiar and specifically trained in those areas. I visited each company and was well receive, and seemed to have impressed each, greatly with my experience and qualifications.

They were familiar with the company back in North Carolina, which I had recently resigned from.

A familiar question that I was asked, and delighted to respond to, was "why did you decide to leave your last employment?"

My answer was easy. "The woman I love, lives in Florida." "And this is the place that I want to make my home, after we are married." And I hope that we can be married, soon!

Wednesday was a good days work, and I had visited four firms that appeared very promising to my possible future in the Medical Insurance Business, some who had operations in other Southern States.

After returning to the hotel, I recorded all of my notes of the days' interviews, as best that I could remember. Then I could wait no longer and called Marilyn.

Marilyn's voice was so wonderful to hear, and after a lot of sweet talk, which we both loved, "I asked if I had received any messages that I had to follow up on. She had been very thorough as I had found her to be, and she had taken all of the information that I would need in following up with, when I returned again to Orlando and Maitland.

We are a great team!!

Early Thursday, I sent out thank you letters for the interviews, that I had not previously acknowledged.

By noon, I called Marilyn to see if there were any calls that I needed to respond to and found out that it was negative. I told her that, "I had now completed my interviews in Orlando and Maitland, and had decided to check out of the hotel and return home to Pensacola and interview there on Friday." I added, that, "I sure was missing her and the children."

Marilyn responded by saying, "it could not be more than we are missing you, darling," and wished me a safe drive home.

I left Orlando in the early afternoon on Thursday and headed for home, in Pensacola. Upon arriving, I checked back into the Holiday Inn and called Marilyn.

She welcomed me home and asked, "if I could come to dinner?"

I graciously accepted, I was looking forward to some good home cooking.

She said that, "I had received three letters, that I had received today, and was quite sure that they were good news."

I told her that, "I would be there at 6:00PM, and was looking forward to review the mail and getting to know her a little bit better."

In the meantime, I planned my visit to two firms in Pensacola that might be a good fit for me in my job search.

At six, I was at Marilyn's door and Jennifer and Matthew came running. I swept them up and asked what they had been doing since I had last seen them on Sunday.

Jennifer, was all excited about school and said that "she had such a good time at school and had wonderful grades, and would show them to me along with some of her work, later."

Matthew, "told me about his teachers in kindergarten and how much he enjoyed the other children."

Marilyn came out of the kitchen and announced, "that dinner would be ready, soon." Before going back into the kitchen, she planted a quick kiss on my appreciative lips.

After dinner, I offered to help with the dishes and she accepted graciously.

The children had already headed to the playroom to read the children' books that I had brought them from Orlando.

Finally, Marilyn and I were in her office and she offered the mail that had come for me. The excitement mounted for both of us as I cut open the first letter. It was from Central Medical Corporation in Orlando.

I remarked to Marilyn that I had been there on Monday.

The letter was from the Director of Human Resources, thanking me for presenting my Resume and Cover Letter and a very fine recommendation of the company you served, prior to leaving North Carolina. "They very graciously gave you an excellent revue and we have reviewed your written information and your verbal presentation, which has been passed on to this office by the reviewer, along with the recommendation that you have the experience and abilities that our company could profit from, here at Central Medical."

"I am happy to reveal to you that you have the type of experience that may be valuable to our company." "Our Vice President of Human Resources, has already advised us that we would like to personally meet with you in our office at the Corporate Headquarters as listed in this letter on next Monday, June 25th at 10:00AM."

"If this is satisfactory with your schedule, please call me at the following number, 407-279-5000, as soon as possible." "If it is not satisfactory for you to come at that time, or if you are no longer interested in a position with our firm, please call and state that at the time you call."

Respectfully,

J. Madison Greenbrough
Director of Human Resources
Central Medical Corporation
Orlando, Florida.

When I put the letter back into the envelope, Marilyn said, "I am so proud of you, Alvin!"

"I told her that I would like to think about this and see what other offers I might be getting, and added that this was just an offer for a second interview, that may or may not lead to an employment with a suitable position and income, that may or may not be satisfactory to me."

Marilyn said, "Alvin, you are such a smart business man, just like my father was, and I am just so proud of you, my darling!"

I just smiled and said, "let's open the second one."

The second letter was not quite as inspiring as the one from Central Medical, as I discovered after opening it. This one was from Florida Medical Corporation. It said, "Thank you for your excellent interview with us on Tuesday of this week. Your qualifications appear to show that you are overqualified for any opening that we may have at this time, or in the near future. However we do appreciate your resume strength and will surely file it for review in the future for any position that we determine suitable for you, at that time."

"In the meantime, we wish you well in your search for suitable employment in your chosen field."

Sincerely,

B. Buxton Myers
Vice President of Human Resources
Florida Medical Corporation
Orlando, Florida.

Marilyn said, "I am so sorry, Alvin, I hope that you are not hurt by this letter of rejection."

"Hey," I said, "I am not hurt at all, I would not have taken a position that I felt would not lead to the type of opportunity that I felt overqualified for, nor unsuitable for mine, and especially, our future."

The third letter was from Southern Medical and Life Services in the city of Maitland, Florida. I mentioned to Marilyn that, "I had been there on Wednesday and was highly impressed with my reception by that company."

The letter began, Dear Mr. Knight,

I certainly enjoyed meeting you and reviewing your splendid Resume and Cover Letter, and marvelous letter of recommendation from your previous employer. "It appears that the type of services that you have been performing fits into our continued plans to install a new program throughout the region of Southeastern, United States. The program would be administered out of our main office here in Maitland, but would require, possibly initial travel, on numerous occasions to cities in the targeted area." "This program would entail setting up offices in eight to twelve cities of operation, hiring, management to recruit agents and your involvement in group training of agents at each location, You appear to have the drive and ability to get this operation established."

"We would like for you to call as soon as possible after receiving this letter to set up a followup appointment. Our offer will include a company car and all driving expenses, and a salary that we agree upon at your arrival. Naturally, insurance licensing for at least ten states in this region will be necessary and programmed by the Corporation."

Sincerely,

J. Andrew Jackson, President
Southern Medical and Life Services
Maitland, Florida.

"Well, what do you think?" asked Marilyn.

I said that, "I had been deeply impressed by the location and the reception that I had had on Wednesday. But I admitted that I was now completely stunned and excited about this offer. I explained to her that this company had exciting ideas about signing up companies and their employees in an appropriate Credit Union." "We would sign up employees and management with the Credit Union and payroll deduct the plans of savings, and possible loans, desired by the employees we signed up."

"In addition to promoting the Credit Union, our agents would be presenting insurance programs, offered by our company, which are designed to protect those employees and their families in case of sickness, need or the possibility of death." We were, also, "offering a plan that provided savings, built in, that could be taken advantage of, prior to death. We will also be offering disability due to an accident, cancer coverage and intensive care programs."

"Our insurance programs in addition to the Credit Union programs were to be payroll deducted by the businesses and forwarded to the service provider, our companies insurance products sold, or the Credit Union services, offered."

"Our agents call on the companies we enrolled on a fixed schedule and would have access to enroll new employees, who were sent to our agents when they arrived on location."

Marilyn, I continued, "this surely looks like the key that I have been looking for to make it possible for us to be together, always. And I continued, Marilyn, I love you very much, and this makes it possible for me to ask for your hand in marriage." "Darling, Will You Marry Me?"

Marilyn threw her arms around me and jumped into my lap and hugged me so long that I could hardly breathe.

Finally she said, "Alvin Knight, as you know, marriage is not new to me. I loved my first husband, but I never saw in him the strength that I see in you. You have made me the happiest woman in the world. I could never have loved David as much as I love you." "Yes! 'Yes! Yes! I will marry you and be the best wife to you and contribute to your strength."

She continued, "can we set the date, please?"

"Hey!" I said, "we can be engaged for a few more days, but when I sign on the dotted line, we can proudly announce our wedding day."

Another long kiss sealed the deal. And after looking at Jennifer's school work, we tucked the children into bed. Then we just sat and hugged and kissed and held each other in our arms in pure contentment.

I must admit that I had never felt this kind of bliss before in my whole life, and I was warm with a feeling of gladness that finally, I felt truly loved.

I went back to the hotel, showered, and tried to go to sleep. The one letter from Southern Medical had made me so hyper with expectation that I had difficulty in falling asleep. I finally realized, I have more work to do tomorrow. I must go through with my plan to hold two interviews here in Pensacola on Friday, so I willed myself to sleep.

In the morning I held the two interviews here, but could not get very excited by either one. Neither one seemed to be very forward thinking as Southern, in Maitland.

I went into both interviews and gave much information and receiving information in return, but did not expect to be convinced that these companies could possibly compare with the opportunities I saw in Southern at Maitland. As customary, I dashed off a thank you letter to the two interviewers, here in Pensacola, thanking them for the kind interviews, they had given me today. I told them that I was now considering another offer and was no longer available.

By Friday afternoon, I was ready to call Central Medical and verify that, I would attend the interview on Monday the 25th at 10:00AM.

Then, I called Southern Medical and Life Services and was able to get an interview at 2:00PM, that same afternoon.

During that call, Mr. Jackson "told me that Southern Medical was prepared to make me an offer, and asked how I felt about that?"

I told him that, "I was excited about the visions of his company and only had one more interview in Orlando that I felt obligated to attend, on Monday morning." "Then, I would be in his office at 2:00PM, and was looking forward to receiving his offer of our future, together."

Mr. Jackson said, "that they were prepared to make an offer that he did not feel I could refuse." "He suggested, in my planning for the week, I should plan on staying in Maitland for the rest of the week."

I agreed to this, and was ready to spend the weekend with wonderful Marilyn, who, I now considered my driving force.

The rest of the weekend was pure bliss and filled with anticipation of discussions for our future. I spent as much time with Marylyn and the two children as I possibly could. This included attending church services at a local Lutheran Church, which Marilyn recommended. She and the children had attended there frequently, before and after David's death. The church members had given Marilyn and the children a lot of love and compassion during the period after David's passing.

The church was small, but beautiful and the children were looking forward to attending Children Sunday School.

Marilyn and I attended a class for young people and fit nicely into the group, as we were well accepted. Marilyn was delighted to show off the beautiful diamond ring that we had just purchased to seal our engagement.

It was asked to announce to all that, we were engaged and the audience, then applauded and wished us much happiness.

Later, we attended the 11:00AM service and were enthusiastically greeted by members of the congregation and the pastors. I noticed that she made a practice of showing her engagement ring with pride at every opportunity. During the service, she softly whispered into my ear, "that our attending gave her greater comfort for our future together."

After lunch, at a quaint restaurant, I took Marilyn and the children home. I was sorry to tell them that, "I was returning to Orlando on Monday, and may be gone for the whole week, but I hoped to return to them by next weekend." "I told them how much I would miss them, but I would be busy creating my business for our future together."

Later, I returned to the hotel room to do some more research in order to prepare for the two interviews that I had scheduled for tomorrow.

Rising early Monday morning, I checked out of the hotel and headed for Orlando. Traffic was light at that time of day. After arrival, I checked into the same hotel that I had stayed the previous week. I showered from the road trip, dressed and was at Central Medical for my 10:00AM appointment. The very professional and efficient Administrative Assistant greeted me and graciously said that Mr. Greenbrough was expecting me and would be with me shortly. She called to announce that I had arrived and Mr. Greenbrough, Director of Human Resources of Central Medical came out of his office to welcome me. I thanked the Administrative Assistant, and accepted Mr. Greenbrough's extended hand as he invited me into his office. Mr. Greenbrough asked me to make myself comfortable, and told me "that he was about to have a cup of coffee, and asked me if I would join him in a cup." I gladly accepted and asked for a little cream in mine. He ordered black coffee and shortly the assistant arrived with our order and we got down to business.

Mr. Greenbrough, said that "he had thoroughly reviewed my record and was very impressed with my credentials." "He offered that he was able to enter employment with me, at this time, as an agent for the company on a commission basis, with an immediate draw from the company of $2000 a month, as I built up my clients." Naturally, I would also be assisting present clients that would be assigned to me with rights to future commissions from those clients that I generated. He acknowledged that "the company covered the Southern half of Florida. I would be provided an allowance, based on the mileage that I reported."

The company offered Medical, Accidental Coverage, and good cancer care.

"They would arrange for me the licensing procedures to sell, in this state the company's products." "He added that a physical examination would be required and paid for by the company at no cost to me."

Mr. Greenbrough said that, "he was authorized to offer me a contract at this time, if I was ready to accept the position and sign the contract."

I told him that, "the offer was very interesting, but I had another interview scheduled for the afternoon, and was not prepared to make a decision at this time, but would continue to consider it."

Mr. Greenbrough insisted on taking me to lunch in the company canteen, and we could meet some of the company management on the way to lunch.

I knew that my appointment with Southern Medical and Life Services was scheduled at 2:00PM, so I accepted his offer to lunch.

On the way to lunch, I was introduced to the Company President, a very distinguished gentleman, and to the manager that I would be assigned to in the event I accepted their offer of employment. The Manager planned to attend lunch with me and Mr. Greenbrough.

I was greatly impressed with the company's lunch facility and the lunch we were served. I was greatly impressed by all of the class being shown toward me, but I knew that I was looking forward to getting to my 2:00PM meeting at Southern Medical and Life Services. The man who Mr. Greenbrough had introduced me to as my prospective Manager was Mr. Ivan Robertson. I was very complementary to the company and "thanked them for the lunch and interview, and informed them that my decision would be given serious consideration and forth coming by the end of the week."

I returned to the hotel to refresh for the interview at 2:00PM, at Southern Medical. I already knew in my mind that, if things went right at Southern Medical, I had found my future that would make all of my dreams come through.

Returning to Maitland and my appointment with J. Andrew Jackson, at Southern Medical, I was ushered into the office by his assistant.

Mr. Jackson took my extended hand in a firm grasp and shook vigorously, saying that, "he was glad to see me and asked how my week end had gone?"

"Very well!" I said and added, "that I had been pleased to hear from him."

He asked, "if I had any questions about the letter, and had I made a decision over the weekend?"

My reply was that, "I had read the letter in detail and was very excited about the plans to add a division that would concentrate on representing Credit Unions by signing up companies and their employees to be able to access benefits of the Credit Union in providing services that they offer and, at the same time, allow our company to provide insurance products that we can provide on a payroll deduction basis." I continued, that, "given the opportunity, I was looking forward to having a large part in making this happen and providing profits for Southern!"

I quickly added that, "I understand that there would be considerable travel required in making this venture happen and I was looking forward to getting started." I added that, "I had studied all of the tactics of this planned operation by the company and I wanted to be a huge part in making it become a profitable venture."

Mr. Jackson said that, "he was glad to hear that I was ready and eager to help develop the program. We initially plan to begin here in Florida and expand into Georgia, South Carolina, North Carolina, Tennessee, Alabama, Mississippi, Louisiana and Texas. We will begin here, and later we will evaluate the program and the profitability to the company, then we can add other states, perhaps Virginia, Kentucky and Arkansas."

"If you accept this proposal, we are prepared to open an expense account.

Your initial salary will be set at $5,000 per month. Naturally, we will assist in building offices or leasing available offices where we decide to set up offices. We will assist in advertising for District Managers and assist in the recruitment of agents." It will be your responsibility to group train those agents as they are hired."

"Financing is to be provided by the company as we form this new division." "In the beginning I can say that finances will be unlimited as long as we see continuing progress."

"As for you, if you accept, we are prepared to offer a $5,000 per month salary plus expenses." "Rest assured that the bonuses will be quite substantial as the division's income from the venture allows us to provide appropriate bonuses."

"How does that sound to you, Mr. Knight"? "Are you prepared to accept our offer?"

Mr. Jackson, "I gladly accept your offer and cannot wait to begin this venture and the creation of this new and exciting division of Southern Medical and Life Services."

"Thank you, Alvin, I will have our lawyers draw up your contract and the dates of employment." "As of now your salary has began."

"Can you come by tomorrow at 2:00PM to sign the contract?" In the meantime, we will begin the process of your licensing for the sale and management in all areas of our products. "Naturally this will be provided at the companies expense."

"The licensing will be for Medical, Life, Cancer and Accidental Care Services." I believe that Life and Accidental Care Services are new to you, and we will schedule your training and testing in those areas. "We will attempt to transfer your existing licenses if that is possible.

Your official salary will begin with your signing at 2:00PM tomorrow."

"Yes Sir!" I said, "Mr. Jackson, my time is your time, and I will prove to you that you have made a wise choice in choosing me to join into this new venture. Thank you, Sir!"

CHAPTER 26

ON RETURNING TO the hotel, I dashed off any thank you notes to the companies that I had not previously done so.

"I thanked them for giving me the opportunity to interview with them, and told them that I had accepted another offer and wished them well in the future."

As for Central Florida Medical, "I thanked them for providing me an interview and kind offer of employment, but that I had accepted another offer that fitted into my plans for the future." "I told them that the offer from Mr. Greenbrough had been very fair, but my decision had been made." I then wished the company success in the future.

My next action was to call Marilyn, "I give her the news of the great offer from Southern Medical and Life and my acceptance and the very future bonuses was well beyond any anticipations that I might have had."

Marilyn just cooed and said, "Alvin, I am so proud of my successful businessman." "This is far more that either of us anticipated and I am so proud of you. Your happiness in your job is just another thing to make me love you so much more. The money has never been that important to me, and added, When are you coming home?" she asked.

"I told her that the company was setting up the licensing schedule, and I would have to stay all week, adding that my salary and training begins immediately, but I hope to be home for the weekend."

"I miss you terribly and love you so very much." "Please give the children my love." By the way, I sure am looking forward to that biggest kiss ever!"

Marilyn just gave her love and added that, "Alvin, I love you so much for you and your strength in the the accomplishment in securing this new job and the security that it provides for both of our new beginning, together, now and forever."

Wow! The call to Marilyn, and her beautiful response, was so very soothing and I went immediately to sleep.

On Tuesday, I arose from a wonderful nights sleep and began by reviewing all of the information that I had about the life and accident insurance programs that Southern offered here in Florida.

Anyway, I knew that I would be studying and preparing for the licensing for those products. At 2:00 PM, I was back in conference with Mr. Jackson and the attorney. Signing was easy and I was assigned to the licensing division for studies, to be licensed.

I was given all of the information that I needed to prepare for the testing preparation to equipe me with all the information needed to successfully pass the exams and licensing. My office was then assigned by Mr. Jackson. I was immediately impressed by my office arrangement and the beautiful view of the surroundings of Maitland, which I immediately loved. I had loved Salisbury, North Caroling, but this was a tropical paradise. The office was large and had tables that would be my study area.

I was assigned a tutor for my studies. His name was Jonathan, who I immediately liked and knew that we would work well together.

Jonathan took me through all of the information that I would need to successfully prepare for licensing of the products by the State of Florida and the ability to sell and train the agents, who would be employed to promote our products. Jonathan was quick to add "that I was a very good student, he anticipated that my studies, testing process and licensing would take several weeks."

After successfully passing the exams, then I would be in a position of helping approach the Credit Unions with our program to represent the credit unions in installation of the program into the manufacturers and organizations, where we installed the payroll deductions for savings that were set up for the employees. Then, the premiums for insurance products that we sold to them, for protection of their families, would be payroll deducted and forwarded to our company.

For the time being, Southern Medical and Life would be accumulating information needed to approach prospective companies in the area that we choose to implement our program. We have already decided to begin the program in manufacturers and other organizations that had at least fifty employees, and have the expertise to provide programs to implement the necessary payroll deductions, that fit the needs for payroll deduction to the credit unions and insurance premiums to our insurance company.

The weekend was fast approaching and I was told that I should use it for as much study as I possibly could, back home in Pensacola. I was pleased to hear that, and called Marilyn to tell her that, "I would arrive home, late Friday night." It was now late Thursday, and "told Marilyn how much I had been missing her, and said that I would be studying a lot during the weekend, and asked her to please understand." I knew she was looking forward to hearing about all the interesting things that were happening for me.

She said that, "she had some more news for me, and hoped that I would understand that she meant well and had not made a devious plot." "She had prepared a bed room for me to stay at her house and would not hear of me going back to my former hotel room in Pensacola." She said that the bedroom was equipped with a large desk, and space for study. She admitted that she was expecting a lot of affection but respected and appreciated the fact that we would honor our agreement of no sex prior to marriage, but please, let's plan our marriage as soon as possible, and before you became too involved in your new job, which was likely to involve a great deal of travel.

I want some of your time, prior to that.

I laughed at her mentioning no sex until marriage and "told her that all I expected at this time was a lot of good snuggling and tons of kisses, that I love so much." "Good night, sweet love! I will see you late Friday."

On Friday night, I arrived at Marilyn's home. The children were already in bed, so I could not give them the gifts that I had purchased for them. Marilyn and I snuggled for a long time and I did get that fabulous kiss that she had promised. I must admit that we were both so hot that we had to be strong to carryout out our agreement of 'no sex prior to marriage.'

Finally I told her that. "I should get some sleep, and prepare for a lot of study on Saturday and Sunday, which she understood." After this,

I held her so close that I could feel her pulse beats, that were much too stimulating. Another quick kiss followed and we went to our separate beds.

Marilyn knew that a lot of study would be going on in my preparation for returning to Maitland on Monday, and she understood.

She hoped that I would get around to planning our marriage while I was here during this weekend.

Morning came with beautiful Florida sunshine and the bluish-green skies. I smelled her wonderful breakfast preparations and that fabulous smell of coffee perking. The children had not yet awakened, and Marilyn and I had an opportunity to talk about our future. I began by, "suggesting we plan our wedding to be held in that little Lutheran Church where we had been attending. I hoped that the pastor could perform the ceremony and, I would like to invite my parents, if they could attend. It was early July, and I suggested the ceremony could be performed on Saturday, August 2nd, 1960." "I told her that I would like for the children to be involved in the ceremony. I would ask someone from my office, yet to be appointed, to be my best man."

Marilyn had waited patiently, but she was so excited that she could hardly stand it any longer. She simply blurted out "Yes!, Yes! Yes!"

and came into my arms. "I am the happiest girl in the world!!" She shouted out, that she would like to invite her parents from Wisconsin.

Of course, I agreed and, "insisted that she invite the members of that little church, make all of the announcements and arrange for the marriage license and any medical exams."

Marilyn said that, "we were a good team and I am so much in love with my strong and wonderful husband and lover, to be."

I smiled, and taking her unto my arms, kissed her long and slurping, and promised her more, later. Then, I said, "enough of this wonderful passion.

I have a lot of studying to do."

Marilyn just smiled coyly and slowly ran her fingers over my lips before I retreated to my room and office to study for my up-coming exam for the various licenses that I would be required to take and successfully pass.

The licensing for life insurance was new to me and I would really have to put more study into that area. I was already feeling very comfortable in the other products, we were offering in the State of Florida. I stopped just long enough for a wonderful creation of sandwiches and sweetened tea and milk, that Marilyn had prepared, along with some exotic nuts. After lunch I gave the children the gifts that I had purchased for them in Maitland. As usual they shrieked with joy and headed to the playroom to enjoy their gifts.

I thought it might be a good time to bring out the diamond wedding ring that I had purchased in Orland during the week.

I told her that the ring was returnable if she did not like it.

The diamond that had cost me an arm and a leg glistened as she took it out of the box and asked me to, "please place it onto her finger."

"I told her that I could not do this until the wedding, my reason for showing it at this time was to allow her to approve it, only if she could wear it with pride at our wedding day."

"Forgive me, my darling, and yes! I love it so much."

"I told her that I would study in the morning during their trip to Sunday School, but I would be joining her for the service prior to eleven."

Sunday morning, I got up early, had breakfast and studied until Marilyn and the children dressed for church and got ready to leave.

I told them that, "I would have loved to go with them, but had to study some more, in order to pass the exams required by my new company and the State of Florida." "I then assured them that I would be sure to attend the 11:00AM service, and join them there."

I was beginning to feel very comfortable with my understanding of the laws governing life insurance in the State of Florida, and the products offered by Southern Medical and Life. My thanks were due to the intense information that the Legal Department had provided me in preparation for my taking of the exam. They had been thorough in providing the likely questions, to be asked, and the answer to those likely questions.

Dressing and preparing for the 11:00AM church services, I departed and arrived a little before the Sunday School Class, that Marilyn was attended, let out. She rushed to me and, "introduced me to the class as the real reason that she was smiling today. She said, I want you to meet the wonderful man that I am now engaged to marry on Saturday the 2nd of August, here in the Sanctuary." And she continued, "you are all invited to the service and the refreshments in the church Fellowship Hall, that follows."

How could I not love this woman who continuously shows her love for me so sweetly? And would you not know it, when we arrived at the 11:00AM services, she asked the pastor, "if we could stand as a family to greet the church members when they arrived?"

After church we drove home and had a light lunch and I settled in to study the rest of the afternoon and evening. When the children were ready to go to bed, Marilyn and I tucked them in, and gave each a good kiss. I had taken a great deal of interest in the children and they were responding in such a wonderful manner to me as their new father to be.

I told her that, "I really cared for the children and after the wedding, if it was alright with her, I would love to adopt them as my own."

She answered that, "she thought that David would have wanted it to be that way." She said that, "David was a career Naval Flier, and as much as he loved the children, he had had to spend much of their lives away on assignments. And she continued, I think that is why they are so responsive to you, Alvin. I know that is one of the reasons that I need you so much, darling."

I kissed her and "apologized that I must retire early and would leave quite early for my trip to Maitland."

On Monday morning, I left to beat the heavy morning traffic and arrived in time to report to my assigned license trainer.

We went over my studies for the exams. He finally said, "that I was ready."

"I had done a great job with my studies and the company was requesting the State Licensing Examiners to receive me this week."

Before the end of the week, I had successfully passed all the licenses for products offered by my company, and "was told the licenses would be processed and forwarded to my company, prior to the end of the week."

Upon assurance that I was now licensed for the products that were provided by the company, Mr. Jackson and I began making the plans to begin contact with the manufacturing companies. Before that, we must receive permission to represent the credit union and to receive the applications we would be required to process in representing the credit unions to plant management, prior to setting up a schedule to visit the plant, and make contact with the employees with the programs, offered by the credit unions and our companies insurance products. These were to be payroll deducted and paid to the credit union or to our company, for products purchased.

The products provided by the credit unions normally, consisted of savings plans and approved loans. The insurance plans we planned to provide were health and accident plans including cancer coverage as well as combined life insurance that provided life protection, and potential growth life savings, through a dividend plan.

Next, we had to plan for setting up District Offices, scattered throughout the state, advertise for District Managers to represent the company in each district office, and advertise for insurance agents who would work out of each District Office. Of course each agent will have to be licensed by the State of Florida for each product we provide.

It was now Thursday morning and Mr. Jackson, "announced that a meeting would be held in his conference room for all managers that had been appointed for this new division for the company." "Each manager would be required to be in his office by 10:00AM, sharp."

At 10:00AM, Mr. Jackson began the meeting by "announcing the reason for the meeting was to make sure that all managers had been introduced to Mr. Alvin Knight. He asked me to, please stand and be recognized as the new head of the division and responsible for establishing this very important new division to begin a relationship with credit unions throughout the state."

Mr. Jackson, also said, "that the relationship with credit unions would allow our company to offer payroll deductions that the credit union offered, such as savings plans and possible employee loans." The plan was devised to allow our company, Southern Medical and Life Services, to offer our products through payroll deduction to employees of companies that we contract with to participate in this program, with our company and the credit unions.

Mr. Jackson, asked me "to divulge the plan of action that he and I had decided upon just this morning."

I began by telling the assembled managers that, "I had reviewed the record of accomplishments of each, and realized that we were all committed to the growth of Southern, and I was very pleased with each of them in this venture of growing Southern and individual growth that each would gain in the progress of this venture in personal, and financial gain."

"Each of you will have a big part in making this new division a tremendous success." Now I would divulge the formation of this project and how we plan to progress. "We will begin by setting up District Offices in the following cities of this state, Tampa, Fort Lauderdale, Miami, Daytona Beach, Jacksonville, Orlando, Gainesville and Tallahassee. We will hire District Managers through advertising as well as agents. Naturally, each District Manager, as well as agents will have to be trained and licensed according to Florida Licensing Regulations. The District Office will be located, furnished and leased. It is hoped that we can find suitable locations that represent our company well, and hire experienced management and agents, if possible. We plan to advertise in reputable television, newspapers and radio, in order to get the most experienced salespeople and administrative personnel that we can get. We will each have our respective responsibilities in this operation and must get onto this beginning tomorrow. I am calling a meeting in this assembly office for tomorrow at 10:00AM. We will all need to help Property Managers, Advertising, Human Resources, Training and Licensing to get this ball rolling as quickly as we possibly can. Product Design must start immediately in order to get them accepted by the Insurance Commissioner of the State of Florida."

Before the meeting was adjourned, "I cautioned all that we must keep all of this private, so as to not alert other insurance companies of our plan to combine credit unions and manufacturing to promote our products." "'We do not want to have any competition from any other insurance companies. We want to sew up the credit unions and the manufacturing plants and any other types of business employees that we may seek to participate in our project for this new concept. Before adjourning, ladies and gentlemen, let me assure that this project can provide a great service to businesses and their employees, the credit unions that we contract with, our company, and, finally, we as individuals. Let us all get rich together! Thank you all for attending, and I will see you all at 10:00AM, tomorrow."

Mr. Jackson, "asked me to meet with him in his office as soon as possible."

"I told him that I was free and would accompany him to his office."

When we arrived in Mr. Jackson's office, he put his left hand on my shoulder grasped my right hand in a firm handshake and exclaimed, "Alvin Knight, you are DAMN GOOD." "After I observed you in that meeting, your monthly salary will be increased to $10,000 per month, we will have your contract changed to that effect. May I please sit in on your meeting, tomorrow?"

"Thank you, Sir, I would be proud to have you," I said.

Well, I floated out of there and returned to my office to call some of the Department Managers, that I deemed must begin immediate action to procure the action that, we must take before finding property to lease suitable office space, Advertising and Human Relations to work together in pursuit of Office Managers, Agents and Office Administration, Licensing to rev up preparations to license those Managers and Agents, Marketing to prepare new products that we wanted to seek approval from the Insurance Commissioner in Florida, and Legal, that may be involved in every area of our projects and training, that must work with all of the agents in group training sessions.

"I reminded each manager that we must work in great haste to get this entire project up and running as quickly as possible in order to keep competition from rushing in, as we wanted no competition in this entire venture." "We wanted it all in order to raise our company and ourselves to greater heights."

Calling another meeting for Friday morning at 10:00AM, to see if there was a full understanding about the duties of each manager in the division, I felt that we all had to be on the right track to have our division and our goals moving in the right direction. "I called Mr. Jackson to ask him if he would open the meeting, even tho I had called for the meeting."

Mr. Jackson said, "that he would be delighted and thanked me for the offer."

Then, he offered that, "he was so pleased that he had brought me on board and had all the confidence in my being able to lead this division, and venture, in this exciting new era of the company. He continued that he had already seen that I had the fire to light this company to the desired heights that they had envisioned."

I took this time to tell him, "that I was going to be wed in Pensacola on the 2nd of August and wanted everything to be settled, and up and running smoothly, at that time." "I told him that I was being very presumptuous, but I was new to Florida and wondered if he would be my 'Best Man' at my wedding?"

He laughed and said that, "sense you are aiding this company in becoming even stronger, I would be proud to get your marriage off to the strong one, that I know it will be."

Sir, "you have honored me very highly and I will see you tomorrow morning at 10:00AM."

At the Division Meeting on Friday morning, Mr. Jackson, "welcomed the Department Managers and thanked them for taking the time out of their busy day to give us news of your progress in implementing this new venture."

"He then told the group that our Division Leader, Mr. Alvin Knight had just informed him of his pending marriage to a wonderful lady in Pensacola on the 2nd of August. Now gentlemen and ladies, we must continue to do all things that we can do to get the program going smoothly so that he can enjoy that wonderful moment. Are you with me? Let's hear it for Mr. Knight!"

A round of congratulations met me as I took the floor to address the group.

"Thank you Mr. Jackson and to all of you ladies and gentlemen." "You have been asked to do a super job in getting this Division active. Now I would like to add that my marriage was not going to take away of my zeal in accomplishing all of the goals, we have set to accomplish in getting running. So, I will call on each Department Manager to tell us about their progress to this point. Property, what progress have you made in securing locations for our operations in the cities that we have chosen?"

"We have been in touch with leading business property real estate companies in the selected cities and they have scoured their inventory in order to fill our advertised needs." "Tampa, Orlando, Jacksonville and Miami have sent us specifics on several desirable locations that we may pursue leasing in the next week. I will keep you advised of our progress on those and other cities when we finish reviewing the other cities."

Very good, now Advertising and Human Relations, "what is your progress on securing District Managers, Agents and office staff."

"The Advertising is complete and the replies are piling into the Human Relations Department at this time, reported the HR Manager."

"We will be doing due diligence in finding the best possible applicants for each area office. We should begin interviewing as early as Monday."

"Thank you, we certainly appreciate your thorough selection of highly qualified personnel to man those offices and sales areas." "Licensing and Training, you will be expected to become fully involved as HR begins to hire the personnel that we need at each location." Product Development, "your job is to quickly add to our product line new policies for Cancer and Accident coverage and the New Combined Life policies that are designed to offer life benefits that offer savings accumulation. These will have to be approved by the Florida Insurance Commissioner and may take a little more time. So I hope you are on top of that."

"We are, sir. As you know, this is a very complicated process and we are proceeding with caution in order to be right the first time," said the Product Manager.

"Marketing, we will be busy next week in contacting Credit Unions and the businesses that we hope to contract with, to provide Credit Union services and payroll deduction for the insurance products that we offer."

Marketing replied, that "they were fully staffed and ready for our marching orders."

Very well, I said. "I am very encouraged with the progress that you have reported." "I am calling another meeting, in this assembly room, for next Monday at 10:00AM. Are there any questions"? And hearing none, announced that this meeting is adjourned.

CHAPTER 27

WHAT A WEEK we had been through at Southern, and after planning for our visits to Credit Unions and businesses that we had selected to persue in the next week, it was now time to call Marilyn of my plans to arrive back home.

"I told her that I was leaving shortly and should arrive before Jennifer and Matthew went to bed. I told her that I sure had missed them and was looking forward to tucking them into bed. And, as for you, I have several pieces of good news. The business planning was going very well and Mr. Jackson, the President of the company, had consented to be my best man for the wedding. And last of all, me, Mr. $5,000 a month, had been increased to $10,000 per month, How does sound to you?"

"Well, Mr. $10,000 per month, I have been used to getting by on $2,000 per month and you will be rewarded when you get home." "How does that sound to you, good sir?"

"Careful now, you living doll. I cannot wait for you to fall into my arms."

"So, I will hurry home to you! I love you!"

The road home was easy as I contemplated seeing the family after a long but successful week at work. The miles passed by quickly and I reached home by 8:00PM and Marilyn greeted me, with a big hug, and a kiss as the children came, so excited to see me, and I stooped and cradled them both in my arms and told them, "how much I had missed them." "I told them that I had a surprise for them in the trunk of the car and would give them the surprise in the morning."

I had purchased a small bike for Jennifer and a training bike for Matthew, and would put them together in the morning, before they awakened.

The children had had their supper and were preparing for bed, so Marilyn and I tucked them in and kissed them a happy good night.

Marilyn had saved supper for she and I, and we quickly downed the fantastic meal and opened the red wine that I had picked up on the way home.

Marilyn smiled and coyly, as we enjoyed our meal and said, "well, what did you bring me?" I could not pass up the moment and turned the phonograph on and selected some slow music, and held her closely, as we danced around the room.

What bliss is this, to be returning to this wonderful woman that I loved so much, and feeling that this was all I wanted at this romantic moment. It seemed that we danced for hours. As you will recall, I had taken dancing lessons while I was in the Navy in Hawaii.

I had wasted so much of my 'BEFORE,' previous life in a way with other women, who could not hold a candle to this precious woman lying in my arms. That life with Loraine and some of the others that I had known was the 'BEFORE.' My life with wonderful Marilyn, who is the 'AFTER,' in my life.

Now, I recall that Marilyn had told me earlier that the boy that she had met in Hawaii had grown up to be a strong man.

Later, we just sat and cuddled, and we both knew that was all that was going to happen, even though our need for breaking our vow of no sex prior to marriage, was driving us wild. It did give me some comfort, just knowing that we were so perfect for each other and our marriage was going to be so secure, and we loved each other so much that it was going to be a respectful, and loving experience, that we would both continue to do and say the things that made us so loving to each other; plus, I adored the children, just as much as if they were my own. I did plan on adopting them if Marilyn agreed to it, which I think she has.

I mentioned that, "I now felt that I knew that money was not really a big thing to her, especially since money had been always available through her fathers early contribution." "It was now comforting that my income for that period would place us able to live a very comfortable life, for the things we needed and the future education of the children." I must admit that when she first wrote to me, my first thought was, I could not have expected to provide for them, as I now can, and very comfortably. I now felt quite secure in our future.

Bringing up my new raise to $10,000 a month, made me feel secure that I could now comfortably provide for my family.

Marilyn just cooed and then, she said the following:

"Oh! Alvin, you just continue to amaze me. Honey, I am yours, forever!"

Marilyn said that, "she had made the scheduling with the pastor and for the chapel, where we would be married on Saturday, the 2nd at 2:00PM, and the reception, right after the service. She had made arrangements for some of the congregation to serve finger food and punch. She was still looking for the right wedding dress and has selected a Made of Honor, and was planning some way to include the children into the service. Jennifer would make a good flower girl and Matthew could possibly be the ring bearer. If that would be alright with me, she could continue with that plan." And, by the way, she was terribly impressed with me for having secured the President of Southern Medical and Life services as my 'Best Man.' She said that her father would be terribly impressed by that action.

And she added that alone should cement my career with Southern Medical and Life Services.

I told her that, "I was going to show how much they needed me, and would continue to pave the way for even added responsibility."

Marilyn continued to show "she was working hard on our marriage service and had purchased lovely and innovative invitations for the special people that we had already discussed, including her parents and my parents, and they were ready to mail." "She had made arrangements with a very talented florist and had made a contract with a popular photographer here in Pensacola."

I told Marilyn that, "she had done a terrific job on our marriage plans and if given a chance, I sure would be glad to hire her for her administrative know how."

She just smiled and "told me that just thinking of spending a short honeymoon with me was what had kept her going so far."

A long kiss was enough for me and I slept well on Friday night in the very anticipation that I had two more days with she and the children. Eager to give the children the gifts of the two bikes, when they awakened, I got up early and had them assembled by the time they came rushing out of the house to greet me, when I was reentering from my chore of pleasure. I can still remember my first bike and how happy I was to go on my first ride.

When Marilyn came out to see what was going on, "she shouted with pleasure."

It was their first bikes and "she gave her quick approval."

I told them that, "after their breakfast, I would help them get on the bikes and hold them as they made their first ride."

Since Matthew was two years younger than Jennifer, his bike was small and easier to ride. The training wheels helped, we sure did not want him to fall.

After breakfast we all went outside to the bikes and I assisted Jennifer on her bike and held her up until, she learned to turn the peddles, in order to carry her foreward. I showed her how to stop by stopping the peddles and putting on the brakes.

She had a few rough starts but quickly she had it down pat. Earlier she had tilted over and almost fell, but I put her back on and she soon had it down pat.

In the meantime, Marilyn was working with Matthew and he quickly was able to master the peddles and the training wheels, giving him comfort that he would not fall. He learned that starting out slowly, helped to master the peddles.

Soon, I put the bombshell on them when, "I said let's go spend the day at the beach." They clapped and said, "mommy, can we go?"

Marilyn said, "sure, I think that would be a lot of fun. Go in and get your swim suits on and your beach balls and sand shovels." "I will pack us a lunch basket and off we will go to the beach."

Suddenly, I realized that I had lost touch with my swim suit, and excused myself to take off to the sporting goods store to secure a new one. I hoped that Marilyn would not notice that I had lost the tan that I had exhibited there in Waikiki when I first met her in Hawaii. I still had a good firm body that I was proud of and I suspected that she would have that beautiful body that I had admired when I first met her. I made sure that the swimsuit would flatter my body and headed home with it. When I pulled up, they were ready to go and I donned my suit and we were off to the beach for the day.

I can honestly say that I cannot remember a day when I enjoyed being with the family any more than I enjoyed this day. Just being together and sharing in the laughter, brought so much contentment in sharing this beautiful sunny day.

Marilyn and I went into the water with them and "told them that they could only go out waist deep, and to watch out for the waves that might engulf them." Of course, Marilyn and I were keeping a watchful eye out for them and they were very disciplined and did not cause us any anxiety. After a brief swim, they were ready to play in the sand with their shovels and make sand castles, which they seemed to do very well. I watched over them very well and soon, Marilyn called us all to have lunch, which was delicious as usual.

After lunch the children went back to their sand castle building and Marilyn just brought out our sand blankets to watch over them, as they played. I could not help but to think about my hopes to adopt them and later to go to work about having our own. As we lay there on the blankets, Marilyn finally caught me admiring her beautiful and curvaceous body.

She had to know what I was thinking, and whispered in a sultry voice. "You are not so bad yourself, buster!"

We just sat thinking how wonderful our loving life was going to be, but we knew that it was worth waiting for.

In the early afternoon, the children seemed to tire and came back to us with their shovels and, "asked us to see what they had built."

Marilyn and I were quite proud of their achievement and told them so.

"Why don't we leave them for others to see their beauty and head home for an early dinner?" "I have something else that I want to tell you about, after dinner."

After dinner, I had preapproved with Marilyn, and "told the children that we are going to the park, after church and lunch tomorrow." "But first, you must get to your studdies that are due on Monday."

We fear that you will be too tired after our stay in the park to study tomorrow afternoon, so you must get to your studies now.

The children screamed with pleasure about going to the park tomorrow and were off to their school studies before going to bed.

On Sunday morning we had another of Marilyn's wonderful Florida breakfast meals of pancakes and syrup, followed by exotic fruits that are well liked by all.

Everyone showered and put on their favorite Sunday best and we headed to Sunday School, deposited the children in their respective class, and then we went to our young couples class. We were welcomed royally as usual and there was a lot of chatter about the upcoming wedding, which, by now seemed to be known by everyone in the class. Marilyn had recruited some of the ladies to serve during the reception. The members seemed so happy for us, because we had shown them that we were head over heels in love, and showed it in so many ways in the things we did and said, especially the way we touched and smiled at one another.

As usual we were greeted as we entered the Sanctuary after picking up the children at their classrooms. As usual, we got the impression that the message from the pastor was being spoken directly to us and our family relations. We did seem to be greeted by almost everyone as we exited the church. The children seemed to be spoiled by all of the attention that they received. We found out that the word had been passed around the church that the children had just been given new bikes and were very excited about them.

After a quick stop at one of the fast food favorites, we went home to change into comfortable clothing for the park. I asked the children, "if they would like to take their bikes and get in some more training, that would give them more confidence in riding their new bikes?" As usual they just squealed their pleasure, as excitedly as always. Marilyn and I got so much pleasure in seeing them hop on their bikes as if they had been riding them always. To be on the safe side, we stayed very close to them and never let them get out of out sight. The park had facilities for catering to birds and small animals that inhabited this area, and we were able to purchase some favorite foods, of the birds and animals, that the children enjoyed feeding to them. They were finally showing that their riding the bikes and romping around was beginning to tire them out. So we loaded up and went home in anticipation that Marilyn would come up with another one of her Sunday night special dinners. They put their bikes up, cleaned up a little, and Marilyn was ready for us to come to the dinner table.

As usual, Marilyn did not disappoint us as we enjoyed a wonderful meal of Jambalaya, mixed vegetables and fruits. Then the children were playfully excused after dinner, and I helped Marilyn clean up the dishes, with a few sweet touches in between. This was one of my happier times of just being near her.

After finishing the dishes we told the children that, "we were sure that they had had a busy and tiring, fun day." "And to get ready for bed, and ready for class tomorrow."

After we tucked them into bed, I told them that, "I would return to work in the morning, but was looking forward to seeing them next weekend."
"I told them, that while I was gone, they could not take the bikes out into the street and into traffic. If they did ride, they should only ride around in the drive way and the back yard."
Marilyn agreed, and "told them that if they were found not obeying, they would lose riding privileges for the entire week."
The children assured us that, "they would obey our instructions, because they knew that we were looking out for their safety."
We hugged them and I "told them that, I had had a wonderful weekend with them."
They were pleasantly exhausted and were quickly asleep.
How much I loved these children. They were so special. But, right now, I just wanted some snuggle time with this wonderful and precious woman that meant so much to me. We both knew that we needed some special time to ourselves. As it turned out, we were so much in need of love, we were not to be disappointed. It went something like this--snuggle, hug and kiss until we had our fill of each other. We knew more than that would not happen now, because we were so much in love with one another.We must have snoozed for a while and I later awoke, and thought I might be in heaven, since my life had changed so much.
Marilyn had seemed to read my thoughts and said, "Alvin, darling I believe you are a poet and it makes me so glad to accept you and your love without any effort, and with great gladness."
"Then you do agree that we should go to bed -- separately and rest our bodies for more promises, later." Yes, things have changed for the better and drastically in a few short months. The study and all of the planning and testing is suddenly gone, and tomorrow, we would begin to see a return for our close planning of the last several weeks. And to top it off, I was beginning to realize the total joy of my new found family.

CHAPTER 28

MONDAY MORNING EARLY, I was on my way to Maitland and the miles quickly flew by, as I easily completed the trip, and went quickly to my office, knowing that I would have a big and successful week, and I was ready to exploit it successfully.

The meeting was scheduled for 10:00AM and I had, as a courtesy, asked Mr. Jackson, "if he would like to attend the meeting?"

"I would not miss the meeting," he said. "I am looking forward to see what progress has been made."

After welcoming the Managers in the Division to the meeting, I said that I would like to make my own report to the group and tell them of the upcoming meetings scheduled with Credit Unions, that were planned for the week. "The first was today at 4:00PM at Orlando Regional Credit Union. The next one was on Tuesday at 1:00PM with Premier Credit Union in Miami, followed by Florida First in Ft. Lauderdale at 4:00PM. Our group takes a day off on Wednesday to catch up with happenings in your department, but we will be in Tallahassee with 1st Choice Credit Union at 10:00AM on Thursday, and then to Gainesville at 2:00PM with Members Credit Union. Members has locations in Tampa and Jacksonville and we hope that one location will suffice for the other."

"We can plan for 10:00AM at Tampa on Friday, and if Jacksonville is necessary, we can schedule that next Monday at 10:00AM, and Daytona Beach at 2:00PM."

"I realize that this is an aggressive schedule, but we must make sacrifices in order to meet our goals." "We are receiving schedules of possible meetings with the manufacturing, and other types of organizations, that we wish to visit in order to promote the opportunities of their attaining contracts with the Credit Unions in their area."

"All of you will not be involved in these visits. I will definitely need the Marketing Manager and their best product specialist, along with the Legal Specialist to handle any contractual commitments that we perform." "We may require others, but they will receive scheduling notices, if they are required to accompany our deligation. Our group will travel together in the company car, unless other arrangements are requested, prior to our departure."

"Thank you, ladies and gentleman for your patience." "Now I would like a review of the progress of the other departments." 'Let's start with Property."

"Mr. Knight, as far as property is concerned, we have now received the specifications from all of the business real estate agencies in each city that we had inquired about locations, that might be available and possible leasing arrangements." "Our staff and Legal are now going over the information and we expect to move on any that we feel are the right opportunities in each city, where we feel that we have the right opportunity to close on, as soon as possible. Naturally, there will be requirements for convenience in location and adaptability for our working personnel."

"Thank you Mr. Adams for your good report." "Let us know if there is any assistance that we can help with."

"Now, Mr. Johnson, how are things going with our advertisements in our search for District Managers?"

"Mr. Knight, we have now received resumes from fifteen applicants, all together, they represent most of the areas that we have advertised for as of today. Currently, Human Relations are going through the process of doing due diligence on all of them to determine experience, qualification and whether they will represent our company and agents, in the professional manner, as we do expect. Naturally, licensing and honesty has to be given special concern." "As for possible agents to man the districts, we have received at least sixty, and again, they represent a vast area and experience, some with no experience and others that are currently licensed in many of the products that we would potentially be offering in our division."

"Thank you Mr. Johnson." "We do appreciate the thoroughness in your report." "Mr. Hudson of Human Relations, do you have anything that you would like to add to Mr. Johnson's report?"

"Not at this time, sir, we are currently somewhat over loaded and we are trying to work through it all."

"Thank you Mr. Hudson." "Mr. King of licensing and Mr. Warren of Product Development, I suppose your departments are awaiting the hiring and the new products we will be offering, but do you have any information for us at this time?"

Mr. Warren, "confirmed that his department had submitted information to The Florida Commissioners Office for their review of the products we had planned to sell, and were awaiting their conformation."

Mr. King said that, "they would be requesting testing and licensing from the state, as the personnel are hired by Human Resources."

"Thank you all for your reports."

Finally, I asked Mr. Jackson for any comments or questions, prior to closing the meeting.

"Yes, all of you gentlemen and ladies are making our company proud.

The professionalism that you are exhibiting, in getting this project off the ground, is amazing. My personal appreciation goes out to all of you."

"We certainly have a lot of can do people in this new division."

"Well done to you all, keep up the good work and we will all grow personally, and financially, as Southern Medical grows," said Mr. Jackson in closing.

"Thank you Mr. Jackson, for your kind comments." "I would like to speak with Mr. Summers of Marketing, Mr. Ray Hudson of Legal, and Miss Marion of Payroll before you leave. This meeting is adjourned." I said.

After the meeting, I met with Mr. Summers, Mr. Ray Hudson and Miss Marion from Payroll. "I asked them to gather anything they would possibly need in meeting Orlando Regional Credit Union, as we ask them to allow us to recruit companies, and work out a contractural relationship, in which we offer services of savings and other services, provided by the Credit Union, through a payroll deduction, as we provide service to all employees."

I also, asked Mr. Summers "to pick out his very best insurance products specialist, who, first of all, knew the products backward and forward, and who had the potential to be the best sales person that we have, to successfully help us sell the opportunity to the Credit Union as a win - win situation for the businesses, employees and the Credit Union." I then, "asked them to meet me at my company car at 2:30PM, in front of the home office, and we would head for Orlando and Orlando Regional Credit Union and our 4:00PM meeting. And, then to plan on meeting me in front of the main office, again on Tuesday at 10:00AM, for our trip to our 1:00PM meeting at Miami, and back to Fort Lauderdale at 4:00PM. I reminded them that we would travel again on Thursday and Friday."

"Thanking them for putting up with some overtime due to our schedule for these meeting in distant cities." "I assured them that we would try to get this job done, and would see that they would be compensated with some time off, as soon as we get the program rolling, and the sales people could take up most of this travel, after that."

I had an early lunch in order to get that out of the way and went over the information that I had secured on Orlando Regional Credit Union. I saw no information that they had ever used a service like this, we would be presenting this afternoon. I suspected that our proposal could potentially double their cashflow position, depending on how many companies and number of employees we were able to bring for them to serve. I had taken the liberty to review the names of their officers, their Board of Directors and other company statements, that Mr. Ray Hudson of legal had previously passed on to me. It was obvious to me from these reports, that we needed them to help us grow and show how, we could help them grow, making a win-win situation for both of us.

After arranging a suitable company car, where we five could be comfortable as we drove to Orlando, some ten miles away, I parked in front of the main office and waited for my traveling associates to appear. I had no doubt that they had done their homework, as I had prepared myself. I especially looked forward to meeting the product specialist that Mr. Summers, of Marketing, would be bringing.

My traveling companions came out to me and, of course I knew the others and Mr. Summers introduce the product specialist to all of us, as Mr. Jonathan Bixby.

Mr. Bixby was a nice looking young man, well dressed and made a very professional impression. Our entire crew seemed to immediately know that we had a winner in Mr. Bixby.

I had prepared a two page cheat sheet on Orlando Regional Credit Union and provided a copy for each of our crew to look over in preparation of making our first sale and bring a big credit union into our joint operation. As I had said before, we had to show them what we could bring to the table for Orlando Regional and, at the same time, explain what we hoped to accomplish by our relationship with them and the businesses that we planned to bring to them. Each of us would have their part in convincing Orlando Regional that they should participate in this new venture with Southern Medical and Life Services.

Our people will introduce themselves and their positions of responsibilities at Southern Medical and Life, when we were ushered into Regional's Board Room to meet Mr. Smith, the President, and his entourage of the group that we had requested to assemble to hear our presentation.

I had requested, at least access to their Product Manager, Receiving Manager of Payments Receivable, to take deposits that came from the businesses, that would be sending payroll deductions for savings plans that Regional sponsored and any loan arrangements that they might provide to the businesses' employees and, finally, Legal, capable of any contractual agreements that we may reach between the three parties.

As we were ushered into the meeting at 4:00PM, Mr. Smith graciously greeted us and introduced us to his managers, who had assembled. I made a mental note of the individuals and their position of responsibility, they were Mr. Grimes of Receivables, Ms. Ledger of Legal and Mr. Terry of Products.

"I introduced myself as Mr. Knight, the Division Manager of this new division, now formed to bring the relationship of payroll deduction of employee savings from employees of area businesses to the Credit Union and solid loan relationships, at the Credit Unions discretion, and perhaps other products that the Credit Union might choose to provide."
"Our company would have the opportunity to provide our insurance products, such as insurance to cover life, cancer and intensive care, accidental and disability, etc."

"Naturally we would have the opportunity to visit the manufacturing and other types of businesses that had enough employees to qualify for this service."

"As new employees are hired, we would have the opportunity to provide these opportunities of services to them, as well. We would go into the plants on a schedule that was mutually convenient, to all concerned."

"The Credit Union would be responsible for providing applications for its products and our company would provide applications and insurance policies for the products that we offer. Naturally, we are just a vehicle to bring the three firms together in these transactions." 'The Legal Departments would make sure that the Credit Union is responsible for its operations and Southern would be responsible for our operations. Neither would be responsible for the other's operations."

"Our company will employ only agents that are licensed by the State of Florida." "Your responsibilities only cover your own activities as you handle receivables of payroll deducted funds, sent to you by those businesses."

"This meeting was called to offer an opportunity for Regional to be able to offer products to dozens of businesses and thousands of employees of those businesses." 'I will close my presentation with our estimate that our company, as well as Regional, may well double its operation and cash flow through an alliance."

"We are available to answer any questions, and have a free flow of ideas between our groups. This is all that I have at this time, Mr. Smith."

"I now ask if any of my group has anything to add to my report? If so, I would welcome you to present that at this time."

Seeing no hands, Mr. Smith, "do you have any questions?"

Mr. Smith spoke to our group with the comment that he, personally was impressed by my comment that you could envision a potential doubling of our company and doubling of our cash flow. "How could we turn down such an intriguing possibility? Up to this point, our business has been built on small companies with maybe ten employees to sign with our company on a payroll deduction basis, and we had to accumulate a lot of them to build our business. Your plan is for your company to furnish the acquisition of the companies and the servicing of the employees in order to bring the business to us through payroll deduction." "I have to agree with you, Mr.Knight, that would be a true win-win situation for both of us."

"I would like for our representatives to retire to my office for a brief discussion of your kind offer in this manner." "Please wait for us in this room, for perhaps thirty minutes, and we may be able to give you an answer at that time. Please excuse us ladies and gentlemen," Mr. Smith finished.

The regional group went into Mr. Smith's office and we had some time to evaluate our situation. "Mr Summers spoke up that it appeared that I had scored a home run with my presentation."

Mr. Ray Hudson confirmed that, "he was ready to begin negotiating the legal aspects of contracting, if Regional's acceptance came at this time."

We all felt very positive that we would secure our first Credit Union! In only fifteen minutes the Regional group returned, and Mr. Smith said that, "we have a deal and that, our Ms.Ledger and your Mr. Ray Hudson would go into Ms. Ledger's office and draw up the legal documents to start the process at this time." "As for the rest of us, shall we proceed to our cafeteria for a light dinner."

Dinner with our new partners was a good time to get acquainted and await the two legal departments to come up with the completed documents.

Shortly, we were called to return to the meeting room as the initial contract was now ready for signing. This was accomplished and we were back at the Home Office by 6:00PM to give Mr. Andrew Jackson the good news that we now have an initial contract signed and our first Credit Union--Orlando Regional Credit Union."

Mr. Jackson congratulated us and was happy to know that we were going on a trip to Miami and Ft. Lauderdale, tomorrow afternoon.

Knowing that we were headed for the long trip to Miami, "I suggested that we call it a day and meet here at 8:00AM, and we would be off to Miami and Premier at 1:00PM, and Florida First Credit Union at 4:00PM in Ft. Lauderdale."

I went back to the hotel and went immediately to sleep for the early arrival at the office at 8:00AM.

Back at the office, I awaited the arrival of the other traveling companions.

All of them quickly arrived and we set out for Miami. On the way we talked about how our meeting with Regional, in Orland, had gone. They said that it was a 'nobrainer.' "I suggested that I wanted to make each, a part of the presentation and would introduce each one of them and their position with Southern and, then ask them to present a brief description of how their department would be involved in carrying out our activities, to bring the large businesses and their employees to Premier on a payroll deduction of funds for savings as well as other services that Premier might offer to them, and their employees." I did say that, "I would give a short description of what we would do in creating this three way arrangement of recruiting the firms and their employees and servicing the accounts that would bring business to Premier through payroll deduction."

Since the product specialist had not had any advanced meetings on what we were offering to the employees of the companies, that we recruited, "I quickly went through the new products that he would be offering to the employees, especially the new combined Life Plan that led to a combination of life and accumulations of growth in savings, as well as the Cancer Plan and the Accidental Plan, to provide for expenses during his or her recovery."

Naturally, "Mr. Summers of Marketing would explain how our agents would service the employees by setting up the savings plans that would be payroll deducted and sent to the Credit Union and the agents selling the insurance policies to the employees, and initiating a payroll deduction for the premiums to be sent to our company, for products purchased."

"Legal would handle the contracts and Payroll would handle the payroll deduction responsibilities."

We arrived in Miami in plenty of time for our 1:00PM meeting with the President of Premier, Mr. Avero. I made the introductions and briefly described how we were desiring to contract with the credit union in order to contract with larger manufacturing or businesses that had twenty five to hundreds of employees in order to enroll employees in the credit unions savings plans, through payment by payroll deduction. "We do the contracting, the servicing of the employees, and the credit union gets the assigned savings or any other product they offered." "I will use the win-win idea of growth to both our company, the business, their employees and the credit union."

I am pleased to say that, "we contracted both Premier in Miami and, also Florida First in Ft. Lauderdale, as Mr. Ray Hudson did his thing and secured the initial contracting."

We were a very tired, but happy crew, and stopped to have dinner prior to driving back to Maitland and the office. As we drove, "I told them that they had been responsible in getting our division off to a great start, and suggested a late arrival at work on Wednesday with no meeting, but that we would start out to Gainesville to arrive at 10:00AM, and go to Tallahassee at 3:00PM on Thursday." On Wednesday I had telephone conversations with Mrs. Gail Hudson, of Human Resources, to see how the search for District Managers was going.

"She confirmed that they had settled on District Managers for Tampa, Miami, Ft. Lauderdale, Orlando, Gainesville, Tallahassee and Jacksonville."

"They had interviewed with several possibilities for Daytona Beach, but had not made a decision at this time."

"I asked if we had made any progress on possible agents for our cities where we would be operating"? And she replied that, "they had about eighty current applicants with various experience. Many of them were already licensed in most of the products that we were planning on selling." She also said, "we could already move on at least thirty of them, who could start work as early as next week, on those products that they were licensed to sell. The licensing for the rest may take another week."

"I thanked Mrs. Hudson for her report, and told her what an important part that she and her department were performing."

Pleased with the way the program was turning out, I knew that our next venture was to start bringing the businesses, that we had promised to the Credit Unions.

"Next, I called Mr. Summers of Marketing and reminded him of our trips to Galveston at 10:00AM on Thursday, and Tallahassee at 3:00PM."

I told him that, "I knew that I was pushing him to the limites, but we must get ready to start calling on the manufacturers and other organizations that we had already agreed, would be our best prospects to contract with, to bring our marketing program, to supply funds from their employees to the Credit Union, while creating sales of our insurance policies for our agents and the company, while we provided needed insurance services to those same employees and their families."

With that in mind, "I asked if he and our product specialist, Mr. Bixby could begin calling on those companies, that we had targeted in the area in and around Orlando on Monday"? "I reminded him that we had already received examples of the required applications from Orlando Regional and our companies application materials that we could show, as necessary, the items that we would be offering to the employees of the targeted companies, which we had previously decided upon."

"I suggested that we call on Florida Steel and Sheeting at 9:00AM, Southern Power at 11:00AM, have lunch and hit Colonial Trucking at1:00PM."

"We could finish up at 3:00PM with Florida Machinery. I reminded him that we would not be able to work with servicing their employees until we sell ownership and high officials on the desirability to provide these services to their employees."

"It should be an easy sell to the management, since we will show it as a benefit for their employees, that does not cost the company anything except their labor while our agents enroll them in the Credit Union's savings plans, and possibly applying for possible loans that the Credit Union may provide."

"These enrollments by our agents will take little time and hopefully, provide our agents with sales, which benefit our company by building our sales."

"Well, we would start visiting the companies around Orlando on Monday, but first, we still had Credit Unions that we needed to bring into the fold, so we would be going to Gainesville at 10:00AM on Thursday and finish at Tallahassee at 3:00PM."

On Thursday, we arrived in Gainesville at the Members Credit Union.

Our crew was the same that had been successful in securing the other Credit Unions earlier in the week. We met with Mrs. Bentley and her team of management, and as usual, it was a slam dunk. They had signed on the dotted line, and we had a quick lunch and were headed to Tallahassee, arriving before 3:00PM for our meeting with Mr. Burton and his team of management. Again we spun our story and they proved to be ready to sign by 4:00PM, and we were headed back to Maitland and the home office.

On the way home, we celebrated the fact that we had secured five Credit Unions in the brief span of only four days: Orlando Regional, in

Orlando, Premier in Miami, Florida First in Ft. Lauderdale, Members in Gainesville and First Choice in Tallahassee.

We still had to schedule and visit Tampa, Jacksonville and Daytona Beach, next week. In the meantime, part of our crew would begin calling on businesses that we had selected for Monday and schedule others throughout the week.

"I told the group that they had performed outstandingly, and that I knew the President, Mr. Andrew Jackson, would be so proud of all of them. And, I told them they were a big part of creating the New Southern Medical and Life Services out of their former company." I questioned them "if they knew what potential changes this might have in their future income. I guessed that it would be substantial. With this encouragement, I suggested that we visit Jacksonville and Daytona Beach tomorrow and schedule Tampa for sometime later in next week. We could visit Jacksonville at 11:00AM and Daytona Beach on the way home by 2:00PM." All agreed to this plan.

On Friday, prior to our departing for Jacksonville, I made a quick call to Mr. Jackson's office and he answered the phone. I gave him the good news that "we had signed with five Credit Unions and were leaving for Jacksonville and Daytona Beach shortly."

Mr Jackson, "shouted out his pleasure and said that all of our crew had earned a promotion!" And, he assured me "he would approach the Board and that he would begin to implement this immediately. You all have my deep gratitude for how hard you all have worked to make this division a success. I and the Board Of Directors, are so amazed and so thankful for what you are doing for Southern."

Our regular Credit Union organizing group left right away to arrive in Jacksonville by 11:00AM. When we arrived, Mr. Johnson was waiting with his management crew and, after our presentation, "he exclaimed that this was a concept that he had been waiting for, and quickly had a brief meeting with his group and they provided selling points for promoting the Credit Union and signed quickly." Returning toward Maitland, we met the same reception at Daytona Beach with Ms.Spangler, and her management group. As she was signing, she exclaimed, "why has no one thought of this type of program before?" Our group just smiled in approval for her appreciation of what we were now going to be doing for her Credit Union, the businesses that we would enroll, and our company.

By the time we got back to the office, most of the employees had left for the weekend. I checked out of the hotel and called Marilyn to tell her that "we had had a very successful week at Southern Medical and Life Services and I was coming home to be with my honey."

She said that, "her thoughts would be with me every mile of the way."

We had a lot to talk about, when I arrived. Hopefully, it would be all good."

"I said for her, to save some real time for smooching and snuggling, and I was on my way."

"Just come home safely, my darling," she said.

The miles from Maitland to Pensacola melted away quickly and all I could think about was taking sweet, sweet, Marilyn into my arms, when I arrived home. I could never even think about another woman when I knew that I had Marilyn waiting for me at home.

Suddenly I realized that I had not had time to buy a gift for the children.

Guess they will just have to take me, I thought. And I knew that that was all that Marilyn wanted, me! Our wedding on August 2nd was only two weeks away.

And, I could not help but think of all the mistakes that I had made with many cheap women in the past, my 'Before'--this was the 'After,' and I have saved a lot of loving for this wonderful Marilyn. Thank you God, for bringing this precious woman into my life, to save me from my past!

CHAPTER 29

FINALLY, THE LIGHTS of Pensacola came into view and, soon I was entering the open door to one of God's most beautiful creatures, sweet Marilyn, and I knew just as soon as I took her into my arms, she felt just the same about me. We made no chatter, we just knew that nothing else mattered at this beautiful time.

This is what love is all about, sweet contentment. We did not have to say or do anything. This was our opportunity to feel undivided love, love, peace.

In the quietness, I felt her pulsing body pleading against me.

Take me now it was saying! I only whispered, "it will only be two more weeks, my darling, and we will be wed." "This has been nearly two years in the awaiting, surely we can wait now."

She just gave a sexual bump against me and said, "you, my darling, are worth waiting for."

By the way, "have you had anything for dinner?"

"No!" I said, "I have not had supper, but all I want is to hold and kiss that pretty face."

"Silly, you, come into my dining room and I will get out the best diner you have had." And pulled a beautiful steak, that she had prepared, and was now warming. She produced tasty, large grapes and orange juice and the steak was one of the tastiest, I can recall having.

I just grinned at her and said, "I believe we will have many of these in the future." "I suspect we are about to have another raise."

"Oh! Mr. Businessman, what have you done now?"

"Well, we contracted with seven Credit Unions to bring businesses and their employees opportunity to save with the Credit Unions and buy the products from our company." "We approached seven and contracted with all seven. The President of our company, my Best Man in our wedding, is seeing dollars coming to our company as well as ourselves. By the way, how are the children?"

"They are great and went to bed early, in hopes of seeing you tomorrow.

They had a good week in school and you should have seen them on their bikes."

"They now get on them and ride without effort or fear of falling. And, they drive with safety in mind. You may not know it, but you have won their little hearts, forever."

"I am sure that you realize that that was not my intent, I am very pleased to hear you say that." "I just remember how I felt about my first bike when I was a kid."

It was just about like the proud moment when you first got your drivers license and mastered the driving of that car."

"Well, what about you?" "What have you been up to, Marilyn?"

"The wedding plans have all been made and all is set with the preacher and the helpers, during our reception, after the wedding. All of the invitations have gone out and we are getting a lot of answers like, this is wonderful, and we will be there. My parents will be here and your parents have said how thrilled they are for us, and will be here. The flowers will be there and the photographer is so excited for us and cannot wait to view and photograph the event." "Matthew is all excited about his duties as the ring bearer and Jennifer can hardly wait to be the flower girl. I have applied for the wedding license which will require a blood test at our convenience. We are the talk of the neighborhood, the Sunday School Class and the church. Literally everyone is so happy for us. I suspect that they think and feel that we are ready for the good things to happen in our life, which we deserve to happen to us."

"We are both worth their hopes for us, and I feel that we are preparing for a great life together, now and forever," I said. And took her into my arms again and held her tight, raining sweet kisses on her wonderful throat, cheek and lips. As for me, I said, "this is the 'Before' and 'After' in my life.

I love you Marilyn, and you are my After."

"Now, one more kiss and we must both get our rest. I must tell you though, I am so proud of what you have accomplished for our wedding plans." "That last kiss, before we both go to bed, just yielded the promises that we would soon lead to our honeymoon, after we are wed."

We were so much into the wonders that we should expect, after that special day of August 2nd 1960. We were now just excited about what would happen in so many ways after that date. We simply knew that we, each, would make it work. Of course, marriage is such a commitment between two people that have had a lifetime of different experiences, hope fullness, and possible disappointments. But, we were now ready to make a total commitment to each other. We had vowed that we were ready to make and have our lives totally heaven on earth.

Saturday began with my spending as much time with the children as they wanted. We played in the yard and I was amazed that they had made so much progress in their bike-riding skills. After they had their fill of the bikes, we joined Marilyn in the house, and they all brought me up to date on what had transpired during the week, back here at home. I was especially interested in the schoolwork that Jennifer and Matthew had been accomplishing. I, then, told them that, "they were two very sharp kids, and it was such a pleasure to see how they were progressing, not only in their schoolwork, but as in every aspect of their lives." I was so proud of them, and hugged each one of them to Marilyn's delight.

Later, when we were alone, she kisses me and "whispered that she was so proud of me for the way I had accepted the children and had shown such fatherly interest in them." She, then, said, "you are going to be a great father to the children, a wonderful husband and leader of our family and a fantastic lover to me." She then came into my arms and laid the best kiss ever on my opened lips, while inserting her tongue into my mouth and ran it around so softly and excitedly.

I pulled away and said softly, "how much do you think that a man can take, you seductress?" "We will continue this after our marriage, for which I can hardly await."

She laughed and said, "you haven't seen all of me yet, lover boy!"

"Hmmm"--I exclaimed, and hugged her again.

Marilyn said, "she was going to prepare for me, and the children, the best lunch, ever. "Give me thirty minutes and meet us at the dining room table," she added.

She was right. It was London broil, new potatoes, an exotic salad, hot biscuits smeared with butter, and desert of vanilla ice cream, with a topping of chocolate syrup. We really chowed down. I believe she was attempting to show me what a wonderful life, with her, that I could be expecting.

After the children had had their fill, they asked to be excused for play on the swings in the back yard.

I asked, "if I could help with the dishes?"

And Marilyn said, "sure, that is always a treat to me, just being with you."

After checking on the children, who, were having a great time at play, in the back yard, she returned to do some household choirs.

I had a little time to myself to go over my schedule for the following week. I decided that it was going to be a busy one, but a highly productive one, for the future of of my position at Southern Medical and Life Services.

Later, in the afternoon, I had researched the local movie schedule to see what was showing, and selected one, which I thought the children would enjoy.

Marilyn said, "this was a lovely way to spend the rest of the afternoon," and the children were very excited when we shared the idea with them.

After a short cleanup and change from their play, we were off to the theater. We stopped in the lobby and loaded up with popcorn and a soft drink.

We entered as the feature was about to start. Naturally, the children were very animated and eyes glued to the screen, they seemed to be lost into the movie.

This allowed Marilyn and me to sit silently and just enjoyed the light touching, that we enjoyed so much. After the feature movie, we stayed for the cartoon that followed. The children just watched, seemingly spellbound.

As we left the theater and realizing it was dinnertime, "I suggested that we give Marilyn a break from the kitchen and head to McDonald's for dinner."

Marilyn gave me an appreciative smile, and we drove to McDonald's.

Everyone got to select their choice and we dinned happily. The children may have overloaded on the onion rings and the french fries, but Marilyn just seemed to shrug it off, since they did not get to do this very often.

On the way home, "I suggested that we go to the park, after church, and a lite lunch." Naturally, we would get into clothes suitable for the romp in the park.

I felt that this would give the family a good chance to continue to bind for the future. We all enjoyed the romp in the park and were tired and ready for some rest.

After all of this excitement, the children went quietly to bed and were immediately asleep.

Marilyn and I were glad to have some quiet time as we snuggled together in quiet contentment as we watched the television features, and later, the evening news.

We both knew that I would be on the road to Maitland, early Monday morning, and we got the most out of just being together.

As sleep began to overtake us, Marilyn checked the children, and weary, I headed to my room, set the alarm for 5:30 AM, and was soon asleep.

5:30 AM came very soon and I had a quiet breakfast and drove to work in Maitland. Upon arrival, I called Mr. Summers and "reminded him of our schedule for calling on businesses all over the state, this week. I told him that we would work together today, but for the rest of the week, we would divide up the rest of the state and get as many of the companies, that we were targeting." Also, we start preparing our agents to call on the companies as soon as the companies were signed up. The companies were advised to prepare employee schedules to review assigned products available by our company and the credit unions. By this time, the District Offices were established in all seven cities, agents had been trained and licenses secured for the products, that they would be offering to businesses, as soon as we contracted with them to have employees ready to be brought in to a meeting with the agents, to make their presentation. Mr. Summers and I, had agreed that, "our agents should be prepared to make a good presentation. However, we would not allow high pressure to be applied. We were merely offering to give good, friendly service, which we knew would create greater demand for our products on future service dates."

As we began in Orlando today, we had procured another company car. This was a requirement for our operation for the rest of the week. My team would consist of Miss Marion from Payroll, Mr. Jonathan Bixby as product specialist and myself. Mr. Summers, of Marketing, would lead the other team and he would bring two new assistants along, Mr. Jamison (another product specialist) and Miss Mary Spires, who was second in command in payroll.

Before the day was up, my team had signed up Coca Cola, Simmons Tooling, Good man Manufacturing, Metronic PI, Central Florida Press and Pepsi Co.

Mr. Summers and his crew had been equally successful and had signed up Poly Two, Cyber Coders, Bimbo Bakeries, Coleman Aerospace and Sebastion Peach Growers.

Totally exhausted, we met back at the home office and made our plans for the rest of the week.

We agreed that Mr. Summers and his group would cover Ft. Lauderdale, on Tuesday. My group would go to Miami. Naturally, both groups would have to get an early start, because of the distance covered. We arrived and began to enroll companies that we were assigned to.

In Miami, my team signed PMG, Florida Viconic, Old Castle Envelopes, Covant Energy Group, Cyber Coders, Diedre Morris Corp, Inline Plastics, Economy Linen and Service, G & K Service Center, Randstand and SVR Micronics.

In Ft. Lauderdale, Mr, Summers and team signed Vital Pharmaceutical, Inc, Bosch, D C Waters, Dayton-Ranger, East Coast Electronics, Powers Diaper Services, National Beverage Corp and Wishbone Safetronics.

And, again we traveled home, tired but very contented that our work had accomplished so very much today. Tomorrow, Wednesday, we will head for Tampa and Mr. Summers and his group will head to Gainesville.

I called Mr. Summers, "to suggest that we stop and have dinner on our way back to Maitland." "He suggested a nice restaurant outside of Ft. Lauderdale."

And, "I announced that the tab would be on me for the entire group." After he had confided to me of the tremendous success that his group had had in Ft. Lauderdale, I said, that they had earned a good meal.

We met at Marconi Steak and Ale, and had a fabulous meal and gloried in our successful day. I told them, "how proud Mr. Jackson was going to be when I reported to him in the morning." We were on our way home and Mr. Summers told his group that, "they were headed to Gainesville on Wednesday." "I revealed our trip to Tampa, and that we would leave at 8:00AM." I am sure that both crews slept well, as I did.

The alarm went off at 6:30 AM, and after a quick breakfast, I arrived at the office. We turned southwest and arrived in Tampa at 9:30AM. Our day was full as we arrived at National Starch and were successful in getting a signed contract, and were off to ALCO for another signing. This was followed by Mecca Farm, Thomas Farm, Georgia Pacific, Textile Factors, Ciba-Gigy, Herculese Powder, Anchor Hocking, Indigo Producers and Phosphorus Deposits.

We were on our way home by 4:00PM and arrived by 6:00PM. I called Mr. Summers to see how they did and found out that they had signed PMG, Phillips, Temp Frame, Adecca Engineering, Berringer Archery, Boltz Bottling and Paradowski Beverages.

On Thursday, our group was headed to Tallahassee, and Mr. Summers went to Jacksonville. His group left at 8:30AM, but our group was on the road at 8:00AM due to the distance.

Again, we had a very successful day at Tallahassee, signing Leon County, Florida Central University, City of Tallahassee, PMG, Old Dominion Carriers, Enterprise Florida, Enterprise Auto Rentals, Northern Florida Tree Products and Florida Steel. We were extremely tired with the long trip of nearly 200 miles.

I told my group, "to sleep in and report for work at 10:00AM and catch up with things in their office, that had accumulated since their long week on the road." "I deeply thanked them for their contribution to this successful venture in establishing this, next to final step in establishing our division, as the new darling of Southern Medical and Life Services." This was now the beginning of agents servicing the businesses, that we had just signed in our relationship with the Credit Unions.

Before I left the office, I called Mr. Summers to inquire about his day in the City of Jacksonville. He told me, "it had been very successful, to the extent that his group may have to go back to pick up some more locations Friday, or possibly Monday."

"He reported completing Acosta Marketing, BAE Systems, Black Publishing Company, City of Jacksonville, Remington Co, Crowley Maritime, Duval County Schools, Ring Power and May Clinic. He said that, there were seven companies, that they could not get to today."

"I congratulated him and his crew for the job well done, and to take Friday off, so that his crew could catch up with work, that they had piling up in their office."

I personally was looking forward to making my report of attaining contracts with eighty one companies, signed up for all of our seven credit unions, at this time.

All properties had been installed in the locations that we had contracted for and the staffs were now in place; the agents were trained and licenses had been completed.

All would begin scheduling for the service agents to begin servicing those eighty one companies by early next week, and I was now ready to be married in Pensacola next Saturday, a week, on August 2nd.

When I met with Mr. Andrew Jackson on Friday morning, I gave him this report. He jumped up and came around his desk to grab and shake my hand. Alvin, he said, "you have only been with our company for eight months, and you are about to double our company in several more months, as this production begins to mount. What possibly could we do to deserve your outstanding work performance? Well, first I am going to be proudly, your best man on August 2nd."

"You are going to take a week off to be with your new family. And then we will chart your next move. Is that clear?"

"Yes sir, thank you very much." "You make me so very proud. I believe we are just getting started!"

Then, Mr. Jackson said, "I can't wait to report to the Board of Directors, what you have accomplished."

CHAPTER 30

THE NEXT TWO weeks were filled with making sure that everything, that needed to be done at Southern was set into motion, running smoothly and accomplishing our goal to see our goal of having every District Office set up and being productive; the sales staff scheduled to make their contacts with the companies that had signed contracts with Southern Medical and Life Services and the Credit Unions in the respected Districts, savings, and other services being directed to the Credit Union and insurance products payments being payroll deducted, and submitted to Southern in a timely fashion.

Most of all, we wanted a smooth transaction of all activity that provided value in each transaction, that was made by the sales force to all involved--happy employees, who felt that they were getting value for their payroll deducted funds. Our goal was employers continuing to feel that their employees were receiving quality service, and was an advantage to the employer at little cost for providing this service; and the Credit Unions were receiving the payroll deductions and applying them in a way that was beneficial to all concerned; our sales agents receiving commissions for their work in making contact with the employees, and promoting the Credit Unions services. Finally, Southern receiving premiums for insurance sold and issued to the buyers of our products. Most of all, our sales agents must never give the impression that they were applying pressure to those companies'

employees in any manner. Also, when the insurance policies were delivered, we wanted to be assured that the employees received their policy with the feeling that they had made a good decision, when making the original purchase. It was known by all at our firm, that an unhappy insurance purchaser was going to result in a lapsed policy. This would cost the employee the premiums lost, when they discontinued payments, causing the policy to lapse. Our company would lose the cost of issuing the insurance policy, and our sales agents would lose the commissions, which they had anticipated receiving.

As Director of the Division, I made sure that ever District Manager, continually stressed the value of sales agents making sure that every sale, that they made, resulted in a happy employee, feeling that they had received a product that was going to provide value to them and family, in the long run.

I personally visited each Division Office in this week and met with sales agents and the District Manager, to stress this very point that a happy purchaser led to continued premiums coming in and continuation of commissions to the sales agents. At each Division Office, every meeting that I held began with a festive meal, which I previously had arranged to be catered, and was indeed a festive event. The meeting was to be informative, but most of all, we were trying to create the feeling of a team effort, that each person there was a big part of the team. At each meeting, I was accompanied by a Product Specialist, who was able to give sales tips and sales methods. Each meeting was to provide opportunities for sales agents to ask questions, that we provided answers, promptly and accurately.

We made sure that each meeting was designed to create the feeling that we were a team and all in this, together. We promised to do everything that we could do to make each sales agent a success, both emotionally and financially.

The meetings went well and began in the Orlando District Office on Monday afternoon. I have scheduled Miami and Ft. Lauderdale for Tuesday.

On Wednesday, I will be in Tampa and Gainesville. Thursday, I will be in Jacksonville, and Daytona Beach. And, Tallahassee is scheduled for Friday at lunch and, finally, I will be headed home to my beautiful new family for the week end.

Well, you know what happens next week, but first I will be meeting with each department head on Monday, and will make sure that everything has been taken care of by Tuesday and Wednesday. On Thursday, I will be heading to Tallahassee for a lunch meeting at the District Office there, and on to Pensacola for a very important meeting with the beautiful Marilyn, to make sure that all is setup for the Friday party at the Marriott.

President Jackson has told me, that "he and Mrs. Jackson are taking an early flight Friday and are looking forward to the events of that day and evening.

He is especially looking forward to meeting Marilyn and both of our parents."

"Mr. Jackson is most excited about being my best man on Saturday, the 2nd of August, coming up nest week."

He said that "everyone back at the Home Office was excited for our wedding, and that he had thought about my offer to return from Nassau on Wednesday from our honeymoon." "For the record, and due to the accomplishments of my hard work over the last two weeks, he was ordering me to take the week whole week off, and arranging our honeymoon as we choose, and return to work on Monday, August 11th."

I thanked him "and assured him, we would put the week to good advantage!"

He acknowledged that, "he was sure we would," as he smiled and gave me a sly wink.

The luncheon meeting, on Thursday at Tallahassee, went well and I really enjoyed being with that whole team. Since I was headed home to Pensacola after the meeting, I had not brought along a product specialist and found that I was able to handle the product line, and any resulting questions from the sales staff, on my own. The meeting was verry positive and I felt secure that this office would be performing, very successfully.

Soon, I would be headed home to plan for the last week of my busy life as a bachelor. I was really looking forward to having my father and mother as well as Marilyn's father and mother at the wedding. I have heard how successful her father, Alan Fitzgerald, had become and how beautiful and articulate her mother, Susanne must be. Marilyn had expressed her excitement in meeting my parents, Laurence and Marianne Knight.

When I finally arrived home, Marilyn showed me all of the acceptances to her invitations, to the Friday night party at the Marriott and the wedding on Saturday. I was pleased to find out that the Summers, Larry and Claudette, had accepted invitations to the party and the wedding. They would be flying up on the same plane as Andrew and Shirley Jackson. No problem, I had reserved a block of rooms at the Marriott and could accommodate many others, who may wish to attend. Marilyn and I certainly plan to make our wonderful event a happy one, for all of our guests.

We already knew that Marilyn, the children, Jennifer and Matthew and myself were looking forward to the events.

The weekend flew by, and the excitement grew and grew. Sunday's church attendees greeted us with smiles and cheers from all who greeted us. Lunch at a nice restaurant saved Marilyn from having any chores, and Marilyn had the opportunity to double check all of the exciting things that were going to happen next weekend.

I could feel the closeness that Marilyn and I were sensing about all that was going to be happening. I know that I could not keep my hands off her, and her flirting was so beautiful to me that we were so right, for what was about to be happening to us, in so many ways. We just knew that this was going to be happiness ever after.

It was now Sunday, July 25, 1960, and Marilyn and I were going over all of the details of the wedding events, to make sure every possibility had been covered. This event had to be perfect as our future was anticipated to be.

Marilyn and I had had our physical, required by state law, and received a glowing report. We had met with the pastor of the church and assured him of our perfect love for each other, and my assurance that I loved the children and hoped to adopt them as soon as possible, after our marriage. After the meeting with him, he confirmed that he and the congregation had seen the love that we had for each other, and all had told him that this was going to be one sweet life together, for us and the children. The marriage license had been issued and he had reviewed it, as in perfect order. We revealed the details of the service in detail, first with the party at the Marriott on Friday evening.

Paster assured us that, he and his wife would be in attendance. He was pleased to hear that the children were serving in their respective duties, Jennifer as flower girl and Matthew as ring bearer. He was looking forward to meeting her parents, the Fitzgeralds, and my parents, the Knights.

I informed him the name of my best man, Mr. Jackson, from my firm, and Marilyn's brides maid, Sabrina Breedlove.

Marilyn confirmed that Sabrina Breedlove, had volunteered to keep the children while we were on our honeymoon. Sabrina and her husband, Bob, had children of their own, and Marilyn had previously kept their children on several occasions, while the Breedloves were away on those occasions.

We discussed the details of the reception, after the service, which had previously been approved to be held in the events room of the church. The members had been invited to the reception, and refreshments would be served.

We were making a special donation to the church to show our appreciation for those who served, from the church.

This concluded our meeting with the pastor and he told us that he was greatly impressed with the planning that we had made and wished us well in our upcoming marriage.

At home, we continued our coverage of details. Her parents, the Fitzgeralds, were flying in late Thursday. My family, the Knights, were, also, flying in on Thursday. I hoped to meet them at the airport. However, Marilyn planned to meet both parties, in case I was detained at my meeting in Tallahassee, on the way home. My parents were due at 7:00PM and Marilyn's were due at 7:38PM.

Marilyn and I, had secured suites at the Marriott for the Jackson's, the Summers and our parents. We reserved several other suites, just in case there were other guests showing up and needing suites. Marilyn had arranged for suitable attire for her father, a black tuxedo, and a lovely gown for Mrs.

Fitzgerald for the wedding. The Fitzgeralds were also staying at the Marriott.

I had arranged for a similar black tuxedo for my father and a lovely gown for my mother, as approved by Marilyn. Actually, both of the gowns for the mothers were selected from available gowns at the best store, here in Pensacola.

Marilyn had already purchased a lovely gown for Jennifer for her duties as flower girl and a fitting outfit for Matthew, as the ring bearer.

We both had gone to the jewelers, where I had purchased her engagement ring, and the wedding ring was just as elegant. I later picked up her ring and she picked out my wedding band, and is holding it for the occasion. Matthew would be presenting them to the paster, when asked for the rings.

We went over all of the details of the Friday night party at the Marriott for both of our parents, the Jackson's and Summers, the pastor and his wife, and any others, who might come from my firm, and the Breedloves, as well as any other special guests that Marilyn might have invited from her neighbors and friends from the church. Naturally, our very special guests--Jennifer and Matthew, will be there as well. I imagine Marilyn and I will dance with both of the children.

We had arranged with the Marriott to serve a delicious meal of London Broil along with baked potato, salad and dessert. We had arranged for a small band and a vocalist to perform, while we all danced. Dinner will be at 7:00PM, preceded by a social hour for all to get acquainted. Beverages of choice will be provided.

Now the really good part-- The Honeymoon, which we have been looking so forward to, and have saved a lot of love for this special and new event. We had carefully selected the Island Paradise Hotel in Nassau for this, now, six-day week of pure pleasure.

Mr.Jackson has insisted that I take a full week for the honeymoon, and we will be flying down to Nassau for a glorious week of getting to know each other---better and better and better!!

As for the party at the Marriott next Friday, the last night of my being a bachelor, I told Marilyn that I planned to stay overnight at the Marriott in order to not see her on Saturday, prior to the wedding. Her father was going to march her up the aisle and I wanted to enjoy this glorious entrance into the rest of my life. When asked by the pastor "who presents this woman to this man?"

Mr. Fitzgerald will proudly say, "her Father, with great pride!"

The procession for the 2:00PM wedding, will be as follows:

- The ushers (already selected) will start seating the congregation as they enter the sanctuary.
- Pianist will start playing a medley of love and wedding music (Marilyn has selected the love and wedding selections, that will be played).

- At 1:55PM the vocalist will sing Marilyn's favorite love song as the pastor, followed by myself and my best man approach the alter and stand facing the center entrance.
- Our pretty little flower girl (our Jennifer) will enter tossing petals as she comes to the alter, to await the bride.
- Our fine son (the ring bearer) will follow the flower girl and stand with me and Mr. Jackson.
- The brides maid advances to the alter and awaits the bride. As the pianist begins the 'Hear Comes The Bride,' Marilyn will start down the aisle, accompanied by her father to the alter, where I have been waiting for my beautiful bride, to be.
- The pastor takes over and here we go. You all know the routine.
- After the service, the pastor directs the congregation to the fellowship hall, for the reception, where we will receive, after all of the photo opts.

Well, we hope it works out like we planned, but this is Sunday, July 27th. I still have a full four day work schedule back at the home office. It would begin with my meeting with each division manager in order to make sure that things in the division, under their responsibility, were going to proceed as scheduled, as if I were there next week (they all knew where I would be). Actually, I was delegating my authority to them to carry out the schedules of sales agents being in the businesses on the scheduled time to visit with the employees, that wished to sign up for the Credit Union benefits, new policies to sign up and policies issued to be delivered, and any other changes, that the employees wished to make. Any payroll deductions to be made to the credit union, and new payroll deductions to be made for the policies, that they make new sales on and issued, which require payroll deductions, to Southern. I had left my car at the airport in Pensacola and flew down to Maitland, knowing that if I needed to travel while in Maitland, I could reserve a company car.

Throughout the week, I met with Mr. Summers in Marketing, Miss Marian in Payroll, Mr. Hudson in Legal, Mr. Adams in Property, Mrs. Hudson in Human Relations, Mr. King in Licensing and Mr. Johnson in Advertising. With each manager, I wanted to know if there was any thing that I needed to do for them, and if there were any problems, that I needed to be aware of, that I could assist in solving the problem, prior to my departure home to Pensacola and my family.

With each one of the managers, I let them know that I would back them up with each decision, they need to make, while I was away. To some extent, each one had some contact with the businesses we had contracted with, the credit union that serviced that business, and internal department activities here at Southern Medical and Life Services.

By Thursday, I had met with President Jackson, and gave him a full report of my meetings with the managers and any necessary undertakings that I had initiated to be happening, while I will be away next week.

Finally, "I told him that I planned to take the same flight to Pensacola that the Jackson's and Summers were taking." Our flight was out of Orlando at 5:05PM.

I had not previously met Mrs. Jackson or Mrs. Summers and was introduced to them before we boarded our flight. I found them quite charming, as I had been expecting that they would be, to be married to these two distinguished gentleman, who, I had grown so fond of, as associates in the firm.

We had a very smooth flight to Pensacola and I had my car stored there in order to finish up any things that I had scheduled to happen in preparation for the Friday party and the wedding on Saturday.

I retrieved my car, and we drove to the auto rental, where Mr. Jackson rented a car for their stay at the Marriott. Then, the Jackson's and the Summers followed me to the Marriott to enter the suites that I had secured for them.

Both families seemed quite pleased with my arrangement for their stay here, until after the ceremonies on Saturday.

I assured them that, "I would be at their disposal on Friday and Saturday, except for the party on Friday and the wedding on Saturday." "I agreed to pick up Mr. Jackson in order to have him fitted for his tuxedo, which I had reserved for him." I told the ladies that I would have Marilyn call them in the morning, in order to see if there was anything that they might need during their stay.

It was near the time for me to go meet my family and the Fitzgeralds, as they exited their flights. I had called Marilyn and she was leaving for the airport when I called. "I told her that I was coming right away and would meet my parents and be with them until the Fitzgeralds arrived."

My parents arrived at 7:00PM on their flight from Winston-Salem, NC, and I was so glad to be there when they exited the plane. I helped them secure their baggage and took them to the coffee shop to await Marilyn and the Fitzgeralds, as Marilyn and I had previously agreed, would be best for all of us.

Me, I was so glad to meet the Fitzgeralds, and proudly introduced them to my parents, the Knights. It appeared to me that everyone was going to be quite congenial. Marilyn had brought the children, so I asked her to bring them and their grandparents to the Marriott and join us. We would get both of our parents settled in their suites there, and we could all have dinner. I thought it would be nice if the Jackson's and Summers were there at dinner, but found that they had had dinner by this time, and settled in for the night. This was fine because it gave me the opportunity to meld with the Fitzgeralds, who were already having a ball with their grandchildren, who they had not seen for many months.

After dinner, we made certain that our families were comfortable in their suites, had everything that they needed, and were aware of the plans for the party here on Friday, and the wedding on Saturday. Both families said "they would be just fine," and we went home with the children to have a good nights sleep and prepare for the events of Friday and Saturday.

On Friday morning, Marilyn reminded me that," I should take my father and her father, Mr. Fitzgerald to the Tuxedo Shop to make sure of the fitting and pick up their tuxedos." I thanked her for reminding me to take care of this, and called them in their suites at the Marriott and arranged to pick them up at 10:00AM.

I called Mr Jackson and made the same arrangement with him. Since it was now 9:00, I headed for the Marriott and got all of them together, and headed for the Tuxedo Shop, and the sizing had been perfect. My tuxedo was perfect, as well, and I went back home, after delivering them back to the hotel.

In the meantime, Marilyn had called all of the ladies to see to their every needs. My mother asked her to take her to the dress shop in order to change the gown that she had previously picked out. While they were there, Marilyn called Sabrina, her maid of honor, to see if she had picked up her gown, and was told that she had picked it up and that it was perfect.

While I was at the Marriott, I checked to make sure that all of the details for the party, here tonight, had been set in motion. I was assured that everything had been covered, and all we had to do was to show up a little after 6:00PM.

Marilyn had assured me, earlier, that the reception, after the wedding, would go very smoothly.

Our flight tickets were in hand for our departure to Nassau at 6:05PM and we had been assured that our stay at the hotel, while there, had been extended to check out next Thursday for our flight, back to Pensacola, arriving at 12:05PM.

By now, Marilyn and I already knew that the memories of our marriage and our honeymoon, would be profound, and would remain with us for the rest of our lives. How wonderful it was going to be!!

As for now, everything that we had planned for the Friday party and the wedding had been carefully thought out, and placed in motion. The Jackson's and Summers had never been to Pensacola, and they toured the town, with plans of arriving at the hotel, in time to arrive at the party.

My parents had, also, toured the town and arrived at the party shortly after the others.

Marilyn and I had discussed the fact that I would be spending the night here at the Marriott, in order to not be seeing her until she came down the aisle at the wedding with her father escorting her, to our heaven sent, wedding!

As for the children, I knew that the Fitzgeralds would be spending time on Saturday with the children, since Marilyn would be preparing with the hair dresser and gown fitting with Sabrina, the maid of honor.

I entered the party room and was pleased with the arrangements that the hotel had provided. My parents came in shortly and we chatted until the other guests arrived. The Jackson's came in with the Summers and the Pastor and his wife, arrived shortly after, as did the Breedloves and their two children. Shortly, after that, Marilyn, Jennifer and Mathew came in grinning, along with the Fitzgerald's.

We all dug into the finger foods that had been provided and the children had punch, while the adults chose wine, red or chardonnay, of choice.

I had hoped that some of the church members would be coming, but Marilyn assured me that, "she knew that many of the congregation would be coming to the reception, after the wedding."

The wedding party seemed to be enjoying the events, and Marilyn and I had planned the seating. I made sure that the Jackson's and Summers were placed with our parents, the Knights and Fitzgeralds.

Marilyn chose the pastor and his wife to sit with the Breedloves, along with their children, and Marilyn and I and our children, sat together. Any other guests were free to sit where they choose. In preparation for the wonderful dinner, that we all knew we would enjoy. The staff quickly provided beverages of choice, and began delivering the entree of London Broil, with potatoes, biscuits, salad and a variety of deserts as well as the beverages.

The band started playing, and the crowd enjoyed their delicious food.

"I announced that we had ordered extra food and hoped that they would ask for seconds, if they so desired."

After the meal had been enjoyed, "I announced that the band and the vocalist would be staying until 10:00PM, and hoped that we would all dance and enjoy ourselves." Marilyn said, "she and I were going to dance with the whole crowd and would be cutting in, to make sure that we enjoyed the whole group of families." The band director was advised that we wanted to enjoy the music of the forties and fifties. We asked that all would request any special songs of choice. I asked that, "Marilyn and I have the last dance, for just the two of us."

I think that, I wound up having danced with most of the guest wives, including my mother, and Marilyn danced with the guest husbands including her father. We made sure to dance with the children, ours and the children of the Breedloves.

Marilyn and I had never had the opportunity to dance with each other, in Hawaii. We had danced at home, at times. I was pleased to show she was a wonderful dancer as she flowed smoothly in my arms, as we danced. I do believe she must have learned at Arthur Murrays, there in Honolulu, as I had, while being stationed there. I could not take my eyes off of her as she gracefully danced with all comers, even Matthew cut in on her.

As for the children, they were persistent, laughed, giggled and did not want to quit. We gave them as much time as we could, but knew that the purpose of this occasion was to let everyone of our guests feel this special and memorable occasion, and, also, feel our appreciation for sharing this night with Marilyn and me in celebration of this night and our wedding tomorrow.

The band had been wonderful in bringing their music to us. We knew that the vocalist had been very special and we were looking forward to having her at our service tomorrow. The crowd had given her a round of applause after each song, which she had performed.

It was nearing 10:00PM, and I reminded the band that the last dance was especially for Marilyn and myself. I chose an all time favorite of mine by asking, "if they could play 'Moonlight Serenade', in the Glenn Miller style?"

And they assured me that, "they loved it as much as I did, and would be quite delighted to play it for us, on this wonderful occasion."

Marilyn flowed into my arms and the crowd gasped at the electricity-charged dance, that we performed for all of us to remember, as we departed in anticipation of what was to become, tomorrow.

CHAPTER 31

I WENT BACK TO the Marriott to my room, and tried to remember all that had transpired during the party. Every one had seemed to enjoy the moment and, hopefully, they would be looking forward to the wedding service, that would begin in about 14 hours, from now.

Most of them would have a part in the wedding service and would be a part of the memories that we would share for the rest of our lives. I had taken this route to the rest of my life, and it was so totally right, and would affect lives of not only me and Marilyn, but the children as well, since I planned to adopt them soon after the wedding. I hoped to be good with the children and try to repair any damage, that the untimely death of their natural father might have caused. They were so young, that I hope that their new life with Marilyn and me, will blot out any unhappy memories that they may have experienced.

Hopefully, they will remember the good things that their father had provided in their lives, and now be willing to accept me as their new and loving father, who will give to them the one thing that I will easily give--my love.

As for Marilyn, she is the best thing that has ever happened to me. I will make sure to show her how much I appreciate her, at every possible opportunity.

The way she flowed into my arms on the dance floor is totally ingrained in my memory, and I am sure that we will have many opportunities to have this feeling on the dance floor in Nassau, on our honeymoon, and any chance we get in the future. This beautiful seductress has been tantalizing me for months and I will make sure that the wait has been worth it for both of us.

As for the wedding, tomorrow, I cannot wait to see her beauty as she walks down the aisle with her father. But for now, I must try to get to sleep and enjoy the big day tomorrow.

On Saturday, I awoke early and had a quite breakfast with my mother and father, in the hotel dining room. We had a lot to talk about--what was going on back home in their daily lives and other things, including my sisters and families, our neighbors and the church where I had attended, and most of all, I wanted to see what they thought about Marilyn and the children.

In unison, they assured me that they were delighted to see how happy I was with Marilyn, and both agreed that the children were a delight. Mother asked, "who would not love Marilyn?" And added, "that Marilyn was the most bubbly woman that she had ever met. She announced that, they were staying over a few days to spend some time in the town and visit the beach, before flying home."

Dad said that, "he was so happy with my business move." He confided that Mr. Jackson and Mr. Summers had expressed their excitement in having me with the company and had added that, your son has a brilliant business mind and a great future with our company! I was glad to hear that. Dad said that "Marilyn was a doll and that I was one lucky fellow to have met her."

I agreed and told them, "that I was crazy about the children." I added that "I hoped to have children of our own in order to grow the family and, maybe to provide them with more grandchildren."

Dad asked me, "how I felt about my future in my business?"

I assured him, "you can rest assured that we will never have needs that we will not be able to provide for!"

My father had planned to wear his tuxedo and mom had her beautiful gown and assured me that, "they would arrive at the church at least thirty minutes prior to the service, and were looking forward to the service and the reception afterward."

We spent a great morning together, and by 11:30 I had spent some time with our other guests here at the hotel. By this time, every one's expectations were extremely high and began dressing for the our visits to the church by 1:30PM.

By 1:30PM, Mr. Jackson and I were entering the church by the side door and waiting in a spot that we could watch the ushers as they ushered in the ladies and their guest. They did a great job of ushering and seating of my parents, Mrs.

Fitzgerald, Mrs. Jackson, Mr. and Mrs. Summers, and Mr. Breedlove and his two children - so beautifully dressed.

At about 1:45, the lovely Jennifer entered and tossed rose petals as she approached the alter and waited for the bridesmaid. Matthew entered and stood by me and Mr. Jackson. The pianist began to play a beautiful love song and the vocalist sang so beautifully, in anticipation of the brides arrival.

The bridesmaid entered and proceeded to her station by Jennifer and the crowd turned to face the glowing--beautiful Marilyn, as she was ushered to the alter by her father, Mr. Fitzgerald.

The vocalist had now completer the lovely wedding song and the pastor stepped up to begin the service.

He began by, "dearly beloved, we are gathered here to honor this couple in Holy Matrimony," and continued, "who gives this woman to this man?"

Mr. Fitzgerald said, "her father, with pride," as he stepped aside. The pastor turned to Marilyn and asked, "do you take this man to be your lawful wedded husband?"

Marilyn turned to me and said, "I do." The paster turned to me and asked," do you take this woman as your lawful wedded wife? "Proudly, I do," I said.

Now the pastor asked, "what token of ring do you offer this man?"

Little Matthew, who has been carefully observing the process, presented his mother a band for her to put on my finger. The paster asked me, "what token of ring do you offered this woman?" And little Matthew performed again.

The paster said to us that, "by the laws of man and God I now pronounce you, Mr. and Mrs. Knight!" Turning to me, "you may now kiss the bride."

This kiss will be remembered by all present. It was electric, and long.

Many in the congregation let out a loud gasp and hmmm.

We now rushed down the aisle and waited for the photo opt, as the pastor announced that, "the congregation was invited to the reception and refreshments, to begin shortly in the fellowship hall, to the left of the sanctuary, and the photos would continue during the reception."

The wedding party had been asked to be present for the photo opt, and it progressed quickly as the congregation began entering the fellowship hall.

The photographer was very professional and quickly assembled the group clustered around Marilyn and me, with all of the children in the front. He next set up shots of Marilyn and me with my parents, her parents and our children.

Next, he set up a photo of me with the Jackson's, Summer's and Marilyn, me, with our children up front. He followed with Marilyn and I with the pastor, and me and then Marilyn with Sabrina Breedlove, with her children.

He had gotten many shots of the service itself, such as me with Mr. Jackson as we entered, the entrance of Jennifer, Matthew, Sabrina, and Marilyn with her father as they entered. We were delighted that he had taken shots of us as the pastor was questioning us about our promises, the exchange of rings, and most especially the best kiss that I have ever had (and hopefully, Marilyn as well). And several shots of the congregation, taken from both sides, from the front.

The photographer agreed to stay around in order to get special shots that he might like in the fellowship hall, perhaps of us feeding the wedding cake to each other, as well as any other shots that he thought were very creative.

Marilyn and I entered the fellowship hall and received many shouts of joy for us and for the happiness that they wished upon us. We were happy to pose for anyone who wanted a special shot with us, either with their camera or the official photographer.

Since we did not have to be at the airport with our tickets and be in line to board until 5:30PM, we mingled with the crowd and accepted many, many words wishing us a wonderful life together, and congratulations in the wedding and a happy honeymoon. We, also fielded a lot of comments about that kiss that we seemed to enjoy so much. Some said that they had taken a photo of that and wanted to adopt our technique. We just laughed and said, "that we hoped that it works for them as it did for us." We added that, "we were looking forward to working on that on our honeymoon, in Nassau!"

We spoke again to our friends, who had participated in the wedding party, the Jackson's, the Summer's, the pastor, who said, "the church appreciated the check for the service and the check for the food preparation in the reception, and the friendship that we had had to the congregation. "He closed with his feelings that he had done such a good job, that he knew it would last our lifetime."

Marilyn and I agreed that, "we also shared this belief."

We made sure that everything would be alright with the Breedloves keeping the children, until we returned on next Friday. They assured us that, "it was going to be good for their children, who were really looking forward to the fun of keeping them." They assured us that, "it was going to be a treat for them and their children."

We promised them that, "we would exchange the favor at a time that they needed a vacation from their children."

Bob Breedlove, "promised to gather up all of the rented clothing, and return them to the rental store on Monday." "He would come by the hotel and collect mine, my fathers and Mr. Jackson's."

I was headed home, but would leave my tuxedo with my father, back at the hotel, prior to our flight.

I spoke to Mr. Jackson and, "assured him that I would return to work, August 11th." In the meantime, "you have my phone number at the Nassau hotel." I am a 24/7 employee, and at your beckon call. Call me if I am needed for anything.'

Mr. Jackson assured me that he knew that I had left directives to my management team, and all would be fine.

As far as my parents, the Knights and Marilyn's parents, the Fitzgeralds, "we wished to thank them for everything that they had ever done for each of us, and wished them a safe passage to their respective home."

We arrived at the airport by 5:10PM, and prepared for boarding, for our flight to Nassau. We believe that every one on that flight recognized us as newly weds. We were still beaming, as we had our passports in hand.

The flight was very comfortable and we would not have noticed it if it had not been. All we wanted to do, was hold on tight to each other. We were going to do a lot of that for the next seven days. After getting through the airport, I rented a comfortable automobile for our stay, and proceeded to the hotel.

When we arrived, we agreed that it was beautiful, and quite appropriate for our honeymoon. We were famished with hunger, after our flight, and headed for the restaurant. I told Marilyn that, "the sky is the limit, order what you want."

We were going to have the best food and the best love while we were here in Nassau.

We ordered a bottle of red wine and toasted ourselves while awaiting our order. We knew that we were going to need a lot of energy and ordered the biggest steak available. In the meantime, we toasted ourselves, Mr. and Mrs. Alvin Knight.

"That, to me, has a beautiful sound, my darling," She cooed.

We were in heaven just being with each other and we would stay this way for the next seven days, and for ever more.

The sizzling steaks were delivered and the plate was decorated with fried tomato, and the best green beans, with added spices, that I had not been served before, baked potato and a wonderful salad, which was well spiced up, was served on the side. Later, we enjoyed rum cake covered by vanilla ice cream.

You would think that by this time we would be ready to sign the check, go up to our room, go to bed and go to sleep, completely exhausted. Not so, you must realize that this is the first opportunity to be in bed and just able to hold this beautiful, desirable woman. As a matter of fact, I was not tired at all.

I just wanted to look into those beautiful eyes and smile my appreciation for this beautiful moment, that I had waited for, so long.

I tenderly touched her cheek, stroked those beautiful blond locks, kissed an exposed ear, her cheek and finally kissed, so tenderly, those inviting lips.

I suddenly realized that we were completely nude and I began by touching one of her pouting breasts, and circled the outer limits, so lightly. Sensing that, by her heaving motion she was saying, "well buster, is that all you got?"

Well, I was not in any hurry, I had waited to long, to not make this the most erotic experience that I have ever had, and hopefully the most erotic experience that she had ever had. I touched her lips with my finger and slowly caressed them.

Moving to her eyes, I planted a light kiss to both of those beauties. Then, I kissed her lovely breasts and finally, moved back to her lips and kissed her long and sweet. She surprised me by inserting her tongue into my opened mouth and circled so slowly and urgently. Suddenly I realized that this was no longer my performance, she wanted more, and now.

A little shocked, I stood up on my knees and surveyed her beautiful body, widely open to be taken in any way that I wanted.

Marilyn just smiled a sensual smile and voiced her approval of my body, as she said, "it is so big!" I did not quite understand what she meant and followed her gaze. I realized that I had the biggest hard on that I could have ever had on my private part.

My macho mood was willing to take that as a terrific complement and planted another ravishing kiss to her lips and enterer her wonderful woman ness, and teasingly began to give her pleasure as she was giving me.

I had wanted to prolonge the moment for both of us, but her heavings continue to pound back at me. Suddenly she gasped and had a large orgasm, that caused me to erupt my load of sperm, that I had been holding for so long, into her receptive vagina.

For a long time we just lay there holding on to each other and enjoying what I will never forget.

Finally, she spoke, "if that does not do it, nothing will."

I asker her what that meant and she replied, "I want your baby and he will grow up to be just like you."

Well, I said, "maybe if we really get this perfected, we can produce a beautiful daughter that looks just like you, my darling."

"Hmmm," she said, "could we do it again?"

"Lets not rush into this," I said. "Lets have another glass of that delicious red wine that we saved from dinner and think about the seriousness of this very important occasion."

Marilyn wanted to put the wine glass to my lips and have me put the other glass to her lips. We both sipped very slowly until the glasses were both empty.

After another glass of wine, we began by caressing each other's body.

I was so happy that this love of my life was going to be a giver, as well as a taker in our love life. We seemed to be perfect for each other-- we loved each other so much and the sex was going to cement our over all relationship. Of course, appreciation for each other's body is a definite plus.

She wanted to lick my chest and I made it available for her as long as she liked. It got to be really good when she got up to my neck, then my ear as she nibbled my earlobe. Then she moved to my forehead and down to my eyelashes.

The tip of her tongue was placed on my lips and began inserting her tongue into my mouth, and gave me the most prolonged kiss, that I could take without keeping us breathless but still able to breath.

I did not know where this was going, so I decided this was going to be her show and to relax and enjoy the trip. She dropped down to my feet and licked the instep of both of my feet and advanced slowly up to the inside of my thigh and saw that this was driving me wild and then took what she wanted.

I surrendered to this wonderful seductress, but soon could take no more She quickly inserted my manliness into her heaving woman ness and laid back for the ride that she knew I was going to give her.

We both took our time, because both of us wanted to prolong the pleasure as long as we could. She continued to bounce up and down like a cowboy on a bucking horse as I bucked up and down with her strokes until she could take no more and surrendered to my probe, with a loud gasp and sigh as she fell into my loving arms and we lay there, totally exhausted until we awoke in the morning.

My first awareness was that she was laying there, just watching me intently and waiting for me to pull her lips into mine. Finally she spoke to me and said "that I must be the most wonderful lover in the world."

I whispered that, "it takes one to know one. But let's go down to breakfast and replenish our energy."

Well, that is the way it went for several days. We did go out dancing and continued our love for feeling our bodies so close, as we swept across the floor.

Every where we went, all eyes continued to be on us and we were loving to show our love for each other and enjoying it at every moment.

I could not take my hands off of her and she responded to my every touch in a receptive manner. What a wonderful honeymoon we were having.

This was pure bliss that we never wanted to end.

We had purchased a good camera and traveled all over the island, often asking someone to take a picture of the two of us together. When no one was available, we both took pictures of each other.

As for our love making, it was as if we were made for each other. We both quickly responded to the wants of the other. Sometimes it was just a touch, or possibly a special look of "I want you now." There was no thought of "not now." Or, I am tired. It was so perfect for each other as we learned more and more about each other's body. I was glad that she had no problem with oral sex, as she had first brought to our pleasure on the first night of our honeymoon. Later, I had returned the favor to her as I drove her wild with pleasure.

So, you see, there was not going to be any negativity in our love life-- we were there to provide pleasure and happiness to each other, and we were very happy and proud to show it in every way possible, to each other.

With this attitude of showing love for each other, we knew that our marriage would endure for the rest of our lives and be an example for others that we come into contact with.

Some may say that what we have is a fairy tale. But to us, we were so glad that we had found our soulmate.

Our stay here in Nassau had been a perfect honeymoon, but Friday did arrive and we were at the airport and ready for our flight back to home and the children. I was glad that we would have the entire weekend to reintroduce ourselves to the children, and the world around us.

We were proud of who we were and always wanted to show it in our relationships with others. The Breedloves' were the first to notice the glow that we were so happy. Sabrina was the first to say that, "that must have been some special honeymoon." We acknowledged that, "yes, it was and thank you and Bob for keeping the children safe and having fun, while we were away."

We told them "how wonderful Nassau was and had been magic. We were glad to be home and getting on with our daily routine."

The children, Jennifer and Matthew were glad to see us and said, "they had had a lot of fun with the Breedloves' children, and were looking forward to tell us about their stay with them." And, that was how it went at home on Friday and Saturday at our house. The children seemed to accept our new relationship as Marilyn an I now slept together. We decided that these were two very smart kids.

On Sunday, we were glad to be going to Sunday School and church.

As usual, we were well accepted by the members of our class, who could tell by our demeanor that this had been some honeymoon. They could see by the glow in us together, that this was a real wedding made in heaven. We were told by the congregation that they had enjoyed our marriage ceremony very much, and the reception that followed in the fellowship hall.

After the service, we were greeted by the pastor, who said, "I can see what a good job I did in marrying you two."

"You sure did, and we appreciate it so much, pastor."

After church we had lunch at McDonald's to treat the children. While there, I asked, "if anyone wanted to go to the park or to the beach?" Getting a resounding, "yes, let's go to the beach." It was decided, so we stopped by the house to retrieve our swimwear and the kids picked up their sand shovels, and off we went for the afternoon. Of course, sunscreen is always a necessity which we always apply and, just in case, we rented a large umbrella so some of us can get out of the sun, if we choose.

While the children were building beach sand castles, Marilyn and I got caught up on some novel reading. Later, after the children tired of their romping in the light surf, we headed home to what Marilyn said, "was going to be a fantastic dinner of hot dogs and hamburgers, that I would grill just right, and she would supply all of the trimmings, including ketchup, mustard, slaw, onions and pickles." "Sounds great," we all exclaimed.

Our honeymoon, away from the children, had been so special, but we were now so glad to be giving back to Jennifer and Matthew. They had been so understanding, that had been fine with them.

After dinner, we devoting all of our time to catching up on what they had been doing, while we were away. We playing games with them and just enjoyed family. Since school had not yet started, we let them stay up until they were exhausted and went to bed.

Marilyn and I took a shower and retired to bed, I think we both knew that we wanted to share our bodies to each other, especially since I would be away, catching up on my business, early Monday morning.

I was eating breakfast by 5:30AM and drove to Maitland, beating the traffic. I met with Mr. Jackson as he arrived for the day and I outlined my plans for the weeks of catching up, where I had left off, prior to the wedding.

Getting up to date on any successes, or problems in our operations here in the office came first, then I wanted to visit each District Office in the field. I personally wanted to talk with some of the agents to see how they were having successes, or possible problems, as they carried out their scheduled visits to the businesses to make changes for their employees, in any manner they wished to make.

Of course, the agents should always take advantage of any opportunity to sell new insurance products that we have to offer, especially if they are meeting with a new employee, that the business had employed since we were last at that site.

As for the agents, I wanted to make sure that we were giving them the training to, not only serve the employees that they came into contact with, but to make them successful in making sales of our products in order to make an income, that was satisfactory in supporting themselves and their families through commissions, received from their sales efforts.

At times I found out that some of the agents needed additional training, to get them back on track to reaching their goals as well as our expectations of them, in their performance. I tried to install in them that we were here to help them achieve their financial goals, while they performed this companies' goals.

With this in mind, I installed a schedule to visit each District Office in the next three weeks. In my discussion with President Jackson, I had told him, "that I wanted to initiate a program that included a luncheon in each District Office, catered by a vendor in that area." He agreed, "to set up a budget enabling the District Manager to handle scheduling a time when most of the agents could be available." I planned to take a supervisor in marketing, a product specialist and, at least one of the managers from the home office, as we have a training session to review all of the products, which we are currently offering, and introduce any new products we decide to add to our product line. We would actually roll play to show how to approach the employee with an introduction of the Credit Union and the services they provide, and finally, do a presentation of the insurance products that we have available to provide security for the employees' family needs.

We, also, want to make sure that the sales agents always have a supply of change forms that the credit union provide for making changes, which the employees of the businesses they are visiting, wish to make. We want to make sure the agents have brochures and applications for all insurance that we sell and change forms to arrange for payroll deduction, to be made for the new sales.

The schedule was now established for our trips. Since it was now Tuesday August 12th, we would begin our visiting with the Orlando District Office, for a late lunch. The meeting went well and we taught a great deal and received very good feedback from the agents. They were thankful that we were trying to give them valuable training, and realized that we were there to back them up and make their job easier, and help them grow their business and financial future. Later, our crew agreed that this meeting provided valuable input that would aid their preparations for the future meetings.

The rest of the schedule was set as follows:
Miami, a late breakfast on Tuesday, August 19th.
Ft. Lauderdale, late lunch on the 19th.
Tampa, lunch on Thursday the 21st.
Jacksonville, late breakfast on Tuesday, August 26th.
Daytona Beach, late lunch on the 26th.
Gainesville, early lunch on Thursday, August 28th.
Tallahassee, dinner on Thursday the 28th.

We always had to have Mr. Summers or a Marketing Supervisor and a product specialist to participate in the roll play with our agents, imitating an employee, willing to hear the presentation of various insurance products that we offer.

The roll play always gave a demonstration of dealing with a new employee desiring to join the Credit Union, and a roll play of the followup of delivering the insurance policies, that were sold in our roll play.

Our emphasis was always that we did not apply heavy pressure that might turn off the new employee, which we were making our presentations to, at that time. We emphasized that if you apply heavy pressure, to sell the product, you will have a customer that would let the insurance policy lapse, very soon. You must show the value that you are providing to the employee and their family by keeping the product and assuring future benefits that justify the premium, that is being payroll deducted from their pay.

The District Managers were delighted that we, in the home office were assisting them in the training of their agents. After all, as sales increased, the District Managers received a bonus on the additional sales that were produced by his or her agents.

The added commissions of extra sales by the agents, provided more means of supporting themselves and their families, bringing greater security and added confidence in their relations with company management.

The rest of the week went fast as I relayed the future schedules to the District Managers, so that they could prepare for the the vendor of foods and scheduling the agents to be there for the meeting. Naturally, agents' schedules had to be taken into consideration in order to get them there.

By Friday afternoon, I had fully revealed the schedule to President Jackson and brought him up to date regarding the results that we had had in Orlando, at Tuesday's meeting. He seemed impressed and "told me that he was confident that we were doing the right thing to greatly make this division as profitable as we had hoped it to be, in our early discussions."

He asked, "if I was returning home to the family for the weekend?" and I replied that, "yes, I was looking forward to a nice weekend with the family."

He asked me to, "give his love to Marilyn and the children." I assured him that I would and asked him to "give our thanks to Mrs. Jackson for her kindness during their stay for our wedding."

On Friday afternoon, I headed for Pensacola and my wonderful family.

I arrived a little after 8:00PM and received a rousing reception from the two children, who had a lot of things to tell me about their weeks activities. I was very attentive to them, but finally realized that Marilyn was wanting to have a lot of my time for herself. I felt a lot of urgency in that wonderful kiss that she gave to me. It was demanding more later, I thought.

The children had eaten previously and were in the game room. They were really enjoying one another, according to the excitement and laughter that was coming from that room.

Marilyn sat at the kitchen table and seemed to take pleasure in the way that I was devouring her wonderful seafood preparations, that she had provided.

This girl was trying to keep me physically well so that I would be ready for what she had planned for the bedroom. We both showered together, put on our bath robes and shed them as we approached the bed.

By this time, we had put the children to bed, and soon knew that they were sleeping soundly.

She literally threw herself up against me and looking me in the eyes, she said, "hold on buster, you are going to get the ride of your life." "But, first I want those wonderful kisses that you always have for me." We began with those slurpy kisses that we had found that we both enjoyed, so very much.

We, then began those licking sensations all over each other's body that seamed to heightened our desire for each other. This may take all night, we both thought, so we just pressed as close to one another as we could, feeling each other's wild heartbeat.

There was no haste, we both knew what we had in each other. We were so well balanced for each other that there was no doubt that we would reach the highest of sensuousness, and dive to the deepest pleasures that our bodies could provide for our pleasure. We had found that we were accessible to trying new means to provide pleasure to each other and would never tire as many couples do, and make our lovemaking become predictable, and therefore mundane.

Finally, she ordered me to lie on my back and spread my legs. She bent over me and took my now erect member in her hands and caressed it, lovingly.

Bending low, she planted kisses on my thighs and gave a loving kiss to my thankful member. I could tell where this was going and she took my member and directed it into her wonderful opening and said, "hold on buster, you are going to give me the ride of my life." And I did. I was bucking like a bull and she was hanging on for her life and we were one----until we were drained of all of our pent up desire, to please each other.

I sighed and said to her, "what a woman you are, my darling."

She whispered a contented "hmmmm." And we slept blissfully, knowing that this was just the beginning to enjoying the wonder of each other.

Saturday, was to all of us a time to relax and do just what each of us wanted to do. Marilyn asked about my work and, "I told her about my travels that would cover the entire state by having meals and training with each District Office." She seemed to be impressed with all of the planning and organizing that I was doing, with the company.

Morning came and we enjoyed a wonderful breakfast of pancakes and syrup. The children had that wonderful Florida orange juice, and we enjoyed coffee. Later, we all showered, dressed and prepared for Sunday School and later, a very good service. The members had not tired of talking about our wedding, and we told them that next Sunday, we would bring all of our wedding pictures, and honeymoon pictures to share with all who chose to see them.

After the service, I treated them to dinner at Mac Donald's and suggested "that we go to the park, and the children could take their bikes and we would just have a pleasant day there." The children let out shouts of joy as my beautiful wife smiled in appreciation for my thoughtfulness. Hey, it was no effort on my part to try to please this family that was so special, and worthy of anything in the world that I could do, for my appreciation of having them in my life.

After a light dinner, I excused myself and went to bed, knowing that morning would come early and I would be on the way to Maitland, very early in order to get the week started off the way that I wanted the week to progress. Our visitation group got together and prepared for our long trip to Miami and, later to Ft. Lauderdale to visit and train the agents, as we had already done at Orlando.

Arriving in the District Office in Miami, I was surprised that many of the agents were Cuban Americans, which did not bother me, since many of the businesses they called on, would have many Cuban Americans working there.

The agents seemed to enjoy the late breakfast that we had, and the training session and opportunity to hear from us and the input that they presented to us, from the home office. We assured them, "that we were proud of them and their hard work to provide good, quality service to those employees they serviced for the Credit Union, and the sales of good quality insurance products, that they were providing to those employees, and their family." We explained "that nothing happened until they made the visit to the employees and provided service that the employees saw good values to them, as they received the services."

Our visit to Ft. Lauderdale for the late lunch and meeting, that followed, contained the same structure that we had presented in our other meetings at Miami and Orlando. The District Manager and the agents were very appreciative of our visit and we all enjoyed our late lunch. After lunch we launched into our training program by, "telling them that we really appreciated their hard work in representing our company and the Credit Union, in their daily calls on the employees of the businesses, that were assigned to them."

"We told them that the company, especially recognized their sales of our company's insurance products and hoped that they were receiving good commissions to support them and their families. One of our purposes in scheduling this event was to provide additional training by roll playing, the best approach to making the employee feel that his or her best interest was why their employer was bringing this benefit program to them to participate in, at this time. The roll play showed the greeting and launched into their purpose of introducing the Credit Union and the benefits that they offered and, finally, the wonderful insurance products we offered to benefit them and their families. We told them that their employer would payroll deduct the savings they chose from the Credit Union, or possibly paying back loans they may seek, plus the cost of insurance programs, purchased from our company.

After the roll play, we gave them an opportunity to comment or ask any questions of us, that they may wish to present. They normally came up with some of the best inquiries that we had received. All in all, our home office group felt that the meeting had been extremely successful. By 3:00PM we were headed back to the home office. On the way we talked about our plans for visiting the Tampa District on Thursday the 21st.

Wednesday morning began with a called meeting by President Jackson for our visitation group to have a private lunch in the cafeteria with him. After lunch, "he thanked us for our hard work in making the visits to the District Offices, and told us that our visits would improve the morale of the sales agents and improved sales for the company, resulting in greater commissions to agents and their own families." "The company was continuing to grow through our hard work."

He announced that "the Board of Directors were fully aware of the progress we were making and applauded us for all that we were doing to further build our company and its profits."

After that special meeting with the President, we almost floated on our trip to Tampa for our District Office luncheon and roll play on Thursday. I personally observed the strongest meeting there of all the visits that we had made, up to this point. The agents really became involved with our roll play and training and gave their appreciation for us coming, and promised even greater effort in their calls on the businesses and employees. They approved with our appeal to create a feeling that, they were not making hard sell presentations, but to create an atmosphere that the employee and their families would benefit greatly from the products offered.

On the trip back to Maitland, we made plans for our visits to Jacksonville and Daytona Beach next Tuesday, the 26th.

Friday was a good day for our visitation group to catch up on things that had piled up on our desks and prepare for the coming week. I knew that I was ready to head out for home, and my wonderful family and was looking forward to learn what Marilyn and the children had been doing this week.

At 5:00PM I was underway and arrived home about 8:00PM. As usual, I received a wonderful welcome as Jennifer and Matthew ran to me and jumped into my loving arms. Marilyn was patiently awaiting her time to have me all to herself.

Coming home was worth all of the hard work that I had been doing during the week. As usual, Marilyn had been preparing a wonderful dinner and this gave me time to play with the children and find out how their week had gone. They were excited, as usual and described school and play activities that they had been enjoying all week. They were always a treat for me to see their excitement. These were fun kids, that I loved so very much.

Soon, Marilyn called for us to wash up and come to the table. We were ready to dig into this marvelous dinner of seafood with all of the trimmings. In my blessing of the food, "I thanked our God for all of the blessings that we had been provided and especially for my appreciation of my wife and children to share my life with." Hopefully, the children would feel the same way, but Marilyn's glow and smile let me know that she appreciated my prayer. She could not appreciate it as much as I appreciated this warm, loving family. I was so lucky that I had made the right decision only a little over a year ago. Life was so very good for me now.

After dinner, I volunteered to do the dishes, while Marilyn read to the kids.

I finished the dishes and Marilyn joined me on the sofa. We listened to good music while Marilyn shared her weeks' events to me. This seemed to be one of our best times to cuddle, tenderly touch and kiss affectionally. I knew that if she wanted more, I would gladly oblige. We were just content in the happiness to be together and enjoy the closeness that we were having at this blissful moment.

The music was right and we got up and moved across the room slowly to the music and paused in each other's arms to enjoy another kiss.

Tomorrow would be another day and we would enjoy it together. We were now in bed and lay in each other's arms, so contented in just holding one another.

Morning came and we enjoyed a quiet breakfast with the children.

After breakfast, the children asked if they could go out into the back yard and play on the swings. We agreed and asked them to make sure that they did not leave the back yard. Marilyn then came into my arms and asked if we could go back to bed. I carried her back to bed and we enjoyed a wonderful early morning romp to a blissful, satisfying climax to our lovemaking.

This wonderful woman never fails to surprise me with her show of happiness in being my wife and wonderful lover. We just cuddled for a moment and I could not hold back my feelings for what she had brought into my life. "I love you, Mrs.

Alvin Knight." To which she just held me tighter as if she never wanted to let me go.

Well, back to reality, we heard the children coming in the back door. I quickly donned my robe and greeted them in the hallway. With a question that I already knew the answer to, "would you guys like to go to the beach?"

"Yes! Yes"! Was their final word.

Donning their swim suits and getting their sand castle spades together happened quickly as I returned to Marilyn, who had regained her composure, put on her swim suit and stood there tantalizing me.

I quickly put on my suit and pressed my manliness up to her and did a mocking bump. "Hmmmm" was her only comment, as we were off to the beach for a wonderful family day. We did not fail to apply sunscreen on all, but we did rent a large beach umbrella, that gave Marilyn and I an opportunity to sit and read our choice of a novel, always alert to what the children were doing. Occasionally, they came in for some lemonade, that Marilyn had brought.

It was a beautiful sunny day, with just a few clouds that occasionally came over to give a little pause of relief from the sun. Lunch time came soon, and we stopped by the refreshment stand to pick up some wonderful hot dogs to go with Marilyn's wonderful cool lemonade. Soon the children were back to their building project at the sun castle. They seemed to really have talent for creative building. I suppose they inherited that from Marilyn's father, Mr. Fitzgerald, who had a wonderful career in the business of constructive building of projects.

Eventually, they finished their sand castle and I could tell by their actions that they were tiring of the beach. I told them, "let's stop by the Dairy Queen and get a wonderful ice cream cone, before we return home."

Jennifer said, "could we go to the park and ride our bicycles?" I turned to Marilyn with a questioning look and she said, "that sounds like fun!"

We stopped by the house to put on some more appropriate clothes, picked up their bikes and Marilyn packed some sandwiches, and off to the park we went. Marilyn and I just walked the trail as the children went ahead on their bikes, but followed our instructions to double back and check in with us on a regular basis for safety precautions. They were such good kids.

Marilyn had trained them well, and I was continuing the process, because I was loving this life as a father. Father, I thought, "I believe I will check with Marilyn to see how she felt about my adoption of these wonderful children."

Of course, I was still hoping that Marilyn and I would soon be having our own children. We certainly had been doing our part to make that happen in a blissful way, and the most wonderful love making that I could have ever experienced.

Sunday morning came and after a wonderful fruit breakfast, we headed out to Sunday School. Marilyn remembered to bring the pictures from the wedding and our fabulous honeymoon in Nassau. The Sunday School group asked if we had brought the photos that we had promised and, after the lesson, we shared them with them. They seemed to be very appreciative and enjoyed the photos, saying that these brought back great memories of their weddings and honeymoon. Some were envious and said that they wanted to take a second honey-moon and go to Nassau. Some of the ladies asked Marilyn if we hoped to have our own children. Marilyn just smiled and said, that we were certainly working on it." The ladies let out a loud giggle and rolled their eyes.

After the church service, others asked to see the pictures and Marilyn was proud to share them. We had lunch at Mac Donald's and spent a wonderful day, just hanging out with the children, playing games that they enjoyed doing.

Marilyn prepared a light dinner and the children were ready for bed as soon as, "they told me what they were going to be doing in school this week."

They certainly had had a very busy weekend and had kept Marilyn and me just running to keep up with them. They were understanding when I told them that I would be up early in the morning, to return to my management position in Maitland, Florida. They asked, "what my management position was?" So I told them that "I was the Director of the Division over eight District Offices that sold insurance policies all over the state of Florida." I am not sure that they understood all of that, but I enjoyed sharing it with them.

But, the children shrugged and said, "Wow!"

I told them that I would return late on Friday and we would have a good weekend together, and left to find Marilyn to see if she was ready to go to bed. I found that she was already in bed with a romance novel that she had been working her way through. She coyly told me that, "the lovers in the novel were novices compared with the wonderful love scenes that we had been having after our wedding."

I asked her, "to describe what she was telling me," and "she revealed that she had become a little hot and bothered by reading the racy scenes and now wanted to play them out." I told her that, "our marriage had grown on the basis that neither of us had ever said no to the other and I think that is a wonderful part of our marriage, that I hope continues for the rest of our lives." Then we fell into each other's arms and our bodies mingled. Yes! I am not sure what she was reading, but I don't think that I had found her so moist and ready for the violent climax that she had as I was depositing my sperm into her hotly aroused body. We were immediately asleep in each other's arms.

I awoke early and showered, ate a light breakfast and headed to Maitland for another busy week. We would be going to Jacksonville for a late breakfast meeting and training session with that District Office. They only get better since we were applying the knowledge that we had attained from our sessions over the past several weeks, since it covered a large industrial base in northern Florida.

Our next stop was for a late lunch and meeting with the Daytona Beach District Office and we found the agents there were some of our best producers.

They had seemed to take off running with the concept of working with the Credit Union as well as insurance sales for our company. We returned to Maitland with many new suggestions, which the sales force there had brought to us. We were looking forward to passing them on to the other District Offices in the Division, especially Gainesville and Tallahassee, where we would finish up our visitation on Thursday.

I visited with President Jackson on Wednesday and told him of the progress we had made, and "would be completing with our current schedule of visitations on Thursday." After that, "we would have complete input of what the Division was capable in adding growth to the companies bottom line." "He told me that the Board of Directors were already saying that our division had doubled the growth that they had expected up to this point in our operations."

He went on to say, "that the Board of Directors had declared a round of bonuses for me as Director of the Division." As a mater of fact, "I was being named as Vice President of our Division and would be responsible for distributing $1.5 Million Dollars in bonuses over the division. He suggested that the District Managers, clerical staff of the District Offices, the division management here in Maitland, as well as myself, receive portions of those bonuses. He was ordering me to receive $150,000, personally, before I make distributions of the balance. He continued, "as Vice President, your new annual income is being set at $250,000 per year and paid on a monthly basis."

I asked him, "to relay my thanks to the Board of Directors, even though I felt that they were being too kind to me and felt unworthy." But, "I assured him that I would accept their generous award and do everything in my power to try to be worthy of this great honor."

"He assured me that I had earned this honor and so much more for the growth that I had already brought to the company." I could only mumble my appreciation for this honor.

By this time, I had given up on staying in the hotel and had rented a very satisfactory apartment in Lake Mary, just north of Maitland. I could not wait to leave work this evening and spend an hour on the telephone to my loving wife and give her the good news.

I called her about 7:00PM and told her, "that I have some very good news.

I met with the President of the company today and he told me that I had been promoted to Vice President within the company." "My title was Vice President of the Division of Credit Union Activity."

She announced that "she was deliriously happy and was so proud of her hard working husband."

I told her that "I was not through yet, and the best news was the promotion came with a salary increase. And would now be $250,000 per year."

"She shrieked her appreciation for me into the telephone."

I had to interrupt, "as a bonus for my division's recent success, I have been awarded a bonus of $150,000 to be awarded to me on September the 1st."

I was afraid that she had fainted with that, because for a short time she was speechless.

Finally, she regained her composure and shouted out "Alvin Knight, I have seen this in you for a very long time. I knew that you were destined for this ever since you came into my life here in Florida. She continued, you are very deserved of anything they could possibly do for you. Would you mind if I call my father and tell him what has happened to you?" I assured her, "that I did admire her father, Mr. Fitzgerald very much, and I hoped that Mr. Fitzgerald would feel that his daughter, sweet Marilyn, was in good hands here in Florida."

"Oh! Alvin, I wish I had you here now. I cannot wait to get you home this weekend." "I am going to want you to hold me in your strong arms and love me forever when you get home."

I told her that, "I loved her and the children, and would hurry home on Friday."

She whispered, "I can't wait, and I love you so much, my darling!"

Good reports kept coming into the home office as sales seemed to be sky rocketing. Our group was looking forward to our visit to Gainesville and with our role playing sales presentations and input from the agents. We would be in Tallahassee for the early supper and the roll playing instructional, followed by the agent's input.

By this time I had sent out a memorandum that I was working on a bonus plan authorized by the President of the company for outstanding performance in our division. "Each District Office Manager would receive $100.000 to share with the salaried employees in that office." "Naturally the sales agents were on the commission plan for their actual production and were not covered by this bonus."

"The home office managers of this division, who had not been involved in the visitation efforts of the District Offices would receive $40,000. These included Mrs. Marian in Payroll, Mr. Adams in Property, Mr. Warren in Product Development, Mrs. Hudson in Human Resources and Mr. Johnson in Advertising."

"The home office managers who had been active in all, or most of the eight visitations would receive $70,000." These consisted of Mr. Summers in Marketing, Mr. Ray Hudson in Legal, Jonathan Bixby as Product Specialist and Mr. King in Licensing.

The rest of the $1.5 Million went to the vendors who provided the food and drinks at the eight District Office meetings.

On Thursday we completed our visitations by going to Gainesville and Tallahassee. You should have seen the emotions of those two District Managers as our team had lunch in Gainesville and then supper at Tallahassee. They had received my memorandum of the $100,000, that they would share with their salaried employees, when received. They emphatically, "gave their thanks to me and resolved that their renewed efforts to make their district the top producing district in the future, would be forthcoming." "They assured me that this kind move of a bonus for their salaried employees was unexpected, but a real morale booster."

The roll play of our agents, as they approached the employees of the businesses they were servicing, was well appreciated. and would help them to get more services for the Credit Union and greater insurance sales for our company, leading to higher commissions, for them to support their families.

"We told them that we were proud of them and their hard work to support the Credit Union and the company's bottom line."

Finally, "we told them that nothing happened until they provided good service to the employees, they were allowed to service."

After we left Tallahassee, on the way home, I asked, "if they had received my memorandum of the bonus they had earned for their efforts in making the visitations of the District Offices the success that the President predicted it to become. I mentioned that the $70,000 would be forthcoming to each of them and they had certainly earned this with their getting up early and going home late on many of these visitations."

I told them, "that the President had asked me to thank them for their hard work on this project and that I too, wished to congratulate them for their service and successful conclusion of this project." "We will see, in the near future, the results of your hard work," I said.

Several hours later, we arrived back at the home office and had earned a good rest for the evening. I had a quick dinner and, before retiring for the night, called my honey to tell her that I would be home by 8:00PM, tomorrow.

This is an important note to my readers of this novel----If you use the methods that I have shone in this novel in dealing with others, either employees, friends or members of your own family, especially your wife or lover, you will receive respect, friendship, and love from all of them. If you have read this far, you know that Alvin Knight has exhibited tolerance in everyone he deals with, and it has enriched his life at every turn and made him a better person for it. This is true, especially after he left the Navy and grew in his manhood. His life now, as a successful business man and his relations with his new wife and children is heaven on earth for him, and the various people that he comes in contact with at any time.

He gives this same courtesy and they respond to him in a positive manner.

Try it, and I believe you will receive the same rewards in life that he has received. You will be the better for it!

The Author.

Friday was a time to review what we had accomplished with our visitations and determine just how successful our efforts had been over the four weeks that we had spent with the District Offices. First, I asked for a report from marketing on the eight District Offices' sales volume of our various insurance products that had been processed on a weekly basis, prior to the time that our visitations began.

Then, I asked for the volume of the present week and was pleased to see that Orlando had increased 28%, Miami was up 26%, and Ft. Lauderdale was up by 30%.

When I received Tampa's report, it was up 24%. The later Districts were lower as Jacksonville up 18%, Daytona up 16% and finally, Gainesville was up 12% and Tallahassee was up15%.

This, I thought, was going to to be good news that I could present to the President at our next opportunity to meet and bring him up to date on this data.

However, I was not through yet. I decided that I wanted to touch base with the Credit Unions that were served by each of the District Offices.

With my position, I had a Vice Presidential contact from each of the Credit Unions that we served. I was able to contact each of those Vice Presidents and "ask for a review of how our Districts were performing in bringing business to their Credit Union, since they granted us the privilege to represent their company to the businesses in their area."

I was especially glad to hear the Credit Union was very pleased with our service and the increase in their bottom line since they contracted with our company had been considerable. I received reports from each and was glad to hear reports from 24% increases for the lowest to just below 50% for the very highest. I now "made the call to President Jackson and requested an opportunity to present my findings with him." "He said that he was very anxious to get the report and said that he was going to request a meeting of the Board of Directors for 3:00PM." He continued, "could you have copies of your report to release to each member of the Board at that time?"

I was very pleased to have that opportunity and told him that, "I would be very pleased to bring those copies to the Board at that time."

It was now 1:10PM and I had my Administrative Assistant get on to typing the reports in the fullest from all of our District Offices, as well as the reports I had received from the Credit Unions, that we represented.

By 2:45PM, I had reviewed the copies of the reports and was headed to the Board Room. Several members of the Board had already arrived and I was pleased to introduce myself to them. I was delighted that they said, "that they had already heard of the fine work that my division was performing for the company."

Just before 3:00PM, President Jackson entered and greeted the Board and called the meeting to order. "He thanked them for coming on such short notice, and added that he felt that they would be delighted to receive the news that Mr. Alvin Knight, our newest Vice President and Director of our newest Division, serving the Credit Unions and businesses in the state, would be presenting."

He called on me and I was pleased to pass out the reports that I had compiled for their review.

"I explained that the first report was a record of the sales record of our insurance products as reported for the week prior to our visitation of our Districts for breakfast, lunch or dinner (depending on the time of our arrival) and the most recent report of increase of sales since our visit."

Then, "I reported the report that I had received for the increase of business that the Credit Union was receiving since the time that we contracted with the Credit Unions to service businesses' employees in bringing the Credit Union products and services in the form of payroll deduction."

The Board seemed pleased that the Credit Unions were receiving anywhere from 24% to 50% increase in their former business income prior to contracting with our companies new division.

"I pledged that our division would strive to continue the growth to our company, the Credit Unions, the businesses that our sales agents call on, and most of all, the employees and families that we are servicing."

Then I asked them, "to review the reports of increased sales by our District Offices that I had previously given to President Jackson."

As they followed my instructions to look at those figures of growth by each District Office, they seemed to pause and then, gave me a rousing ovation for the accomplishments of my Division.

CHAPTER 32

GETTING OFF ON Friday afternoon, I hurried home since I could not bear being away from my family any longer. I knew what to expect when I arrived---the children would run out to greet me as I arrived, wanting to tell me everything that they had done, while I was away. I would listen patiently and tell them that I had missed being with them and we would have a very nice weekend, together.

I told them that I had had a very successful week at work and had a very nice promotion! I was now a Vice President of my company and this would give us a future of financial security. They asked what that meant? So I told them that it may provide funding in order to buy a new house and a college education for them, if they chose to go to college.

They just said, "that is good" and quickly tired of the conversation and went into the playroom to play. The beautiful Marilyn had been observing my conversation with the children and was smiling a "you are good" smile at me.

So I took that as a compliment and swooped her into my arms and carried her into the house and laid an appreciative kiss on those beautiful lips. She did not want to leave my embrace, but finally asked, "if I was ready to enjoy the fabulous dinner she had prepared for us." I said, "well, that is the best offer I have had today," as I was gathering up the children to wash their hands and take them to the dining room.

She was right, not only had she prepared my favorite seafood (flounder and baby shrimp), she had fried a small piece of juicy steak for me.

Then she opened a bottle of our favorite red wine, for she and I, as I served the children a glass of fresh milk, along with their seafood. After dinner, the children headed for the playroom and Marilyn wanted to hear every word of what had happened to me during the week, at work.

I began with the successful completion of the visits we had made to the last of our District Office meals, and training for our agents. I "told her, again, about the wonderful promotion to Vice President and the change in income to $250,000

per year, (paid on a monthly basis). The Presidents awarding me with a $150,000

bonus (to be paid immediately). Also, the President had awarded a $1.5 million bonus to the employees of my division." She raised an eye brow and said, "is that all you have done"? I said, "I have rented an apartment in Lake Mary, in order to get out of that expensive hotel, where I have been staying, in Orlando, "the savings I get from that will pay for the apartment with some left over." Jot down my new phone number, I said, as I handed it to her.

She seemed glad that I had made that move and said, "I am glad that you got out of there, where there must have been a lot of very beautiful women hanging around."

I took her into my arms and whispered in her ear, "honey, when a man has what I have waiting for me to come home to, he can hardly notice those other beautiful women, that are out there."

"Darling, Alvin, that is all I needed to hear from you. I will give you all the love and pleasure that you could possibly need in your life." "And, at the same time, you will be rewarded with the best wife that a man ever had."

"I know, I know, you have already made me the happiest man alive, and you can bet on that." "Now get the children in bed and I will show you the appreciation I have for you in our love nest."

"My lover, the famous Vice President," she said. "I will be in with you shortly.

I have never made love to a Vice President," she whispered.

I knew then that we would have a weekend of contentment in our full sex life, too good to tell you about at this time. We know what we have and if you truly give yourself to your lover without reservation, you will have this bliss, also!

We were so happy with each other, and over the weekend we developed a special look at each other that said, "I cannot get enough of you, let's do it now!" Of course, we had to be very discrete around the children, they may have been a little suspicious, but, I guess it all seemed natural to them. We were very good parents and let them know that they were special and that we loved them, so very much. Marilyn and I really tried to make life for them fun, and know that they could depend on us to protect, and care for them, in all special ways.

We were never obvious to the children in our love making, but we sure did give that look to each other quite a lot on this weekend, as we carried out our motherly and fatherly obligations to the children, in the usual manner, by going to the park, watching them ride their bikes, play with them and read stories to them, before they slept. On Sunday, we enjoyed church, as usual, and had some great meals, together.

We were just a happy family together and all of us knew that we had it made. We had everything that we needed to live life, to it's fullest.

As for church and our church family, they had been so supportive to the children and Marilyn, but I began asking myself a question, how long could I continue commuting from Pensacola and my work in Maitland? I wanted to be in a position that I could carryout my responsibilities to my position in the company, and go home to my wonderful family after work on a daily basis. The past five months had been grueling. The trip from Maitland to Pensacola, and back to Maitland on Monday mornings, was at least 800 miles, round trip.

Obviously, my new responsibilities of Vice President was going to require a lot of trips to the District Offices, throughout the state, as well as visiting current businesses, and the Credit Unions, that we represented for them.

I knew that my income was now quite substantial and I could easily afford a new home in a very nice neighborhood, near quality schools for the children.

How would Marilyn feel about a move that would take us away from the church, that had been so good for the entire family? I thought.

Dreading to mention the possibility of a move from our current home in Pensacola by Marilyn and the children, had been a burden that soon became very obvious to Marilyn, and finally she said, "is something bothering you, darling?"

"You seem to be in deep thought!"

I began by saying that, "we were financially sound and building or buying the right house near my work in Maitland may be a sound thing to do, at this time."

"I would so much like to be coming home to you and the children every day after work, instead of only on the weekend. From a practical standpoint, the round trip is now 800 miles and does not seem practical to continue, for the long run."

I continued by saying, "I know how much this community and the church has meant to you, the children and myself." "And I have hated to bring all of this up.

But, it has been rather trying, and I have to get it off my chest."

"Alvin Knight, I told you when you first came that I loved you and would follow you anywhere you wanted to go. That has not changed and I feel even more the love and need you have expressed in wanting to come home to us on a nightly basis." "Now, the children are asleep and you need comforting and I want to give you all of the love and understanding that you truly deserve.

So carry me to bed and I will show you what you will be coming home to every night, you kind and wonderful lover!"

The early trip to Maitland, on Monday morning, was with a light heart to know that I was going to have to find time to look for a home or condo in the Orlando area. Things, at this time, were going so easy for me in my position as Vice President, that I had a lot of time after work to begin looking for our new home. I was not in a real hurry and knew that I would want to bring Marilyn and the children down for a weekend, after I had settled on about a dozen possible sites, which I felt would be suitable for our family. Especially, since there was always a possibility that our family might expand, soon.

What a pleasant thought!

I began scouting out several homes in great neighborhoods in Maitland and at least four in various sections in Orlando. I continued looking and considering the advantages of some homes in Kissimmee (south of Orlando), and the area west the road to Tampa.

During my search, I found at least two tracts of land in that area which I felt would make great locations to build the home of our dreams in some of the most beautiful surroundings that I had seen in these parts. They both, sported the most beautiful lakes that I had seen in this area, of many beautiful lakes.

My thoughts were now racing, and by Thursday, I called Marilyn to see how things were going back home, and to ask "if she and the children could return with me during the weekend to the Orlando area, and (perhaps) view some of the homes and property that I had been looking at for the purpose of buying an existing home, or buying property, where we could build our dream home."

Marilyn told me that, "she had already put our house up for sale and placed an ad in the newspaper. Our family would be delighted to return with me to those areas that you had mentioned." She asked, "if my apartment in Lake Mary was big enough for them to stay there with me, for a few days?"

I said, "it would be a little tight," but, "we would make it do, for possibly a week, or at least long enough for us to scout the properties, that I had selected, for us to look at their possibilities."

So the stage was set for us to be together in this area for possibly a good week. The week hurried by and I handled my work to the fullest, and was ready to drive to Pensacola and pick them up to return on Saturday, to begin touring the areas, that I had selected.

Marilyn and the children liked all of the locations that I had first mapped out for them to visit. But, "I told them that on Sunday we would visit the land that I saw west of Kissimmee, that would be a great place to build the house of our dreams."

It was Sunday morning and I took the family to those two tracts of property, west of Kissimmee. I did not want to tire the children, by too much walking, so I drove through each of the tracts. As the family looked at their beauty, they saw the many small lakes and the wonderful birds that inhabited them. We saw just about every type of bird that you would normally expect to see near the sea. But they were here in Central Florida, due to the many lakes, which contained many types of fish and other creatures. Many birds sit and await the opportunity of a quick meal, there.

Often we stopped to observe an area that seemed appealing to us and I took the opportunity to take a photo with my camera. The children were running to and fro, just enjoying the beauty of the areas.

We stayed on these locations until the children seemed to tire and we decided that it was time for lunch. During lunch, Marilyn asked, "if I had an outline or form of advertisement for the tracts that we had just visited"?

"Yes," I replied and went back to the car to retrieve them.

Not knowing what she had on her mind, I opened the information on both, and spread them out on the table. Tract one contained nine acres, and was priced at $125, 000, and showed the locations of the one lake and possible building sites.

Tract two contained twenty one acres and contained two lakes, that were outlined along with possible building sites. It was priced as $189,000. Marilyn spent a lot of time going from one tract to the other and finally, asked me, "which one I preferred?" "I told her that I would be happy with either one, but I said that I believe we could afford either one, since I seemed to be well established in my business.

I added that, "I anticipated the cost of a very nice home on the sites would range from $110,000 to $150,000 at current prices."

Her next question was "how long would it take a contractor to build a home on either of these sites?" I told her that, "it would take up to six months to build the type of home that we would require."

The restaurant had a play area, and Marilyn, "asked the children if they would like to go play for a little while?" They let out a big, "yes," and went off to play.

As soon as they were gone, Marilyn placed her hand on mine and said, **"I think we will have to add another bedroom for our new child!"**

I looked at her in amazement, and with a questioning look. She continued, "I have missed my period and my gynecologist suspects that I am pregnant!"

I let out a hoot and took her into my arms and kissed her right there in this public place as we both nearly cried with happiness.

Marilyn said that, "she would like to make sure and get a confirmation prior to telling anyone, including the children, that they were going to have a new brother or sister."

She then added that, "she had put the current home up for sale and would proudly contribute the proceeds to the purchase of either one of these sites."

"The realestate agent had told her that she believes the home would sell quickly and had set a price of $90,000 for the sale of the property."

I asked Marilyn, "if she and the children could stay over for a few days in my apartment in Lake Mary"? Marilyn said that, "Jennifer would be starting the fourth grade at school in Pensacola in two weeks, but yes, they could stay a few days here, if it was necessary."

"You have already seen my apartment in Lake Mary, it does have two bed rooms and we will be a little crowded," I said. "I need to ask you now if you could be happy if we purchased track 2, (the 21 acre lot)? It is on a little higher ground and would be more suitable for building a home, where the whole family would be proud to live there." How does that sound to you?

"It sounds wonderful, but can we afford it at this time?" Marilyn asked.

Then she added, "it may take a little time to sell my house, but the proceeds can go toward the purchase of tract 2."

"We will not have any close neighbors to our property if we buy it, will that be a problem for you and the children?" I asked.

"Of course not," she said. "We have been very crowded there in our home in Pensacola and I suspect that this privacy would be very welcomed by all."

"Very well," I said. "I will make an offer for the property tomorrow. We may be able to close shortly, and hopefully at a reduced price but, if not, I think we should proceed, immediately."

"Alvin, you are such a good businessman. I trust your judgment." "This is such an exciting decision for our future. On the way back to your apartment, let's see if we can find some house plans, that might fit on this tract."

I told Marilyn that, "we may have to perform some financial planning for a loan, in the event we are not able to pay cash for the property, and then, the finished home of our choice."

We did find several magazines with house plans for Florida-type homes, and could hardly wait to get home and go through them. We arrived in the early afternoon and all sat at the kitchen table. Then we confided with the children that we were planning to build a home on the large tract of property that we had visited today.

Anything was O.K. with Matthew, but Jennifer took it in stride and agreed that, "she would be very happy, if we built a beautiful home there near the two lakes."

Then, I confided in the children that I wanted the family to move there, so that it would be near my work and I would be able to come home almost every night, to be with them, instead of having to work all week, and only be able to come home on the weekends.

Jennifer and Matthew thought that was neat, that I would be able to be with them almost every night.

With their O.K. out of the way, Marilyn and I set out to fully review the homes in the magazines. First, we agreed that the home must have at least four bedrooms and three bathrooms. We were thinking about having at least 3,000 square feet of total living space. A two-car garage would be a necessity, a large patio out back, a living room with raised ceiling to entertain guests and a spacious dining room to relax and enjoy our meals, which Marilyn produced in the attractive kitchen, close by.

"We may not immediately have a pool to swim, but it could be added, later."

With twenty one acres, there would be plenty of space for bike trails for the children to ride at their leisure, with the understanding that the two lakes were to be respected. The children would be able to view and enjoy the wildlife, but could never, ever, venture into the lakes. That was forbidden! And they had to realize the possible dangers that may possibly lurk, there. To this we all agreed.

But, first we had to be able to purchase the property that we had now settled upon, as our goal. With that secured, we could then finalize the house plans and secure a builder to carry out our plans, in a reasonable time frame.

Well, it was getting later and we went to a fast food restaurant and had a filling meal. We returned to my apartment and realized that we had had a full day but had made a lot of good decisions for our future.

The children had had a busy day and retired to the smaller bedroom, and after a big glass of milk, were quickly asleep.

Marilyn and I popped the cork on a great red wine and sat on the sofa to contemplate all of the decisions that we had made, today. The biggest one was that Marilyn may be pregnant with our first child. And then, the decision to purchase a fantastic piece of property, that could be the location for our dream home, in the near future. I told Marilyn that, "I hoped that she and the children would not be too sad in the possibility of moving from Pensacola to Kissimmee, in order for me to be able to spend more time with the family."

Marilyn, sort of cooed and said, "that was the best part. She was going to really enjoy the fact of having her lover near her much of the time."

She pressed against me and let me know that she wanted to have me now.

I remembered that she was possibly pregnant, and asked her, "if this was wise, due to her condition?"

"Silly, you! the gynecologist had assured me that sex would still be very pleasurable until late in my pregnancy," she informed me.

I picked her up and carried her to my bedroom and made sure that she did receive all of the sexual pleasure that I could give and take, until she gasped with the pleasure of it all, and I quickly came into her wonderful receptive body.

We both went to sleep immediately, entangled in each others arms.

Monday came and Marilyn and the children were staying over for a couple of days. The children were still in bed, and Marilyn and I had breakfast and planned some more details into our dream home in that property.

My first intent, after reporting to work, was to contact the realestate company that was advertising the tract of property, that we were interested in purchasing.

They were located in Orlando, and my inquiry was for information on the history of the two tracts, we had visited.

The Realtor said, "that those two tracts were part of an orange grove that had been in a family for many years and no longer had the patience that it took, in order to make a profit in continuing that business." "I asked about any possible contamination that may have existed on the property," and was assured that none had ever existed on those tracts. The owner has assured them, that no pesticides were ever used on those tracts, since there were never any actual peach trees placed on those tracts.

"I asked the price of both tracts and was given the prices that I already had."

My next question was, "are the prices negotiable?" And was told that they would entertain the possibility of an offer and would present it to the owners of the property. I next asked, if a cash offer was made, would that affect the final price of the properties?

The answer was that, "this indeed was a possibility."

I left my name and contact information with the agent and immediately left the office and went to the county office of the register of deeds in order to verify the information that the realestate agent had given me about the two properties.

The information was confirmed by the records retained there, and I was able to get a copy of those records.

Checking with my administrative assistant, at the office to determine if I was needed at the office, came back negative, and "I told her that I was looking at some property and would be out for several more hours."

"No problem! Everything is fine here," she added.

I next went to my banker and discussed the possibility of a temporary loan in order to pay cash for some property, that I was interested in purchasing. "The answer confirmed that my record of cash on hand in my account showed that I would have no problem receiving up to $200,000 for a temporary loan for that purpose, and possibly more, if I needed it." The funds could be available immediately I was told.

My next visit was to the realestate agent that was handling the two tracts.

"I informed him that I wished to place a cash bid of $175,000 for tract 2, the 21 acre plot west of Kissimmee."

He immediately called the owner of that tract and, "gave the message that he had no other offers for that property at this time, but he had a cash offer of $175,000 for the tract that was 21 acres." The owner confirmed that "since it was a cash offer of $175,000, it would be accepted and asked to speak with me."

I introduced myself and we negotiated the location for the deed to be drawn up and cash payment to be presented at 1:00PM, tomorrow, with my attorney present at the proceedings. All information was exchanged for the preparation of the deed to be registered with the Registered of Deeds in the county, after the transaction was completed, tomorrow.

I immediately went to the banker and had a check drawn up to be presented for the property at tomorrows meeting.

Everything was now set for the closing on the tract 2 property, and I had the check for $175,000 ready to present to the seller. When I got back to the office, I called my apartment in Lake Mary, hoping that Marilyn would answer. We did need to talk about what I had accomplished today and what was expected to happen tomorrow at 1:00PM, at the closing.

Marilyn did answer, and I told her everything. "We were paying not the asking price, but $175,000, which was a saving of $14,000." "I had borrowed the $175,000 on a temporary loan from my bank and will have a check for that amount to pay cash at closing, tomorrow at 1:00PM."

I asked her, "to be available for the signing, since the deed would read that the property was in the name of Alvin Knight and Marilyn Knight. So, she may be required to sign some of the documents along with me."

"Alvin," she said, "you never cease to amaze me in what you are capable of accomplishing." 'You have only been working on this for three days and look what you have accomplished, in that time. Of course, I will be available for the closing."

"Very well," I said. "When I get home tonight, we can go get a rental car, so that you and the children can drive home, tomorrow after the signing, and I will join you in Pensacola on Friday night for the weekend."

I took care of any loose ends at the office and went home to my apartment to be with the family. Marilyn and I really got serious about what we wanted in a home that we could, immediately present our needs and desires to a respected contractor, as to our specifications.

While I had been in the office this afternoon, I took the liberty to call Mr. Adams from our property department, here in our main office. "I told him what we were doing and asked if he was in the position to introduce us to a reliable and imaginative home builder, that we might offer our plans for the home of our dreams, on the site that we are purchasing." Mr. Adams did recommend a Mr. Wesley, owner of Orange County Construction Corporation.

Mr. Adams said that, "Mr. Wesley's company was in demand and that, I would have to wait my turn in getting his firm as General Contractor for our home.

You would be very pleased with the results, if you did get him and his corporation.

'They had a reputation in the area for producing quality and sound homes in a reasonable price range. Mr. Adams said that, Mr. Wesley and his sub contactors received very few requests to make corrections, once the job was done. And the homes they constructed had a definite look of quality and always stand out when compared with other home builders' work."

Mr. Adams, "volunteered to have Mr. Wesley call me in the morning, at my office, in order to see if we can get together to show him our plans, so that he could draw up the official plans and get our requirements in order, to draw up a contract."

"I thanked Mr. Adams and told him that I deeply appreciated his assistance in this very personal matter." I added that, "I owed him one."

So, Marilyn and I had a lot of homework to do in preparation for a meeting with Mr. Wesley.

But, the first order of business was to get a rental car, so that Marilyn and the children could drive back to Pensacola, tomorrow (if we can complete all of our plans), or leave sometime after completion on Wednesday. We did have a lot to accomplish before she left. Tonight, we would work overtime in order to make a firm decisions about the specifications on the home construction.

Of course, we knew that we would have to leave many details up to the contractor, because of their knowledge of the site requirements, and the materials that are long lasting in the environmental conditions, here in Central Florida.

Also, the contractor understands what the area building codes require. "I am sure that we do not want to create problems that could slow down the process of construction," I said.

We had been very thorough in outlining our requirements. One major change that we decided upon was to add a little living space to the size of the home. We now realized that in order to provide for growth in our family, we needed to get at least 3,500 square feet of living space. This would, also, give Mr.Wesley a lot of leverage in creating a home that we could be really proud of, and in addition, be easier to sell in the future, if we were required to move into another area, that the company may decide to open, and require my locating into that area.

Another thought that we had, was to have a very large and private master bedroom, especially since we two were so sexually active and needed privacy from the children. Also, we wanted the children to be comfortable in their sleeping quarters and playroom activity.

By this time, Marilyn had been making a list of all of these changes in the house plan, that we were prepared to present to Mr. Wesley. It was, also, obvious to us that we may need to rethink the idea of being able to pay cash for the home, we were building. We now suspected the cost to be around $200,000 and would have to utilize a home loan, for the financing of that larger amount.

We enjoyed breakfast and I decided to report to the office early in anticipation of a call from Mr. Wesley, the contractor. While I waited, I was able to get caught up on a lot of reports that I had received from the District Offices. I was pleased to see that there were no obvious problems, and the production was continuing to grow in all of the districts.

At 9:30AM, the call came from Mr. Wesley.

Mr. Wesley said that, "they were caught up on their building obligations at the moment, and was glad to hear from Mr. Adams that a very important member of his company was desiring a quality home for his family, on a beautiful piece of property, West of Kissimmee." "Have you closed on the property?"

I told him that, "I was closing today at 1:00PM and would be paying cash for the property in order to not have a delay in the plans for construction, of a home, utilizing an illustration that we liked very much and would like for him to see if he could use those plans, with minor changes which we wish to suggest." Naturally, we wish his input on anything that would increase the livability and quality of the home on the property, we have selected. I added that, "I had been told that his company was very creative and we certainly did not want to interfere in his ability to provide that creativity."

Mr. Wesley said that, "my source was very complimentary, and he appreciated the source." "Do you think you and Mrs. Knight would be available by 3:00PM in order to meet with me in my office in downtown Orlando?"

I certainly believe that "the closing will be routine for the property and can join you by 3:00PM. Mrs. Knight and I will be looking forward to work with you in order to get a contract with you, moving forward."

Mr. Wesley gave me directions to his office and said that, "he was looking forward to working with us."

A call to my apartment gave the good news to Marilyn and she was extremely pleased that we might get all of this taken care of, today or tomorrow. "She really needed to get back to Pensacola by Thursday." "On the other hand, she knew how important it was to have all of this business taken care of, before she and the children drove back home to Pensacola."

By 1:00PM, we and my lawyer were in the office of the realty office and ready to close on the property. My lawyer had checked everything out and assured us that the sale and purchase could be legally deeded to us.

The owner was there with his lawyer and the transaction went smoothly. The presentation of the my check for $175,000 and the closing documents that transferred the property to us completed. We were out of there. "I asked my attorney to take the closing documents and prepared deed of trust awarded to Marilyn and myself to the county office and the Register of Deeds Office." This he did, and we were now the proud owners of 21 acres of prime property, west of Kissimmee.

This allowed me to call Mr. Wesley and "tell him that Marilyn and I were now having lunch and would be in his office at 3:00PM."

We were able to do all of this because my Administrative Assistant had made arrangements for a trusted friend to stay with the children, while Marilyn and I were conducting the business, that we were trying to complete, today.

Before 3:00PM we were in Mr.Wesley's office with the proposed plans and our list of changes that we were choosing to make, in them.

Mr. Wesley came out of his office and greeted us. Marilyn and I immediately liked him and felt comfortable that he was going to make us proud that we had chosen his firm to build our dream house. He ordered refreshments to be brought in to all, and immediately emersed himself in the plans that we presented.

"He asked to see the list of changes that we had indicated our desire to change."

He was delighted to see that we had indicated the addition up to 3,500 square feet of living space, and said "that this would allow him to make changes that would fit well with other quality homes that carried the Central Florida look, that fits well in this area." The plans that we had presented were not specific with Florida and would require the roof covering and look, that most quality homes in Florida display." He loved the changes that we had recommended in the master bedroom and noted the additional bedroom, which would be our nursery, and placed close to the Master Bedroom. He said, he could do some creative work with the playroom for the children and was adding a forth bath room.

He suggested a curved driveway that curved around the front of the house and included an entrance and an exit back into the road that stood in front of the property.

We especially liked that idea and the two-car enclosed garage that he suggested.

He continued going over the changes that we had suggested and even expanded some of them, and recommended a specific type of airconditioning. "He told us that most homes did not have heating in Florida," but he said that he would like to add a gas log heating element in the large living room, just in case the weather becomes cold. He quickly said that "this is a rarity, but a good thing, especially because of the children."

Mr. Wesley had been generous with his time. But he knew that we were on limited time, and asked if there was anything else that we wanted to add.

"I told him that we would like an awning over the terrace in the back, since the sun going down in the west was directed onto the terrace area."

"He said that that was a very good request. He began to close by saying that his company put in quality plumbing fixtures and kitchen appliances and I can now say that I think we can do a turnkey job for you for189,000 at todays prices."

"I told him that I had originally planned to pay cash for the home, but now realized that I would have to seek a loan program of possibly fifteen years." I added that we planned to start doubling up on the monthly payments and expected to repay the loan in possibly half that time."

No problem he said, "we will be delighted with what ever method you choose to pay for the home once it is finished and accepted by you." "I like the way you two work and will be delighted to create your dream home."

With the actions today. Marilyn and I felt that we had entered another stage of our lives. Everything was coming up roses. We were working at easing the need for weekend trips from Maitland to Pensacola, and my long workweeks of being totally away from my family. Of course, we were still going to have to continue that routine for the four to six months that it would take to build our dream home. But, we now knew that the wait would be worth it, once the contractor finished his work and turned the finished structure over to us.

You have to know that this was my first home, that I could say, this is mine.

Marilyn had been a joy to work with throughout this five or six days of planning that we were able to set in motion. It seemed like a dream that all of this has been opened to us in such a timely fashion. I realize that we were now in debt, created by the loan that we were establishing, but it certainly was an answer to our prayers. We had been in a temporary lifestyle that we knew we had to tolerate in order to get to where we were making the changes, to put us into positive pleasure, that we would now be able to really enjoy life as a family in our new home, that we have put so much thought into making it a happy home for all of our family, and hopefully our expected love child for Marilyn and myself.

Now, I had to get back to work and Marilyn had headed home to Pensacola.

I had had a key cut for her, so she was able to load up the kids and off she went to her home. She had about five hours of daylight to drive safely home and promised to call me at my apartment, when they were safely home. She did call shortly after 9:00PM, and we spent more time on the phone than we should, but we were so happy with what we had accomplished in such a short time span.

Marilyn said, "that the children were so happy to hear what we had been able to accomplish and even though they were too young to understand all of it, one thing that they really understood, was that they were going to have their loving father, you, home on most nights." They were really excited about that, Marilyn said.

They were also, excited about their new home in Florida and kept asking her to describe what it would look like. "They also, liked the idea of having all of the space they would have to go exploring. They kept asking me to describe what twenty one acres looked like and the two lakes. I cautioned them again, that they could never go into the lakes and must avoid any of the animals and other creatures that may be there."

Life is good, I thought. My life has changed so much in such a short period of time since Marilyn came back into my life, only about one year ago. I felt that I had been lost and now I am found. My life was changed by meeting this wonderful Marilyn, who showed me what a real, strong woman she really was, and is now as, my wife, my love and my happiness.

I went to sleep knowing that I had to be the luckiest, and happiest man alive.

I was looking forward to a lifetime of pure wedded bliss.

Morning came, and I went to the office refreshed and rededicated to being the best executive that Southern had, to continue develop products and services for it's customers and Board of Directors. I appreciated the time that I had been permitted to prepare for a more stabilized life of having my family near me here in Central Florida. I knew that the entire division, that I had helped create and now directed, depended on my input and devotion to it's continued success.

For the next two days, I directed my attention to the reports from each of our eight District Offices. Each one of them were doing well, but I knew that if we were not continuing to build up our districts, by adding new businesses to the districts, we would stay where we currently were in production for the Credit Unions, as well as sales of insurance products that we offered.

I sent a memo to all District Offices that we were interested in receiving information on any new business, that we were not currently serving, so that we could send a visitation group from the home office in hopes of enrolling a number of new businesses into the Credit Union, and contract for our agents to begin schedules of calling on the employees, of those businesses.

My theory was if you do not continue to grow, you face the possibility of other insurance companies attempting to develop their own program and compete with our business. We suggested that our existing District Office agents, on the route that they were currently covering, note any large business to their District Manager, who would report referred businesses to my office. If we visit and sign a contract with that referred business, we would make sure that that agent would receive the right to take over any businesses that we were able to contract. This could add a great deal of incentive for the agent to provide names of potential new businesses, that they would eventually take over and start getting the commissions for new insurance, that was needed for themselves and their families.

I was positive that this memo would bring in suggestions of ten to twenty new businesses for us to approach for the purpose of placing the credit unions and our insurance products, sold by our agents.

I was confident that we could set up a schedule that at least two groups, from the main office, could begin calling on right away. I asked Mr. Summers, as Marketing Manager, to head one of the groups and I would personally head the other group.

It was now Friday afternoon and I called Marilyn to let her know that I was leaving for home in Pensacola, and would arrive around 8:30PM.

Marilyn said that "the realestate agent had brought several families to visit and see the home as a potential purchase. The agent had said that one of the families liked the house very much and thought the advertised price of $90,000 was fair to them and were attempting to get a loan to purchase the house."

I told her that, "if the sale came through quickly, we could rent a satisfactory home in the Orlando area until our new home was completed." I told her, "that Mr. Wesley had already started grading our site and laying out the boundaries that would eventually be our completed dream home."

For now, "we would be together for the weekend and we had a lot of catching up to do." The trip to Pensacola was uneventful and I arrived home around 8:30PM.

That little bundle of love, Marilyn, greeted me at the door and flew into my arms and would not let me go. What a way for me to be greeted when I come home from being away for a few days. This is the most lovable woman that I have ever known. How lucky could I be to have this wonderful creature waiting for me?

Well, I decided to do something very special for her tonight, when we went to bed. Right now, all I wanted to do was just hold her in my arms and plant pouty kisses all over her face. There was no surface that was left out, not the eyes, nor the ears, the back of her neck. I decided then, that the rest of her body would be rewarded, later. I believe I must have been a good boy to deserve this heavenly reception. Well, it had been a good week for all of us in the family, and business wise, in my company.

With Marilyn's encouragement, the bank, which made our purchase of the property, the loan vendor, and finally the contractor, we had accomplished in several days what many buyers, of those services normally, take months.

I just laid the biggest kiss, ever on Marilyn's luscious lips and said "honey, we did it, didn't we"? She just moaned and said, "we are so fortunate to have found each other."

Well we had consumed a half hour of my, at home time, since I had arrived.

Who cares, this is the way that we want to spend the rest of our lives.

Marilyn finally came down to earth and said, "you must be famished for dinner and I certainly want you to have your energy, tonight." "What would you like me to fix you? I ate with the children, earlier and they are already in bed in deep, deep sleep."

"Honey, I would just like to have some of your famous grilled cheese spread on a toasted bun and a glass of cold milk." "You can tell me about your week while I am finishing my sandwich."

"Darling," she said, "I don't know how I could possibly improve on all of the good news that you have provided, this week!"

"If you have finished eating, why don't we leave the dishes until morning, and go to bed. I believe you have made some promises that you should now keep."

And that is the way that it went. We headed for the bath tub and lay soaking up the warm water and the bubble bath, and sponged off each other. We knew that we would have no need for clothes, tonight.

We were in our soft bed and I was full aware of the promises that I had made when I first came home tonight. I began by throwing aside the top sheet and the light blanket that we normally slept under, then took a long, slow look at the beautiful work of art that I had to work with. I decided that I had done an incomplete job earlier, and would attempt to correct any pouting jealously that her body may have. I took my hand and drew my fingers from one cheek to the other, passing over her luscious lips and taunting them, that more was to come. I thrust my lips upon hers and and used my tongue to explore her mouth. Then, I planted a moist, lingering kiss upon her lips.

Moving down to her throat, I nibbled a little and planted light kisses all around from the front to the back, and around the other side. I raised up and viewed her pouting breasts and uttered my approval of the beauty that I was beholding, I gave light caressing moves with my fingers around each beautiful breast and finally planted my lips in a rotation which circled each globe and stopped to sip, tenderly on each nipple. There were other parts that had been too long neglected and I kissed a beautiful bellybutton, appreciatively. Venturing further south to her thighs, I then started licking from each knee to the top of her thighs. Pausing to view that very special place, and looked into her eyes for approval. She left no doubt that she wanted me to proceed, and I inserted my tongue into the heat that she was offering. With licks with my tongue all around, I began to rotate my tongue all around on her measure of pleasure. By this time she was grinding her body into my face in utter pleasure, seemingly to get all of the pleasure she felt entitled too.

Suddenly she gave a light gasp and took my member and took it all into her body and kept thrusting with her back arched in order to drain in all of the pleasure she was receiving. I could hold off no longer and began pounding, faster and faster until she fell back, totally exhausted, and drained as I gave up my load of love for her.

We lay there perfectly fulfilled in our love for each other. Life was good, and with this wonderful family and my continuing success with my company, I believe I can finally say it---"how can it get better than this?" But, I believe it will!

Morning came and the children jumped all over me. They seemed so glad to have me home, if only for the weekend. They asked so many questions, such as "when are we going to move"? And "have they started on our new home, yet? and answered themselves by 'ill bet it is going to be really pretty.'" I answered each in order, "we will move just as soon as the contractor finishes the home and we accept it as completed satisfactorily." And, yes, the most important of all, "it will be built in a manner that all of us will have our own little area, that is functional and create a happy home for each of us. Finally, 'I assure you, it will be pretty, you will be very proud."

The rest of the weekend consisted of doing every thing for the children that they wanted to do, consisting of many games, trips to the park, where they could ride their bicycles. I had purchased a small fishing pole for each of them and we fished in the small pond, there in the middle of the park. They caught a few small fish, which I made sure, they threw back in for some other lucky fisherman to catch, at a later time.

Naturally, we went to Sunday School and church service on Sunday and just enjoyed being a family. While at church, several people mentioned that they had noticed our advertisement for the selling of our home. They said, "they hoped that we were not moving away." We were forced to say that, "we had purchased property south of Orlando and our new home would be completed in about six months time. We added that the move was necessary to have the family near my work in that area. We assured them that we would continue to attend this church until our move. However, we were looking forward to having the family be able to be together most of the time. "We told them that we would miss our wonderful church family, who had been so very special to us, during our stay, here."

Monday morning, very early, I was on the road again to my work. I knew this would be a very busy week and had expected my memo to start showing results of reports from the District Offices, containing names of prospective companies that may wish to have our services in contract with the Credit Unions, in that area.

By Tuesday we were beginning to receive prospects, and by Thursday, we had received multiple prospects from all of the eight District Offices. Our job now was to start evaluating the prospects to determine if those companies would fit into a mold of profitable ventures for those companies, the Credit Union and our companies sales force.

We wanted to do a thorough review and honor our District Offices and the sales agents for making the recommendations. In our review, we were looking for businesses that had, at least, fifty employees, a sound record of being fair to their employee base, a solid reputation of being creative in their business of providing quality products (or providing valuable services to their customers).

Naturally, they would have to allow payroll deduction for the the products and services provided by the Credit Union and our insurance products.

As you will recall, Mr. Summers in Marketing and I had established two marketing visitation groups and began calling on businesses that were recommended by our sales agents in the respective District Offices.

Mr. Summers began taking his group to the Northern Florida areas of Daytona, Jacksonville, Gainesville and Tallahassee and contracted with The Port Authority and Jacksonville Boat Builders in Jacksonville and The Greyhound Race Trainers and the Daytona Inn Keepers Association in Daytona, by Thursday.

I took my crew to Orlando, Tampa, Miami and Fort Lauderdale. By Friday morning, we had contracted with Baugh Distributing Company and The Fresh Vegetable Markets in Tampa, EZ Printing and Balboa Beer Bottlers in Orlando, Burton Oil Distributors and Fort Lauderdale Boat Builders in Fort Lauderdale and Genissee Poultry Producers and The Miami Electric Distributors of Miami.

Later on Friday, we realized that we had contracted all of the businesses that we had gone after for Credit Union services and our ability to seek payroll deduction for our insurance products. Our agents would be scheduled to begin servicing all of these new businesses in the coming weeks, along with the businesses they currently were servicing.

Before our groups left work on Friday afternoon, President Andrew Jackson had commended our groups in his private office with making an outstanding work effort for our companies continued successes by our division. This was an outstanding send off as we departed for our weekend with our families.

Before leaving, I called Marilyn and told her that I was looking forward to spending the weekend with my wonderful family.

Marilyn said that your loving family has been saving up a lot of love for the returning hero, father and lover.

Another long trip back to Pensacola, but I knew that my most precious things were awaiting there for me to spend a wonderful weekend with them. The week had been extremely profitable and we had just added to the strength of Southern Medical and Life's bottom line. The company was continuing to grow in a vibrant way.

I was proud to have been a part of this growth and vowed that I was going to continue living up to the huge expectations of my division. As I thought of this, the miles passed along quickly and my excitement of the wonder that awaited me at home, continued to rise.

The outskirts of Pensacola appeared and then I was home. The lights of our house came on and two precious children literally jumped into my arms. I held those precious two and kissed each one with great affection as they wanted to know what exciting news I might have, about our new home in Central Florida.

Proudly, I told them that I had taken some photos of the property, as it was prior to any construction and the progress that had been made this week. I added, "that I would be showing them to them tonight."

Suddenly, Marilyn burst into view and wanted to get into the hugging action.

There we were, the four of us just hugging and hugging.

Marilyn said that, "she had just finished dinner and we should all wash up and come to the table." We were all anxious to hear that, and quickly were back to the dining room. It was obvious that she had made the table decorations and the meal to be a very special occasion. She said that, "she had some very special news that we would share after enjoying our dinner."

We ate the wonderful meal and were looking forward to the special news that Marilyn has announced. She began by saying, "I have been to my Gynecologist and he has told me that we are going to have an addition to our family, you children are going to have a new brother or sister." As we all clapped in approval, she continued, "the doctor has said that he believes, there is a possibility that there may be twins, two boys or two girls, and just maybe a boy and a girl."

Well, I was the first to hug her and kiss her and the children joined in to the exhilaration. There was joy all around and I asked, "when was she expecting to deliver?"

"It is now mid September and I should deliver in early to mid May, next year." She continued for the purpose of the children that, "it takes nine months from the inception of a child or children, in case of twins, to be born in normal births. Inception comes from the union of a man and a woman in love," she continued to explain to the children.

Marilyn had hoped that the children were old enough to understand what she had described. She now said, "I have more exciting news to share."

The children and I were wondering what other exciting news could come after the bombshell that she had just announced, it would be hard to top what she had just divulged.

Again, she said, "I have another good news to tell all of you, as you may know, I have advertised our home here for sale and have received several offers, one for $90,000 and another for $102,000." "I have accepted the $102,000 offer, and we will be closing on that offer in the next week."

"The reason that I am telling all of you, is that the new owners will want to take possession of this house shortly after closing, we will have to move to another location at that time."

I spoke up at that time and said, "that is wonderful news, would you like to move to Central Florida, near our home that is being built?" "Or would you like to rent something near here?"

A loud chorus said, "we want to move to Central Florida!"

"No problem, I said. I will find a good home or condominium that is rentable until our new home is finished, perhaps in April of next year," and added, "we may have to change our home plan to add another room if the doctor's prediction of twins for your mother are accurate."

"But now," she said, "you children brush your teeth and get ready for bed, it is getting late, and we can talk some more about this, tomorrow."

After the children were in bed, Marilyn turned to me and said, "now I want you to take me to bed for very little talk and a lot of action."

I was glad to follow her instruction, or was it a demand that I was glad to respond to with action! What a life, we were sharing with each other!

Author's note--- if you are not sharing this kind of love and life with your mate you are missing out on so much joy in life!

If you are interested in knowing what was going on, it is not any of your business! Do your own thing!

The rest of the weekend went by with my making the rest of the family know that I wanted to share my love for the family and was willing to do what made them happy. I knew that my being away from the family all week would come to an end when Marilyn's home was sold and they moved to the Orlando area. That reminded me that, when I returned to work on Monday, house hunting was going to take part of my time when workdays were over. Of course, some of my working hours could provide time to do some research provided by the news-paper advertisements, as well as calling realestate companies that specialized in rental properties.

But first, I needed to determine if any new recommendations were coming from the District Offices. I knew that this was going to be an ongoing method of building our company's business, and I wanted to make it my priority to be constantly in the forefront of making that happen.

President Jackson had sent personal letters to Mr. Summers and myself, saying, "how much the Board of Directors were recognizing our hard work and dedication to continuing growth in our Division."

I made it a habit, after work each day, to go by the site of our home construction and photo the progress that was being made. Naturally, the work being performed could not possibly keep up with my desire to get the home completed. It was not that I was disappointed in what was being done, but I was in a hurry to have the home completed. I would never express any displeasure in any way to Mr. Wesley and his construction crew, for the work performed; in my way of thinking, that would become counter productive. I just continued my picture taking so that I could show my family what was happening to our home, to be. I was happy to see that the layout was beginning to show what the home would eventually look like.

It was now Wednesday and, after work, I went out to take my photos of the construction. When I returned to my apartment, I continued to check the newspapers to see if there were any homes or condos very promising. I cut out several of the advertisements and decided to drive by and check them out.

One of the qualifications would be, location near our new home, being built.

I was hoping to find something in the school district that our children would eventually be attending. I was aware that the public schools had already started this school year, and Marilyn and I would want to place the children in the schools that they would be attending, once our home was completed.

The second qualification would pertain to size of the facility to be rented; it would have to be large enough to accommodate the family that we presently have and allow for the increase in family that we were anticipating. A room that we could arrange a nursery for one, and possibly two children must be taken into consideration.

A third consideration would be our ability to not have to sign a longterm rental or lease agreement. We would have to be able to vacate the property when our home is completed. Cost of rental is not a big consideration, I am sure that we will be able to find what we need for less than five hundred dollars a month, which would not dent our financial situation.

A final consideration would be finding a neighborhood, where we could feel comfortable and safe, especially for the children.

I took my trusted camera and took photos of several that I felt may be of some interest to Marilyn. We will review them when I returned to Pensacola over the weekend.

The reports from the District Offices continued to come in very positive; an increase in sales seemed to be the norm and most sales agents were making good commissions in order to support them and their families. Our District Managers had an ongoing training program and seldom have we been asked to assist in that retraining. The District Managers, who receive a bonus for increased sales were making more money than they had ever made, prior to their appointment with our company, and continued to work with the agents in order to keep the morale very high, and growing.

So, it seems, our programs were all working well for everyone involved----the businesses we served and their employees, the Credit Unions were pleased that their business had increased greatly, our sales agents earning more commission, and Southern Medical and Life was growing to new heights and overall profits.

As for me, I was completely happy that I had been permitted to be involved as Director of this Division and was giving it all that I had.

CHAPTER 33

IT WAS NOW Friday evening and I was headed home to Marilyn and the children for another relaxing weekend. I had called Marilyn prior to my leaving.

She was excited that I was coming home and told me to hurry home, safely. She said that she had news and would tell me about it when I arrived home in Pensacola.

The miles sped by quickly, and I arrived about 9:00PM. Since I was arriving a little later than usual, the children were already in bed and sound asleep. I was disappointed that I did not get to have their usual, excited welcome, but that was alright, I knew that I would have the entire weekend to enjoy playing with them and enjoying their excitement.

Marilyn did not disappoint me and came into my arms and let me know that she had missed me so very much. She did not want to be let go and continued to cling to me, but finally let me know that she had prepared dinner, for she and I, to quietly enjoy, and tell each other about how our week had gone.

As we ate, I reminded her that she had said that she had news to tell me and I had anxiously awaited what that was all about.

She did not disappoint me and went to the office and brought back a receipt deposit to her bank account for $102,000 from the sale of her home. She said, "that was the good news, the bad news was that she needed to vacate the home in one week, so that the new buyer could take possession of it."

I just held her and said, "we will abide with the request for us to vacate the home in one week." Then continued, "I have been looking for houses and condos that are advertised for rent and I have brought some photos for you to look over to determine if they would suffice until our home is finished."

Bringing out the photos, I showed them to her and described them as best I could. The advertisements had given a description of the number of rooms and bath rooms, and total square footage. All of the homes I showed her had over twenty five hundred square feet of space. I estimated her square footage here to be no more that eighteen hundred square feet of space.

"If you like what you see in any of these photos, I can make the rental arrangements as soon as I get back to the Orlando area on Monday." "Most of these, you have seen, are in the school district where the children will be attending. I kept in mind that it would be unwise to rent in any other area, than the area that our new home occupies."

Marilyn agreed that this would be best for the children.

I continued, "once we decide on a home to rent, we can arrange for a moving company from here in Pensacola to come, package, ship to the new rental and place the furniture and other items, where you determine is the place you want them to remain, until our new home is completed." "Then we will have to repeat the process of moving to our new home. I continued, with your condition, you should not be involved in the moves except acting as a supervisor in providing instructions of how the packing here should be, and the unpacking and placing in the rental home should be done after arriving at the Central Florida location we choose."

"If you wish, I will make all of the arrangements." On the other hand, "if you would prefer, you can make the arrangements. I just don't want you to worry your pretty head, as you know, you are carrying very valuable cargo in that lovely body of yours. What do you think?"

"I will accept your decision on the temporary location that you settle on there."

"Go ahead as soon as possible and nail down the location you believe best for us.

After you chose the location, call me and give me the address and I will contract with the most reputable long distance mover in this area, to pack and deliver all of our possessions to that address. Believe me, I will supervise the entire project of the move and unpacking, there," she concluded.

"This is good, after all, we will expect to be in that location no more than six months and then, we will be in our dream home," I assured her.

We made the best of what might be our last weekend in Pensacola by going to the park on Saturday and to the church on Sunday. It was somewhat of a going away from the church, which we all had loved and had so many memories, especially of the kindness they had shown to Marilyn and the children, after David's death and during our marriage, where we had been truly blessed by the entire congregation. At Sunday school and before, and after the service, we spoke to all of our closer friends and thanked them for being part of our lives, up to this time. We all shared a few tears that we would be parting, but reminded them, if they were ever in the Orlando area, to be sure to look us up.

They assured us that they would take us up on that offer.

We were parting with regret, but we knew that our future was assured by the actions that we had already set in motion.

Early Monday morning came and Marilyn insisted in getting up with me, gave me a big kiss and fixed a great breakfast for me to enjoy, prior to my departure, with another lingering hug and a wonderful kiss for both of us to remember, until we were together, again. We knew that we would be set up in our new rental property, before the next weekend.

By lunchtime on Monday, I had signed the rental agreement and paid the first monthly payment for renting 1020 Bayview Court, in West Kissimmee, Florida. I had been assured that our home, when built, would be in the same School District and our children would not have to move from the schools they were to enroll in, when they arrived.

With that assurance, I immediately called Marilyn and gave her the address to ship the furniture. She said that "the children were in school and that she would have them checked out of school and load them, and some personal items in the car on Wednesday morning, and follow the moving van, after the loading. They expected to arrive around 4:00PM Wednesday, afternoon."

"I assured her that the telephone, power and water would be installed when they arrived."

Marilyn just cooed and said, "my important business man just always comes through on every occasion, and I love him for that."

Immediately, I made arrangements for the utilities to be installed in the rental home and paid for any installation fees.

Wednesday afternoon came, and I checked out of the office at 3:00PM and arrived at our new rental home to make sure everything had been taken care of by the utilities. Everything was great, and I looked over the yard to determine what needed to be done to make everyone feel welcome, when they arrived.

Marilyn had moved ahead of the moving van when they passed Orlando, and they arrived prior to the moving van. I greeted them, hugged the children, laid a big kiss on Marilyn and began to show them through the house and out into the spacious back yard, which the children immediately fell in love with all the room where they would be spending a lot of play time, after school each day.

Later, after the van had arrived, unpacked and settled the furniture in the locations selected by Marilyn, we made certain everything was OK and approved to our satisfaction, I suggested that we drive by the schools, were the children would be installed on Thursday morning.

Marilyn and the children loved it immediately; to my great satisfaction, I knew that I had liked them when I first checked them out, earlier.

It was getting late, and I knew that all of us were getting hungry, so I suggested that we find a good family-food restaurant, that I had previously visited.

All were in agreement to that, and we chowed down.

Later, we stopped and purchased the necessary groceries that we would need in beginning our stay in our new location, and headed home to sort out where everything should be placed in it's final position. The movers had done a fine job and we only had to make a few minor changes. Marilyn was not allowed to do anything that could possibly strain her in any way, because of her pregnancy.

That reminded me that I had requested my administrative assistant do some research on the best doctor in Orlando, who would be experienced in possible birth of twins. She had come up with James K. McDonald, of the Woman's Center in Orlando, this information I now reported to Marilyn.

She said, "this was great news, it confirmed the recommendation that her doctor had recommended when asked for a good doctor to visit in Orlando, when I arrived there." She continued, "you have opened so many doors for me prior to my arriving here. Here is a big kiss that you have earned for being so protective of me, my darling. Tonight we will see how receptive this house is to two of the best lovers, after the children have played themselves out in the playroom and go to sleep." This came very soon and we were one.

I believe we did have the best sex that we had had, ever. But, of course, they had all been great.

On Thursday morning, we got the children up early and took them to school.

After seeing that everything was going to work out, I went on to work. This had all worked out so well, and the children seemed to be very happy with their new school arrangements.

Having the family here in the Orlando area was certainly going to be a blessing to me. I was looking forward to coming home at the end of the day, to the family I loved, so very much.

When I arrived home at 5:30PM, Marilyn had prepared a wonderful dinner for the family to enjoy. She had set up an appointment with Dr. McDonald, found all of the stores that she wanted to shop, and a wonderful store where she could buy maternity clothing, when the need arose.

The children told us all about school and how much they liked their new teachers. We had known that they would have some catching up to do, but the teachers had given Marilyn material that the children would have to address, in order to catch up. The new teachers had expressed their belief that these two were very smart children, and should catch up and quickly surpass most of the other students, who had been in their classes since the school year began.

Marilyn let the school administrators know that she wanted to be involved in attending as a parent supporter at meetings, called by the administration, seeking parental attendance.

Now that we were settled into the community, we began looking for the things that everyone takes advantage of, such as the best shopping centers, the best grocery stores, pharmacies and churches.

During the first week there, we had been so busy in getting the house set up to our liking, we had not thought of attending church; nor did we have any idea where we would like to attend. We realized that we needed to get the children involved in church, as they had always been, especially in Pensacola.

When Saturday arrived, we got the family in the car and drove by all of the area Lutheran Churches, that were listed in the telephone directory, as well as the local newspaper announcements, that had caught our attention. The criteria that we were looking for was a well established congregation, pastor that catered to attracting young families, programs that the children could participate in, such as summer school, and camp activities.

Our drive gave us a place that we decided to start our visitations; we planed to visiting as many as four churches on consecutive weeks. After a visit, we took great lengths in evaluating how each of us felt about the church and our visit. Marilyn and I made sure that the children participated in the evaluation.

These visits, and the evaluation that followed, went on for the next five weeks, with the final one being as far away as Orlando, about five miles away.

Then, we brought out our evaluation sheets and went back over each one and discussed how we had felt after each visit. Of course each of us had our likes and dislikes, and we vocalized each of these.

Finally, we all agreed, we settled on Saint John's Lutheran Church. It was located only three miles from where our permanent home was being built, at this very moment. Our evaluation was that it had an outstanding young pastor, not yet forty five years old; he was a compassionate speaker who knew how and when to entertain, yet brought a spiritual message that we all need to hear and feel in our daily and spiritual life, our family life and obligations to others.

The children agreed that Saint Johns had the best Sunday School and programs that they enjoyed. They especially liked the teachers of their class.

Marilyn and I decided that we felt extremely happy in the young couples class, that we were attending, here at Saint Johns. We agreed that we missed that great group back in Pensacola, and said that after our new child (or children) were born, we would like to go back and visit our old friends, which we had left, there.

After church each week, we usually visited a carry-out deli and picnicked at our now rising home. We were delighted in the progress that was being made and could not wait until it was finished. Our visits gave the children a great chance to run and play. They always loved to go near our great lake and see the birds that always frequented it's shore. For safety sake, Marilyn and I always monitored by visiting with them, at least in the beginning, to make sure that no danger was present, there. We were so proud of these well adjusted children, who obeyed our instructions of safety precautions.

Marilyn and I were happy with what progress Mr. Wesley was making.

It was evident that the location was well laid out, foundations sound and the brick work was nearing completion. Windows had not yet been installed. But the openings indicated where they would be placed. The rooms were showing progress, as the interior lumber was being installed to give an outline where the rooms would begin to show. The roof was yet to be established and the roofing placed, but all in all, our home was beginning to look inviting.

Later, Marilyn prepared a wonderful dinner for us to enjoy and we made sure that their studies had been prepared for school on Monday morning, and allowed them to go to the playroom and then bedtime.

Marilyn and I were looking forward to a glass of red wine and some couch time, before we went to bed. I could tell that her nibbling kisses were telling me that cuddling was not going to be enough, and I said, "are you sure that the doctor would approve, because of your condition?"

She just got that gleam in her eye and said, "big guy, I have had conversation with my doctor, and he tells me that sex is permissible, if desired, until the sixth or seventh month of pregnancy. We have three our four months to enjoy our favorite pastime. Please, let's enjoy ourselves as long as we can, now take care of my lover's obligation."

And I did as I was told, much to both of our great satisfaction!

Monday came and when I reported to the office, my Administrative Assistant told me to return a call at President Jackson's request.

I called him immediately and and he asked me if I could come to his office, at my convenience. I assured him that I was free at the moment and would be there immediately.

When I arrived, he greeted me with a firm handshake and asked me if I would share a cup of coffee, since he was ready to ask his secretary to bring them in. "You do take cream and sugar, I believe."

"Yes, sir," I replied.

Mr. Jackson called in our request and it arrived immediately. We began to enjoy our coffee and he said that, "he had been getting splendid reports of my divisions growth and the Board of Directors had been following my progress in the company and were very impressed." "I want to speak to you in complete confidence that must not go out of this room. I must tell you that I have been contemplating my retirement and have reported to them, that I would like to see our company move into one more state prior to my official retirement, by inserting your division into the state of Georgia. Now, I must ask you about some news that I have been hearing about your private family life. I understand that you have just moved your family to Central Florida in order to be near you here. Is that correct?"

"Yes sir, we are currently building a new home, south of Orlando, and are currently renting a home near the construction site. My wife, Marilyn, has sold her home in Pensacola and moved her family in with me here. We are now expecting what could be twins in six to seven months. But I assure you that my family life will not inhibit my enthusiasm for my work in my division. The division is currently operating smoothly, and my taking on added responsibilities will not be a problem."

"I am pleased to hear that, he said. I want to tell you that I have recommended you as my replacement as President of Southern Medical and Life Services, once the State of Georgia is fully implemented into our company." "At that time, my retirement will take place and Mr. Alvin Knight will be elected as President of Southern in both Florida and Georgia. Naturally, we realize that traveling to business in that state will be cumbersome by car. We are prepared to make an allowance for you to travel by plane to the operations, that are to be set up in Georgia. Are you in agreement with that arrangement?"

"Yes, sir," I said. "Have you considered the cities where we could set up District Offices?"

"I believe we will leave that final decision to you, Alvin." "Do you have any suggestions?"

"I would like to suggest that, for the time being, we set up District Offices in Atlanta, Athens, Augusta, Savannah and possibly, one more to be decided upon." "How does that sound to you, Mr. President?"

"Excellent choices, Alvin. We will set the move in motion by the end of the Month. Our first job will be to contact the Insurance Commissioner of Georgia and seek permission to offer our insurance products in the state. After that is accomplished, it will be your responsibility to set up a team from our office here in Florida to assist you in establishing the District Offices and personnel to man the offices, and hire a sales force of agents." "You are the man who knows how to do those things best, you have already shown us that, with your performance here in Florida."

"Sir, I would like to request that Mr. Summers assist me with this project.

We already have teams that have proven successful in the marketing area. I will need to have the services of Properties, Human Resources, Advertising, Legal, Licensing, Payroll (for payroll deduction), Product Development, and Product Specialists." "We have all done this here in Florida, and now we are prepared to create a similar success in the State of Georgia. Of course we will need approval of all of the heads of those departments. I firmly believe we will get the support of these managers, as we did here in Florida."

"Now, Alvin, I believe you know why I recommended you for this venture.

We will go forward immediately." "Please call a meeting as soon as you get assurances from those Department Managers that they are committed to this project. I would like to attend that meeting, if you do not mind."

"Absolutely, sir." "I will call on you to make the formal announcement and answer any questions that they have of concern, especially about methods of travel."

"Thank you, Alvin. Give my love to the family and let them know that I support you and respect their needs for your time." "That is why I have recommended you and respect their needs for your time. That is why I have recommended air travel, in order for you to be available for the family needs of your time."

One might think that Mr. Jackson's request of me to undergo another huge campaign in the state of Georgia was coming at a bad time, with Marilyn's pregnancy and the continued building activity on our new home. But, I knew that the opportunity that Mr. Jackson had said would come my way as a result of his retirement, was too huge to resist.

After leaving the presidents office, I returned to my office and immediately began scheduling meetings in my office with the managers of departments that I had revealed to Mr. Jackson, as needed to carry out this Georgia project. My first call was to Mr. Summers of Marketing. Mr. Summers came immediately and after he received the news, graciously accepted my request to help lead the project as we had begun in Florida, with great success. Mr. Ray Hudson of legal was my next contact and said that he would be available immediately.

Mr. Hudson listened intently, as I revealed the Georgia expansion, and very quickly said, "he had wondered when we would plan this move, and assured me that he was available to serve at my favor."

My success continued in the affirmative as Property, Licensing, Payroll, Human Resources, Advertising, Product Development and the Product Specialists were brought aboard.

Elated in the vast support of these key players, I called a meeting for 3:00PM in the conference room and informed President Jackson that, "I had been effective in securing the support of all Managers, that we needed to begin the expansion into Georgia, and asked if he could be present in the conference at 3:00PM."

Mr. Jackson was delighted that we were moving so fast, and would be pleased to attend the meeting.

By 2:50, when President Jackson walked into the conference room, everyone was there, and I called the meeting to order, and thanked everyone for attending the meeting. My first comment was that, "it was so good to see the team together again, that had worked so hard in getting our Division started, and to bring it to the very successful position that we were now enjoying."

I continued by saying that, "according to my latest reports, the company had doubled in size in the past six months, since our inception. With that in mind, today we have been asked to take the company forward once more, as we finally venture into another state, the state of Georgia."

"It was the vision of our great President, Mr. Jackson, who first envisioned this move, and I would like to call on him to speak of that vision, and after that, I will announce the cities that we will be selecting for the District Offices for this undertaking."

"President Jackson, will you bring us up to date on your expectations for what, you have envisioned, and then, I will announce what is now six cities, where we would like to cover the state in order to maximize our probabilities of the greatest potential, for fulfilling our President's vision for our expansion."

"President Jackson, the floor is all yours."

Mr. Jackson began by "telling our group of Managers, that the Board of Directors came up with the original idea of working with the Credit Unions to offer their services to businesses here in Florida; a method of providing benefits to their employees that Credit Unions offered on a payroll deduction basis, such as a saving opportunity and the possibility of offering loans to the businesses'
employees." "As a service to the businesses and the Credit Unions and now our business of providing various medical insurance to the employees and possibly offering Straight Life Insurance, as well as a Life Insurance that was designed to grow in value, without the employee having to die and leave funds to the deceased' families."
"The rest is history, all of you gentlemen and ladies, under the direction of Mr. Knight, now a Vice President of our company, took that idea, that I was just speaking about, and has more than doubled our company and its revenue in a very short year, since the formation of this division." "In closing, I can possibly see that you, in adopting this program, may conceivably double our company again, with this venture."
Now, gentlemen and ladies, I must ask you, "are you more financially successful than you were before we began this division?"
A resounding "yes"! came from the managers after hearing this question.
They all knew that the company had been very generous in providing better salaries and overall benefits, since the inception of this business, employee, Credit Union and Southern Medical and Life contract agreements.
Mr. Jackson yielded the floor and, I said, "that the process would begin with Legal, Licensing, and Product Development being successful in getting our company licensed and accepted in the state of Georgia by the Insurance Commissioner of Georgia." "We will then, send in Properties, Advertising and Human Resources to set up district offices in the cities of Atlanta, Athens, Savannah, Augusta, Columbus and Macon, (not necessarily in that order).

Advertising, Legal, Properties and Human Resources will secure the properties for the District Offices and the District Office Managers, and hire sales agents.

Then Training, Licensing, Product Specialists and Payroll will work with getting our sales agents fully equipped to serve the employees of the businesses, that we are able to contract with, to allow us to represent the Credit Union."

"Are there any questions? I asked, and seeing none, I made a final statement, ladies and gentlemen, I am with you all the way in this new venture, and my time is your time. I will be available to you at any time you wish for me to accompany you in any of these steps, necessary to complete any phase of the completion of this program." "I will set a goal of three months to have the program up and running, with trained sales agents to begin following a schedule in their visitations of employees of the contracted businesses."

"Finally, please recall the steps I outlined for each phase of the program and let me know what your plan is for implementing your initial actions in starting your program." "Thank you very much for your commitment to participate in this progressive move for our company's growth."

Later, I thanked President Jackson for his participation in the meeting and told him "that in my three month timeline to complete this project, I was in no way wanting to rush him into retirement. I wanted to assure him, his timing was at his discretion, only."

He assured me that, "he was quite pleased with my success in setting up the alignment of the program, and continued to be amazed at my ability to handle each challenge, that had been thrown my way, to carry out to a successful completion."

He added, "There is only one other thing that I have to say, take time for that precious family that you have!"

After returning to my office, I called Mr. Summers and told him that "I hoped that I could depend upon his working with me on the various phases that we had shared when we set up the division, specifically in contracting with the Credit Unions, the businesses and finally the training visitations at the District Offices with the newly employed sales agents." "I added that, I had already started a process of selecting both the businesses and Credit Unions that would be our best contacts."

Mr. Summers assured me that, "he had thoroughly enjoyed our working together in our successful creation of the Florida operation, and would be proud to serve with me at my bidding."

By this time, it was time to leave the office for home, and upon my arriving there, I was treated to all of the love that I could possibly expect. It was good to be home.

Later, when Marilyn and I were alone, I had to tell her the good news and what may be considered as the bad news, that I would be on the road again. I knew that she would understand, and especially, after "I told her about President Jackson's announcement to me privately of his pending retirement plans and the approval of my selection as his successor." "I made sure that she understood that this must be for her ears only, at this time."

Marilyn said, "there is no bad news here, how many times have I told you that I would follow you anywhere?" "I see this as a win - win situation and I am so proud of you! How could we have ever envisioned that this man (you), who went to work, with this large insurance company for $5,000 per month, could possibly be being considered as the President of this expanding insurance company in only a years time? It is totally surreal, and you are so blessed."

"I want you to know that a lot of my work, in dealing with the Georgia expansion, will be made easier, since I will have flight privileges, eliminating most of those long drives to and from Georgia." "There will be a lot of time when my work will be done here in our Maitland office. At those times, I will be coming home to you and the children after work, each day." I wanted her to know that I would be monitoring her progress with her pregnancy as well as the ongoing, construction of our home to its conclusion, and made sure that she understood this.

"Yes, I understand and appreciate you so much." "Now, could I have a few loving moments as you make love to me and drive me wild, as you always do"?

"Hummmm," was all that I needed to say as we reached for the stars of perfect bliss!

Morning came and I could not wait to become involved in our Georgia expansion. The next two days, I was in touch with Legal, Product Development and Licensing, as they began making progress with the Georgia Insurance Commissioner. The Commissioner seemed intrigued by the possibility of adding this new concept to his state's, allowable product availability, and said, "that he would survey all of the information, that we had provided to him, and make a determination whether or not to allow our company and the presented products to proceed to a final licensing."

By Thursday we received the Commissioner's final approval and all department heads began their assigned activities. Advertising, Legal and Property began their operations to secure sites in the cities, where we were going to establish our District Offices. Mr. Summers, of Marketing and I met to decide which Credit Unions we would begin calling on to present our program, and ask for their desire to contract with our firm, as we approached businesses in or near the District Offices ability, to service contracted accounts.

Mr. Summers and I used all of the information available to come up with a list to approach. First we would approach the Credit Unions with our proposal.

Of course we were prepared to sell them on contracting by our successes in Florida.

Our next project, would approach the businesses that we decided would be the best fit to make employees available, for our service schedule in bringing our products to their employees. We, first knew, that the products and services provided by the Credit Union would be a huge draw in the minds of the business leaders decision to contract. Our sales agents and the service they would provide in promoting the Credit Union and bringing our insurance products would, then, be the icing on the cake, in bringing the businesses to contract with our project.

It was decided that Mr. Summers would lead one team and I would lead the other team as we began approaching the Credit Unions in the next week. After we had secured the Credit Unions, we could then begin contacting the businesses, that we had selected as our targets.

We anticipated the same successes that we had received when we began the Florida program, and this eventually was the results, we expected, since we were all veterans of the formation of our division in Florida.

Our Advertising, Human Resources and Licensing were in full action in securing District Office Managers and sales agents for the respective District Offices, and once that was completed, Mr. Summers and I would take over the visitations to the District Offices, as we had handled so well in establishing the sales agents as becoming very successful and profitable producers, for our company, as well as they and their families financial needs.

Mr. Summers and I split into two groups and went after the Credit Unions that were already operating in Georgia, but not yet involved in operating within the large businesses, that we had picked to present to the Credit Unions, as we contracted with them in serving the companies, that we would call on, just as soon as we were able to contract, bringing their products to the business' employees.

I drew the cities of Atlanta, Savannah and Athens and selected the team, that would fly with me to approached the Credit Unions working in those three cities. We spent four days in Northern Georgia and secured contracts with three Credit Unions active in those areas.

Mr. Summers and his crew visited the Credit Unions active in Columbus Augusta and Macon, and came through, successfully in those in a four-day period.

To celebrate our amazing success in securing every Credit Union that we went after, we took several days off and returned to the home office in Maitland, to share the good news with Mr. Jackson and other management.

Driven by our success, we split up the sixty eight larger businesses and we wound up securing contracts with sixty of those, in the next four days. Since Mr. Summers was heavily involved in the overall program, he spent the next week making sure that the Human Relations Department had employed the District Managers for the six cities, and staffed the district with sales agents, who began training for the purpose of visiting the businesses, and offering the service and products that the Credit Unions offered, while selling our company's products on a commission basis. The company, through mine and Mr. Summer's training efforts were now established and providing services to the employees of those companies, that had seen the opportunity, to provide a benefit to their employees.

It had been a rough three or flour weeks as we established the State of Georgia into our Credit Union, business employees and our insurance sales program, and it would take another month or more to see the results, from our work, showing up into Credit Union profits, and insurance policy premiums, adding to our company's overall growth.

President Jackson and the Board of Directors were able to call all of the Department Managers together for a celebration dinner, and "announcement that our company had grown by another 25% with our successful drive in bringing Georgia into our business operations." Sales were booming and "it was announced that more businesses were finding out about our affiliation with Credit Unions to provide company benefits to employees."

Since management's families had given so much of their time that they would normally have for their families, wives were also invited and it gave President Jackson the opportunity to "praise the wives for their service in keeping the families together, while their warriors were out making a lot of money for themselves, their families and this company."

In his praises for the work performed, he said that, "he was pleased to now announce a good bonus for the management, who performed in this drive, which had added another 25%, officially to the overall growth of our company."

"The bonus would be presented at the end of the month, which was November."

Our children had spent the night with neighbors, that we had great confidence in their care. I was so pleased to show her off, especially, since she was, now "beginning to show her forth month pregnancy."

After we arrived home and retrieved the children, who were so glad to see me home for a few solid days, they went happily to bed and Marilyn and I took the opportunity to get in some great snuggling time, before we went peacefully to sleep in each other's arms.

In the morning, before the children got up from their sleep, Marilyn, caught me up on what had been going on for her and the children. She had been keeping her medical appointments and was doing very well.

She said that, "they were not yet positive, but they were pretty sure, we were expecting a boy and a girl."

I let out a yell, which I hoped did not awaken the children and took her into my arms and did not want to let her go. She felt so good to me as I held her in my arms. I told her, "that I had gotten just what I wanted, that was a girl that would look just like her, and a brother for Matthew."

She, "told me about the school progress for the children and said that their teachers had shown a lot of praise for the work they were performing," they said that, "they were outstanding students and were setting examples for the other children."

I assured her that, "I would be able to be home after work on most nights and weekends," to which she just purred like a contented cat. The children must have awakened when I let out that yell and wandered into our bedroom to see what the yell was all about. "I assured them that their mother had just given me some wonderful news about her pregnancy and their school progress. I gave them the news that I would be able to come home after work in the evenings and would be here on weekends, looking forward to having more time to share with them."

They ran to me, and let me hug them, which meant a lot to me. I knew I was going to ask Marilyn if she minded my formal adoption of both Jennifer and Matthew. After breakfast they asked, "if we could go visit our home to see how much work had been performed." Marilyn and I said, "that was such a wonderful idea." And, we set that into the plans for the day. Marilyn packed a wonderful lunch, and we set out to our new home, to be.

The children had asked to bring their bikes, which we did and spent a glorious day. They rode and frolicked all over the property. We all liked the progress being made. It was really beginning to look like a house, the roof was on, and the interior work was going on in forming the rooms.

The odor of fresh lumber permeated the area and made us feel that a lot of quality was being built into this home. The driveway, which resembled a half moon, had been poured and allowed entrance and circular exit back into the road, without having to back out into the road. This was a good move, since this road could eventually carry heavy traffic as the area developed.

After the children checked out the lay of the house, and were able to see which room would be theres, when the house was completed, they were ready to take a ride around the property. As usual, we gave the children our safety advice of making sure that there were no dangerous animals hanging around the lake.

While the children were riding, Marilyn and I were busy planning how we were going to decorate the rooms and what furniture we planned to place in each room. We had asked for the large living room with the raised ceiling, and were delighted, he had made the dining room a little more spacious.

After all, we had to plan for six of us (assuming there were twins on the way), plus the opportunity to entertain guests that we expected to be coming, once I become in a Presidential role. When the Presidential role was mentioned, Marilyn asked, "how soon did I expect that to come about?" I told her that I certainly was not in the position to contemplate that happening." "I had told President Jackson that it was his call and I, in no way, would want to influence that move, whatsoever." 'I was so involved in the Georgia expansion that I hoped that President Jackson would delay his retirement until we were solid in the expansion.

The children came back and asked, "when were we going to have lunch?"

Marilyn and I had been so engrossed in our room and furniture planning that we had forgotten about lunch. The children had not, and were ready to enjoy the wonderful lunch that Marilyn had brought.

I suggested, "that we set lunch out right in the area that would eventually be the dining room." And, we imagined how good things were going to be in the dining room.

Later, when we were leaving our property, we all spoke of the things that we were going to enjoy, once the palm trees and the garden was developed.

The children had already said that, "they were looking forward to fishing in our lake." I made a note in my mind that we needed to stock it with fish that were native to this area.

On the way home, we talked about the church where we had decided to attend and make it our church. The children said that they were looking forward to going there, tomorrow. The children had made some new friends at the church and were looking forward to seeing them, there.

Since we had had such a big lunch in our new home, to be, Marilyn prepared a light, but filling dinner that was very fitting. Afterward, the children retired to their playroom and Marilyn and I spent some quiet time together, which was a makeup for all of the days that I had been away, working in Georgia.

Later, after the children tired and went to sleep, Marilyn and I were so satisfied, just getting together. Marilyn kept planting lingering kisses all over me and pressing against me in a yearning way and let me know that she really wanted to have me take her right there, on the couch. "I was a little concerned about her condition" and told her so. She answered that, "we could be careful and not be so wild in our lovemaking, as we often had been. She said that, she wanted it to last a long time and just build up our emotions until we just could not wait to have our climax, hopefully together. She said that, she would let me know when she wanted me to fly her to the moon." I assured her "that we would fly to the moon, together." And so it was, just another heavenly moment with this wonderful woman, the love of my life.

We must have slept for hours after our sharing of love for one another, finally, we went to bed and slept in each others arms.

We were up early and began preparing breakfast. "I wanted to know how she rated our loving session last night," and she just said, "hmmmm," and added "we can do that, anytime." "I was glad to hear that," and pressed against her in a knowing manner.

Soon, the children came running and we had a great Florida breakfast, and got ready for Sunday School.

At Sunday School, we, as well as the children, were beginning to enjoy new friends as we had while we were in Pensacola. We now felt that we had found a home in this church. Jennifer is ready to perform in a choir for eight to nine year-olds that performs as the service begins, and Matthew is working on drawing in his Sunday School class. Marilyn and I are really enjoying the 'Young Couples Class', that deals with raising children in a spiritual manner in today's society.

So, you can see that being a christian family is very important to us, and we are loving it.

After the service, which we found to be very inspiring, we stopped at McDonald's for a light meal in order to keep Marilyn out of the kitchen. Each ordered what they really wanted and every one was contented to have a quiet afternoon at home, just relaxing and getting ready for the events of next week, where each would be involved.

The children spent a great deal of time in the back yard together, either riding their bikes or playing imaginary games that they thought up, at any given time.

Marilyn was getting very involved in the PTA at school and was content in doing some work on how to teach your children in creative ways to improve their progress in their study habits.

Me, I thought it would be a good time to do some planning in methods of "how to inspire your staff to want to over achieve, in their work activities." I realized that employees in my division wanted to achieve a better economic life for their family.

And, if I could inspire them to work smarter, as well as harder, they could begin to realize those things in life, that they sought, while helping my division and the company to increase in overall value.

Suddenly, I realized that each employee will grow at their own level, if incentives are made available to provide them a purpose to strive to go after attaining those incentives. As for the agents, they already have incentives, 'a commission status on the sale of our insurance products.' And the company was occasionally giving bonuses to management, including me, that had inspired us to work harder for the company. I knew that it is still true that 'nothing happens until somebody sold something.'

And, so, I had to begin with that thought in mind in order to try to inspire our sales agents onward and upward in their careers. In one way, the memo that I had written, that asked the sales agents to provide a list of businesses in their daily travels, which were not being serviced by us and the Credit Union at this time. We had told them that, "if they submitted a business name and we were able to contract with that company to provide our services to that company and their employees, that sales agent, who submitted that business name, would receive the right of calling on those employees for a chance to make sales and receive commissions from those sales."

So that had already begun to add value to those sales agents. It is now my job to come up with other methods that can bring these same results.

I will continue to search for other incentives to increase added production from our sales force. Suddenly, I began to realize that I was beginning to think like a President of a major company, even tho I may have some time to go before I am actually promoted to President of my company.

For the rest of Sunday afternoon and evening, I kept thinking about what type of incentive we could offer to the sales agents that would create a spark and increase sales and profits for the sales agents as well as the company.

Later, after diner and putting the children to bed had been accomplished, I decided to sleep and see if I could come up with the sales incentive that had been churning in my thoughts.

Marilyn came easily into my arms and I held her until she and I fell asleep.

Morning came, and suddenly I realized that I did not have that terrible rush from Pensacola to Maitland, that I had had in the past. What a relief! I could have a leisurely drive to Maitland after a good breakfast with my family before Marilyn took the children to school.

I was anxious to meet with President Jackson to discus a plan that had occurred to me overnight. After arriving at work, I called his office and asked to speak with Mr. Jackson. He took my call immediately, and I asked him, "if I could have a few minutes with him in his office?"

He said, "certainly, please come right up."

When I arrived, I was rushed into his office and he greeted me warmly, as he always has. "He suggested a cup of coffee," which I graciously accepted. He called his assistant to deliver, and we chatted while awaiting the coffee to arrive. He, "asked about my family," and I told him that, "they were fine and enjoyed having me for the weekend." I, "asked about Mrs. Jackson," and he said that, "she was anxiously awaiting my retirement so that we can do some long awaited travel, which we have been putting off."

The coffee came and we got down to the purpose of my visit. As we enjoyed the coffee, I began by telling him that, "I had been thinking about our sales agents, and how we could possibly offer some incentive that would inspire competition within our District Offices in both Florida, and our new sites in Georgia."

I told him that "prior to this time the management of our company had made several incentives available to members of Management and the District Offices, that I felt had increased morale and had increased the push to greater increases in the value of our company." I continued by saying that, "in this division, nothing happens until a sales agent makes a sale. I said that, a sale by the agent has here-to-for been rewarded with a commission, that will stop being paid if the policy lapses, due to non payment by that business employee."

I paused to let that be absorbed by Mr. Jackson, and began again. "My thought dwells on, first of all, making sure that that agent is fully trained to sell products in a manner that will make the employee want to continue their police coverage and, perhaps, purchase other coverage for their families protection."

"Here is my plan, I would like to start a competition in each District Office for the 'Sales Agent of The Month' in all eight District Offices in Florida and the six District Offices in Georgia." "The top salesman, monthly, in each district would be awarded a two hundred dollar bonus for being Salesman of The Month."

It is that simple. To keep an agent from making sales just to become 'Salesman of The Month,' and failing to make quality sales, that stay on the books and premiums paid, we would subtract lapses from the production of new business, negating his status as 'Salesman of The Month', and possibly awarding the title to someone else, due to making sales that were not lapsed.

We would increase training to make sure that producing quality sales means that business was sold properly in the first place and not, just to pad the agent's record.

The bottom line to the company cost could be only $2,800 or $200 times fourteen District Offices on a monthly basis.

I believe the income from increased sales and improvement to agent morale will net the company significantly more in the long run in quality sales, employee retention, and employee morale.

"Alvin I have heard you completely and I am more certain that Alvin Knight will soon be President of Southern Medical and Life

Services, you have been right on every proposal that you have brought to me since you have been with our company."

"I authorize this project and want you to send a directive to each Division Manager to install this program on the first day of next month." "Thank you for suggesting this worthy project."

"Thank you, Mr. Jackson." "I will send out a directive to all fourteen District Offices." Of course, "we will present a full explanation, since lapses of previous policies written by the agent are counted against new business during the month.

And I continued, we are trying to discourage sales agents from creating high pressure on a business employee, who does not want the protection, or perhaps cannot afford the premium in the first place." I assured the President that I would copy him with a copy of the directive. And everything possible, will be done to make this a positive benefit that the 'Salesman of The Month' winner, can take great pride in, as well as bringing additional income to the monthly winner. 'It is my hope, that all sales agents will strive to be a winner at some point."

The directive was sent out to all District Offices immediately, along with a followup call to the District Manager in order to answer any questions. All of the District Managers assured me that, "they were on board with this program and felt that this would be a tremendous incentive to the agents, as well as increasing district production."

Production exploded almost immediately, and lapsed policies seemed to be slowing down at the same time. This trend would tremendously increase the income to the agents as well as having a positive influence on the bottom line of our company's assets.

Mr. Jackson, "told me personally that The Board Of Directors were extremely pleased with the new life in the company, and had accepted his decision to retire on June 30, 1961, and his recommendation that Mr. Alvin Knight be announced as the new President of Southern Medical and Life Services." "It was also, expected that Mr. Larry Summers, now serving as Marketing Manager, will fill the position of Director of the Division now being vacated on June 30, 1961, by Mr. Knight as he assumes the Presidency of Southern Medical and Life Services."

Mr. Jackson "asked me to keep this in confidence until it is revealed on June 30th.

I assured him that, "this was fine by me and I would strive to serve the company as well as he has so professionally done."

And, so, there were many new and exciting things that were about to happen in my life. My wonderful wife, Marilyn and I were expecting twins in mid May;

I was seeking to adopt Marilyn's two children by deceased David; our new home should be completely finished and allowing us to move in by early May; I plan to ask the company to enter at least two new states and be operational there in North Carolina and South Carolina by March, 1962.

All of these happenings was a great pleasure to me, and I looked forward to every one of them, enriching my life. Of course, I had come a long way from that young sailor who met Marilyn. Marilyn had been the strength that I needed, at that time, to stabilize my life. There had been the young sailor who had been looking for women for all of the wrong reasons. Marilyn had been the one who said to me, "I love my husband who is serving in the Navy as a young pilot in the far west. I do get lonely, but I am not looking to have cheap sex with you or anyone else."

We saw each other at Wakiki on the beach and she even invited me to dinner in her home. That is as far as it ever got, but I saw the strength of a good woman, who was very beautiful, loved her husband and would not have cheap sex.

Later, after I was discharged from the Navy and returned to my home state of North Carolina, and settled into a good job. I received a letter from Marilyn, telling me that, "she was living in Pensacola, Florida. Her husband, David had crashed off of Florida, and was deceased." Later, as she still grieved, she remembered me and kept thinking of me. "Would I like to see her?" she had asked.

I had thought of her often as being the stabilizing thing, that had saved me from a life of sorrow and possibly big trouble.

Marilyn had shown me what kind of life I had been living, which I really did not like the possible consequences, that might develope. The other women before her had indeed been the 'Before In My Life.' Once I dropped my life in North Carolina and went to Pensacola to find a new, very successful job that immediately brought me success and had kept a pact with Marilyn of 'no sex before marriage.'

We were married. "Now, life with my new family has been pure heaven on earth.

And at the same time, I have achieved success beyond my possible imagination, or could have hoped for myself."

Marilyn has brought the 'After In My Life.' Praise God for bringing her into my life! She is everything that I could ever hope for in a wife, and the wonderful thing is that, She Is Crazy For Me.' What a life! What a life!'

CHAPTER 34

THE TIME IS now April, 1961. December and Christmas was very special at our rental home. The children had been on Christmas break and Marilyn was now glowing in her pregnancy. I loved it when we were home together and she asked me to touch her tummy, where we were sure I could feel the outline of two beautiful babies. They were becoming very active and moved around quite a lot. It was good to be home after my travels to North Carolina for a few days in order to determine the best locations for the the four District Offices that we were going to locate there.

Our Legal Department had been successful in getting the North Carolina Department of Insurance to allow our company to sell our major products in that state and Advertising, Properties and Human Resources were at work in making our company there a reality. I had selected Raleigh, Winston-Salem, Charlotte and Asheville as the sites to house our new District Offices, there.

We had determined that we wanted to be rather aggressive and move into South Carolina, next. The Department of Insurance in South Carolina seemed quite happy to have us, once he saw our successes in Florida and Georgia.

Quickly we had determined that Columbia, Greenville and Myrtle Beach would be ideal for locations for our District Offices and soon we had established offices there. Our by now, professional department heads, carried out their usual successes, and by the end of April we had made contracts with the Credit Unions in or near those locations that we had selected in both North Carolina and South Carolina.

We quickly made contracts with the tremendously successful companies in both states. And, Human Resources, Licensing and Training very quickly had the District Managers and sales agents that began visitations with employees in the companies, that we had contracted with.

This had become a new concept for the businesses to provide good employee services through the Credit Unions. The Credit Unions were so pleased that we, through our sales agents, had been successful in nearly doubling their former business, and in many cases, done so at very little, or in other cases, no cost.

We had found that some of the Credit Unions that we had contracted with in Florida and Georgia, also had offices in North Carolina and South Carolina.

As for the businesses that we enrolled, many of them were branches of companies, we had been successful in enrolling in prior states.

Our whole process was now made easier with the hard work that we had done in the original states, we had successfully enrolled. The beauty of it was that, we had learned to duplicate our successes that we had had at earlier times.

We had become a very large company, compared with what the original Southern Florida Medical had been. Of course, we had now expanded more than quadrupled from our humble beginning in Central Florida. As for me I had for some time taken college credits in Florida and had now received my college degree and by July 1 of this year, I will be awarded my Masters Degree, to the delight of the President and also the Board of Directors.

They said that, "I was becoming more Presidential all of the time."

The one that I wanted to please, was the very beautiful mother of my children to be, as well as her two talented children that I have now adopted as my very own.

In case you are wondering, I still get to spend a lot of time with my family, due to the arrangement of being flying privileged. Otherwise, it would not have been possible to accomplish all that I have been able to do for the company in these several years.

I will bet that you are wondering what progress has been done on our home, to be. Well, we still take our weekend visits to view what now looks like the house that we had designed six months ago.

It is now early May, and we will be moving into our beautiful home next week.

It is everything that we had hoped, that it would be in the beginning. It now has five bedrooms, including the large master bedroom, my love and I will be preparing for our exotic love life, that we had been enjoying so very much up until three months ago. Don't get me wrong, we were able to become very innovative as we still keep our juices flowing and the tender touches have continued to promise more, in the not too distant future.

We loved it when I was able to bring tender touches to her stomach and kisses to the constant movements of our gorgeous twins. By the way, the doctor has now confirmed that there is a boy and a girl, that we will be blessed with, very soon. Marilyn has just been glowing in her pregnancy and she is just as beautiful, at least in my mind, as she has ever been.

I know that the girl will grow up to be just as beautiful as Marilyn. And, she has said that she wanted the boy to look just like me, whatever that means.

I received a call from Mr. Wesley, our contractor, saying that "he had very good news for us and our new home. He asked, if we could meet with him at the site and review the current status, which he felt was now complete, except for the installation of kitchen appliances." "He was pleased to announce that our requested appliances would be installed today."

He reported that the painting had been completed, as to the requests that we had made in a previous discussion.

I assured him that my bank had approved the financing of a fifteen year mortgage agreement, when Marilyn and I accept the home as finished to our satisfaction, with the knowledge that your company promises our satisfaction.

Mr. Wesley assured me that there would be a one year warranty against possible defects discovered and presented in that time frame. He said, "they would assure any changes that we wished to make, at this point, could be done now or implemented after we moved in the home, early next week."

After telling him that I would call him back, shortly. I immediately called Marilyn to see when would be a good time for us to visit the home with Mr. Wesley and approve the finished product.

Marilyn was delighted and said, "since this is Tuesday, let's do it tomorrow morning, around 10:00AM," and added, "this is so thrilling."

I quickly called Mr. Wesley and "told him that we could meet with him at 10AM tomorrow, and if everything works out, we can proceed to my bank and finalize the loan at that time."

He was delighted and "assured me that we were going to be very happy with what we would be seeing, especially, now that all of the planting, that we had requested had been planted, with palms included."

I checked out of the office and met Marilyn and Mr. Wesley, early, and we went through the home, carefully. Quite frankly, we were in awe of all that we saw and told him so. Marilyn was so pleased with everything. She had arrived early and had been amazed with the outside appearance that the home presented from the road.

She had pulled all of the way around the circular drive and had traversed the yard, enjoying the decorative plantings.

When Mr. Wesley and I arrived, we happily entered the front door and were escorted through every room, one by one. We almost gasped at the beauty of the living room, with its elevated ceiling and discovered that it was even more than we had hoped for, in our planning. Progressing to the dining room, next, we knew that the furniture we had already picked out would be perfect. The kitchen was next and Marilyn gave a knowing grin as to what she would be able to do with this jewel.

Then to the bedrooms, there were now five, including the master bedroom. I knew what Marilyn meant, with that wiggle she showed, when we entered there.

Marilyn asked to go back to the nursery, to get a feel of how the newborns were to be placed, when they were expected in the next few weeks. She and I were using our imagination, as to how all of the furniture, that we had already purchased was going to look like, when installed.

Before exiting to the back, we knew that we were going to enjoy the beautiful sun room, that all quality Florida homes must have.

Marilyn and I huddled and agreed that this was even more than we had expected, and returned to Mr. Wesley and said, "thank you so very much, we are home. Let's go to my bank and close the deal, now. You have done a very splendid job for us to enjoy, for a long time."

Our arrival at the bank was expected and the financial arrangements were completed, and the keys were now ours.

The furniture would be delivered, later this afternoon, and we would be moving in for the rest of the week.

By the weekend, we brought the children over to see the finished product.

They could not have been any happier, and when they saw their playroom, they were now lost in play.

We had moved anything that was salvageable from our rental house and placed them in use in our new home. Marilyn and I had picked out special, new furniture for our master bed room. The new bed for that room was a thing to see.

I had to restrain Marilyn from wanting to use it right now. "I told her we must wait until our twins are born, and the doctor approves. Then, we will put it to regular, wonderful use!"

The children tired of play in the playroom and wanted to get on their bikes and go visit the two lakes. I told them that "mother needed rest and was going to sleep for a while. But, I would be glad to go with them to the lakes."

It was a very pleasant day. There were just a few clouds gliding by to keep the bright sun from bringing too much heat. I walked briskly, while they rode their bikes and we visited the smaller lake, that was close by. The smaller bird life were there to make their fill of small insects. And, there were always a couple of Blue Herons, who stood in anticipation of gobbling up a small fish that happened by. Shrub Jays were always there, hoping to get their fill.

I was pleased that no danger presented itself and I had been assured that there had never been any alligators spotted near there. Occasional flocks of ducks were known to visit, dive and dine on the food found in and around the lake.

The children wanted to go to the larger lake, located about two hundred yards away, saying that they had not been there on any visits before to our property. We went over to case it out to see what kind of inhabitants frequented there. We saw that there was a lot of marsh vegetation and we were delighted to see that a family of swans were there at this time, and possibly made the lake their home. What a pleasant thought, I said to myself.

There were several large trees that overlooked the lake, and I spotted a large nest. Upon further observation, I realized that a mother bald eagle was sitting on the nest, while her male observed from a nearby tree. I called the children to me and pointed out the mother eagle on the nest and her mate, who looked on to protect his family.

I told the children that, "it would be alright to observe the eagle family from a distance, but they could never get close enough to provoke either adult."

While we were there, the children clapped their hands and frightened a group of ducks that took up flight. The children were having an experience that they would share with their mother, and any other children that they came into contact with at school and at church. This was such a good educational experience, that they would long remember.

After we returned back to our new home, the children were ready to have a late afternoon rest period in their new beds. I took the opportunity to climb in beside Marilyn. She awoke and snuggled into my arms, pausing occasionally to place a light kiss and a lot of nibbling on my face, as I did hers.

We both felt that it would be soon for her to say that she believed we better go to the hospital to deliver two very special children, to add to our family.

Well you might wonder how things were going with my job, during this brief time that we were moving into our new home. Things at work were almost automatic.

I had surrounded myself with highly qualified personnel, who knew their positions, and what was expected of them in carrying out our responsibilities to the businesses, we serviced, and the Credit Unions that we provided services too, in our daily activities.

The District Offices in North Carolina and South Carolina were fully functional, sales agents had been trained and assigned to service the employees of the businesses that we contracted with, to provide employees the benefits of the Credit Union, and sales of our insurance products, which continued to build value in our company, and the families of the the sales agents, who were working hard to become the Salesman Of The Month.

My position was to direct the continuing growth of our business and provide value to the Credit Union, and the businesses we served, while providing value to the employees of those businesses through the products we were offering.

As you will recall, I had been brought on board with Southern, knowing that the longterm goal of our company was to continue to grow throughout the South Eastern, United States. At this time, we are ready to start working to expand into a few more states, namely, Alabama and Mississippi.

The time was now May 10, 1961, and it had been one week since we had moved into our beautiful home. I was in my office in Maitland finalizing our plans to extend our business into the states of Alabama and Mississippi. I was having a meeting with Mr. Larry Summers from Marketing, Mr. King, from Licensing, Mr. Roy Hudson from Legal, and Mr. Adams from Properties.

I had just given each of them a timeline for moving into those two states in order to set things in motion for securing a license to sell our products in those states. Naturally, nothing final could be done until the licensing was secured for each product that we planned to market in each state. Once the licensing was secured, we could then ask Mr. Adams to secure property for each District Office, advertise for a District Office Manager and sales agents.

The assignments had been agreed upon and time tables set to call upon the Credit Unions and businesses that we chose to serve their employees. My loyal Administrative Assistant came in and whispered that "she had received a call that I should come to the hospital in Orlando. My wife was getting ready to go into labor."

"I thanked my meeting group for coming and told them to proceed with the timeline that we had agreed on." "I must see to an important situation at this time and will call you when I return."

I rushed to Orange County Medical and asked to be directed to my wifes' side. She appeared a little strained and said, "that Dr. James K. Mac Donald had been called and was headed to the hospital." Before she came to the hospital, she had gotten the children out of school and had taken them to a friend for safe keeping, and came here to be on the safe side.

I kissed her on the cheek and "told her that she had done all of the right things and I would be right here by her side until the children were delivered."

Within minutes, Doctor Mac Donald arrived and took over. He noted that her water had broken and "called for the nurse to take her to the delivery room, immediately."

"I told Dr. Mac Donald that I would like to be near my wifes' side during the delivery."

Dr. Mac Donald instructed the nurse to have an assistant scrub me down and provide a gown that I could wear in the delivery room and deliver me to the delivery room.

When I arrived, Dr. Mac Donald had all of his assistants prepared for delivery and I was allowed to watch.

Within a few minutes, he had her in labor and instructing her to "push, push, push." He pulled out a wrinkled body that was very beautiful to me and applied a light spank on the appropriate place and a faint cry came in objection.

Doctor quickly tied the cord and handed the little child to a nurse and went back to work. Within a few minutes, he was asking Marilyn to "push, push" again.

Marilyn appeared glad to get this over and responded beautifully.

Dr. Mac Donald quickly tied the cord, gave a little spank, receiving the little protest.

The doctor passed the second child to an assistant and asked the nurse to make Marilyn comfortable.

He scrubbed off and smiled at me and announced, "Mr. Knight, you are the proud father of two healthy children." And added, "the first one was a boy and the second one was a beautiful girl. Congratulations, sir!" he said.

Dr. MacDonald asked me, "to wait in the waiting room outside, with the explanation that they would clean Marilyn up and make her comfortable and then, bring her to her room. I would be able to spend a few minutes with her and then, she would need some rest."

While I was waiting in the waiting room, I thanked God that the twins did appear healthy and that Marilyn had came through the delivery safely.

The doctor came to me and said that, "it would be necessary for Marilyn to spend a few days in the hospital in recovery, and the children would be in the nursery for that amount of time. I would be able to visit as much as I liked, but he assured me that she and the children were going to be just fine!"

After a few minutes with Marilyn, I realized that she needed rest.

I kissed her on the cheek and "whispered that she had done a splendid job in delivering the children, a boy and a beautiful girl." "Now, get the much needed rest that you deserve, darling."

I went to visit the friend that was attending to the children and asked, "if they could spend a few days with her?"

She said "that would be fine and Marilyn had brought everything the children would need, and not to worry."

I told she and the children that, "they now had a brother and a sister that they would be able to love and spend a lot of time enjoying."

Both said that, "they could not wait to see them and play with them."

The next morning, I went by the school and explained to the Principal why the children would be out of school for a few days. "He assured me that they would be able to catch up when they returned."

Next, I stopped into the hospital to see if I could have a little time with Marilyn and the two perfect babies.

The nurse said that, "I could stay for about thirty minutes, but after that, the doctor would be in to evaluate Marilyn, and make her as comfortable as possible."

The nurse told me that "they had brought the two babies in to visit Marilyn. They said that, the scene was beautiful to behold. They added that, Marilyn was going to be a wonderful mother."

Marilyn awakened when I entered and gave me a beautiful smile and held out her arms for me to snuggle into them, then she said, "I have seen and held our two beautiful children, and they could not have been any more perfect." "How are Jennifer and Matthew doing?" she asked.

I replied that, "she had done a beautiful job in finding a friend to keep them while she was in the hospital." "I had gone by and asked her to keep the children until you are able to leave the hospital with our Alvin and Susan."

Alvin and Susan, I thought to myself. Marilyn had insisted on naming the boy Alvin after me (of course he will be Alvin, Jr.). Susan had been her choice for the girl, and I agreed that it was a beautiful name for her.

Marilyn asked, "if I had seen our twins after they had been cleaned?"

I told her that, "I had not seen them, but I was going to visit the nursery as soon as I left, to let the doctor check her recovery."

"They are so precious," Dr. MacDonald, said. "Marilyn was going to be just fine, but he suggested that he needed to complete a few tests. Why don't you visit the twins and perhaps come by later this afternoon, to spend some more time with Mrs. Knight?"

I agreed and went to the nursery to visit the twins. When I arrived, the nursery staff congratulated me and brought both of them out for me to hold. I was overjoyed to see and hold them. They were going to add so very much to our family life, when we were allowed to take them home.

The nurse did not want them to be out of the nursery but a few minutes and soon came to take them back to their beds.

With time on my hands, I went to a cigar store and purchased several boxes of quality cigars and took them back to my office, where I spent a half day catching up with my managers to review where, we left off, at my departure, yesterday.

Everyone gave me the glad hand and congratulations, as I offered one of the cigars to anyone who would like them. I did contact the group that I had formed yesterday to start working on the states of Alabama and Mississippi. I knew that I could depend on them carrying out my instructions. After all, these guys had been through this before when we extended into Georgia and North and South Carolina, after forming our operations in Florida. These ladies and gentlemen were professionals and excelled in performing their duties to grow Southern Medical and Life Services.

Within a matter of several weeks, Alabama and Mississippi would be receiving the same great services that we had previously installed in our other states.

I was delighted to have a discussion with President Jackson. He was quick to given me his congratulations and asked "about Marilyn and the children?" I assured him that they were fine and added that, "I hoped to invite a group to visit our new home, (that we had just moved into over the week), after I get the family out of the hospital and settled back home."

He graciously accepted one of the cigars, as I brought him up to date on our expected move into Alabama and Mississippi.

He told me, "that he just continued to be amazed in how fast I was moving to make his original dream a reality."

"I told him to hold onto his hat, we would be into Louisiana and Texas in the next several months."

He said, "well, by that time I will have retired and you, sir, will be the new President of this wonderful company."

"Thank you, sir." "By the end of next year, we will be in Virginia, Tennessee and Kentucky."

Mr. Jackson just voiced that, "hiring me had been one of the best moves and accomplishments he had made in his long career with Southern Medical." "He wished me a long career with the company and remarked that he had been made aware of my completing college and soon my masters degree. All in the time that I was accomplishing great growth in Southern. I am extremely proud of you, Alvin, and I wish you and your family a great future."

"Thank you so much, Mr. President. You have helped make me the luckiest man that I feel I have become."

Since it was now Friday afternoon, I left the office and drove back to the hospital to visit Marilyn and the twins and see if I could get them released and take them home.

The doctor, who was on call, "suggested that it was too late to receive the permission of Dr. Mac Donald and the nursing staff in the nursery. He did say that the reports were excellent and felt that a release of 1:00PM on Saturday could be arranged, and asked me to make proper care at home and return, tomorrow."

This seemed reasonable to me, and I certainly did not want to take the family home until they were safe to be released. I went into Marilyn's room and was greeted by a sight that will always remain in my memory, forever.

Marilyn was sitting up and holding the twins in her arms. She had the most motherly smile as she looked from one to the other. Susan was quite content, but Alvin, Jr. seemed to be a little bit fidgety.

Marilyn just grinned and asked me, "well, how did I do?"

"You did good, darling, and I am so proud of all of you!"

"By the way, I have been assured that I will be able to take all of you home, tomorrow at 1:00. I will pick up Jennifer and Matthew on the way home after that, and the family will be back together."

Then I continued, "I have arranged for a retired nurse to visit, on occasion, to assist you with the care of the twins, until you have fully recovered. I hope that you do not mind, darling!"

"That just shows that, you are the sweetest husband, ever, and I love you for your thoughtfulness."

Soon, the nurse returned to take the twins back to the nursery and Marilyn and I had a few tender moments together, before I returned home, to make sure that everything was ready for all of the family, tomorrow.

Tomorrow could not come soon enough for me, and at 12:00 noon, I was back at the hospital to check out my love ones.

Dr. Mac Donald had made all arrangements and the attendants helped get the family into the car and comfortable with the blankets, I had brought from home.

As planned, we picked up Jennifer and Matthew from Marilyn's friend, who had been keeping them. Marilyn was so happy that I had brought her friend out to the car to 'oh and ah' over the twins, as Marilyn beamed her pride in the twins.

Marilyn, "asked Jennifer and Matthew to thank her friend for caring for them, while mother was in the hospital."

They did thank her very nicely and said, "that they had had a good time being with she and her family."

Marilyn thanked her and "asked her to visit our home, soon, when the family gets settled in."

After the children were settled in, Marilyn gave me an order for things the doctor and nursing staff had said we would need, and dispatched me to the grocery store and pharmacy. On the way home, I stopped by the pizza store and picked up a couple of hot ones, that the children enjoyed so much. I knew that Marilyn would be nursing the twins when I arrived home. She had just finished, and the twins were now sleeping contentedly, when I arrived.

Marilyn had decorated the nursery so beautifully for the twins before going to the hospital.

While the twins slept, we chowed down on the pizzas and milk shakes that I had brought.

I asked the children, "what they thought of the twins?"

They both exclaimed that, "they were so very small, but they were looking forward to playing with them, later."

Later, after the children went to bed, Marilyn and I looked in at the twins, who were still sleeping peacefully, and Marilyn showed me how to change the diapers, just in case she needed me to help." "That was OK with me," I assured her.

It was so nice to have Marilyn back in our bed, of course it was too soon for us to enjoy our great sexual activities, but I just wanted to hold her close to me and our wonderful kisses were just as passionate as ever. For the other, we could wait for further action.

I was finding that I was getting pretty good at changing diapers!

On Sunday, I took Jennifer and Matthew to Sunday School and church, word was getting around that the church was going to have two more attendees.

Monday, I took Jennifer and Matthew to school, and stopped by after school to take them home. Marilyn could not leave the twins at this time, so this action continued for another week, until she could take back those duties. As for me, it was fun to take over these fatherly duties.

We had purchased a doublewide carriage, and Marilyn took back the job of transporting Jennifer and Matthew, to and from school, so I could get back to directing my crew as they went about bringing our Credit Union activities to the states of Mississippi and Louisiana. We, Mr. Larry Summers and I, had been training one of his assistants to work with him in taking over a lot of the activities that I had formerly been working to set up the Credit Unions and businesses to create our relationships in Alabama and Mississippi. I let Mr. Summers know that I was "on call to administer any assistance that was needed to make those states fully functional in the program that had brought so much success to our programs, in the other states, that we had developed." I also, let Mr. Summers know that there may be a time when he would be promoted to become Director of this Division. I am sure that Mr. Summers assumed that our division was now becoming so large that the Division would require an assistant director. I had now established a method of him being promoted to Director of our Division when I become President of Southern.

When I am promoted to President, I want Alabama and Mississippi to be up and running efficiently at that time. If you recall, I had already told President Jackson that I planned to have Louisiana and Texas fully operating by the end of this year. I had already told Mr. Summers that he had been approved for flight privileges in his out of state activities, to set states up for our company.

As you can see, things were changing very rapidly in my life. I have now adopted two children, fathered two twins and am now only one month away from being named the 'former Director of Credit Union and Business Operations', who is being promoted to 'President of Southern Medical and Life Services of the Southeast.'

Can I handle it? You bet, I can, and will perform it well, especially since I will be receiving my Masters in Business Administration, within another month.

Right now I have to show Marilyn that I am a good father, husband and lover in my obligations to her and care for my family.

At this time, I believe she already knows that I have proved to her, the above. In addition, I am a very good homeowner, bread winner (assured at this time), earning at my young age, over two hundred fifty thousand dollars a year, with the surety of promotion to president and possibly earning one million dollars a year or more.

Well, back down to earth. it is time to change the twins diapers. "I can do that!"

I have now purchased a touring car, that is large enough to transport my growing family; it is a black-colored Mercedes. Marilyn and the children love it and enjoy all of the safety features that it brings to my family.

Marilyn is getting back to all of her regular activities and proudly shows the twins in addition to Jennifer and Matthew, wherever she goes.

Jennifer and Matthew realize that mother has to be very protective of the twins.

But, both Marilyn and I are very careful to let them know that every child is special, in their own way, and we do not show preference to one and not to the others. We love them all!

Marilyn is more active than she has been before and has let me know that it is now time that we regain our loving sex life again.

I told her that I had not lost any desire for her, and she is now, to me, the sexiest woman alive, and tonight, I wanted to show her what she had been missing.

I purely devoured her with my eyes and touched every part of her body, that was now even more appealing to me than ever. I rained kisses on every inch of her alluring body and pulled her to me and rendered all of the desire that I had held during her pregnancy, perhaps a little more softly and tenderly.

Suddenly, she said "Yes!Yes! It is better than it has ever been!"

"Now! Now! Hmmmmmmm," as she surrendered her all."

"Me too, darling!" I whispered.

A month passed and the news announcements said. "The Board Of Directors of Southern Medical and Life Services, sadly announce the much deserved retirement of former President, Andrew Jackson as of June 30, 1961." "We are pleased to announce that we have selected Alvin Knight, the former Division Director of Operations, to Presidency of Southern Medical and Life Services as of July 1, 1961." "Mr. Larry Summers, former Marketing Manager has been appointed as Division Director of Operations, the former position held by the new President, Mr. Alvin Knight."

"Southern Medical and Life Services is currently doing business in the states of Georgia, North Carolina, South Carolina, Alabama and Mississippi, as well as Florida. The Home Office is in Maitland, Florida. The company originated in Florida and has expanded across the South East. Southern Medical and Life Services has grown into a five billion dollar business, since its inception in July 1951."

Well, Mr. Summers, along with his assistant were in final stages of building production in Alabama and Mississippi, and soon he and I would start pushing for the expansion into Louisiana and Texas.

After that, we would sit tight and concentrate on adding more businesses and Credit Unions in the states, where we are then, successfully in operation.

Mr. Andrew Jackson reports that he is really enjoying retirement and plans for he and Mrs. Jackson to take a lot of trips that they had been putting off, while he was president.

In September, Marilyn and I threw a big open house party to show off our new home. We invited Mr. and Mrs. Jackson (now in retirement), Mr. And Mrs.

Larry Summers and his assistant (who would soon be appointed as Marketing Manager) and the Department Managers, who had helped us grow so very much in the last years, plus their wives or guests.

All of Department Managers were being honored for their hard work in our expansion up to this time. Of course, they all had new contracts and were now making more money than they had ever made in their careers.

Later, I have plans to extend our invites to all of the District Office Managers, who are working so hard in managing and training all of those sales agents, who have now grown to nearly five hundred. They work tirelessly with the employees of the businesses, we have developed working relations with. As our sales agents visit their employees on a regular schedule, the business employees take advantage of the services offered by the Credit Union and purchase our insurance policies that has caused our company to grow so strong.

As I said, we invited all of the Department Managers on the first Saturday of September to our open house and I had a tent put up in the back yard and set up several Port-O-Johns for comfort. We hired a local cook and crew to serve up hot dogs, hamburgers and BBQ (like we served back in North Carolina), ice tea, coffee and soft drinks, I had quite a few cases of my favorite soft drink, (Cheerwine).

Alcoholic drinks were available, but we did not encourage drinking, certainly not in excess. We had hired a bartender and suggested he go light on the drinks.

We wanted to show off our new home, but took care to protect the carpeting in high access areas and wanted to share a view of our children on a limited basis.

One of Marilyn's friends saw that the children were protected from tiring, especially the twins, who were only four months old, now.

Everyone seemed to be having a great time and said that our home and the surroundings were one of the most beautiful around. We thanked them and I took the liberty to announce that this party was in appreciation of the hard work that they had been doing for the past years to make our company the success that it has become, and continued to grow. I told them "that the Board Of Directors had asked me to thank them for their untiring support in building Southern to the stage that we were enjoying at this time."

I had thoughtfully brought in a local band with a vocalist. They performed until nine in the evening and the visitors even had the opportunity to dance to the popular songs of the day.

Naturally, Marilyn and I had the first dance and the last dance at nine.

I was so happy to show off our ability to dance, and especially Marilyn. If they had not thought about us being a cool couple, they knew it now. That last dance and a very romantic kiss was a clincher.

As you must have figured by now, this whole event was an effort to be a 'Morale Builder' within our team of players, present.

It was my hopes to keep that morale building and building.

During the party, Larry Summers introduced me to his assistant, who had been instrumental in getting Alabama and Mississippi up and running so very efficiently and productively. Larry introduced him as Benjamin Avery. "Benjamin," Larry said, "had been in the Marketing Division for about four years and had been with Larry on their successful development in North Carolina and South Carolina, and most recently Alabama and Mississippi." Larry continued, "I have been very impressed with his attention to detail and very strong salesmanship in his approach to businesses and Credit Unions in the states, we have been growing with."

I had an opportunity to talk with Larry in private and reminded him that his former position of Marketing Manager was still vacant and wondered if he had considered Benjamin Avery, in filling that position?

He replied in the affirmative, "that he had been meaning to talk with me about doing just that, but knew that I had been very busy and he had thought it could wait for a more opportune moment to ask you for approval."

"Larry, I said, you are the Director of Division Operations. You do not have to get my approval in making changes in your department." "I have the upmost confidence in your ability to make appointments in your division. I suggest that you make the announcement, the first thing on Monday morning."

"Thank you, Mr. President, for setting me straight!"
"Request his salary at the level you feel appropriate, Larry. I will approve and enable flight privileges, as we authorized for you." I continued, "let's talk about the move into Louisiana and Texas when you feel that we are extremely stable in Alabama and Mississippi."

Everyone seemed to have had a good time at the party, many of the early arrivals, in the afternoon had asked if they could visit the lakes and view the birds and other wildlife. In anticipation of this request, I had made a tour of those areas, prior to any guest arrival. My only caution was that they try not to disturb our nesting Bald Eagles, and not to get too close to the waters' edge.

Everyone had departed by ten and Marilyn and I were coming down, just knowing what we had accomplished. We looked in on Jennifer and Matthew and discovered that they were sound asleep. Marilyn's friend, who had been looking out for them, as well as the twins, had left after saying, "how much fun she had had."

The twins had been diapered and fed from the bottles that Marilyn had pre prepared.

"She would be available anytime we might need a night out by ourselves."

Marilyn and I had a glass of red wine and were reminiscing that last dance and the exciting kiss that came at the end. It had just happened as many of the wonderful moments that we have shared. We both knew what was going to happen when we went to bed. We were so excited and did not want this feeling to die in just going to sleep. A simple touch was all that it took to bring us to the heights of excitement, that we had to have our fill of touching, kissing and taking all of the love that we had shared--so many times before. We finally experienced one of the most wonderful climaxes that we had experienced before. It was simultaneous and so electrical, we were literally trembling in the beauty of our love as we clung to each other in the happiness that we shared.

We slept, knowing that we would be alerted when one or both of the twins needed our attention. That was an honor to be cherished and not a chore. It was a labor of love.

Sunday morning came and we slept right through the hour of going to Sunday School. We did get the children up and ready to get to the 11:00AM Service. We tried to be so cool and showed surprise when someone did 'ooh and awe' over our beautiful children.

On Monday, I told Marilyn that, "I would take over taking Jennifer and Matthew to school in order to give her time with the twins." Due to the many duties that I now had as President of the company, Marilyn would have to get the twins dressed and pick up the school kids when school lets out.

I was doing a lot of the shopping after I got off in the evening, so she was not overburdened and could spend more time with our precious children.

Things were going well in all of the states, where our Credit Union partners remained very pleased, with the business we were bringing to them, from the employees of businesses, we had contracted with.

The Sales Agent of the Month program was keeping our sales of insurance at a high level, agents morale was at an all time high, prompting me to congratulate Mr. Summers and Benjamin Avery, the new Marketing Manager for keeping things moving in the right direction. I told them that, "we would give them added support by adding on more training from the Main Office here at Maitland."

Mr. Summers, in his position of Director of the Division of Credit Union Activity was now ready to move into Louisiana and Texas and requested Legal to make approaches to the Insurance Commissioners in those states to approve our products and permission to operate in those states. I assured him that Legal would get on that right away, but to expect a two to four week delay in their confirmation.

As President, I was now deeply involved in every aspect of our business and realized that our Credit Union Division was generating

80% of our generated income. This information was brought to the attention of the Board Of Directors and they acknowledged that, "we should continue supporting every member of that division at every opportunity."

The members of the Board of Directors asked how far we expected to expand?

And, I advised them, "that after Louisiana and Texas, we should add on Tennessee and Kentucky, then wait a few years before taking on any other acquisitions." I told them that I thought it unwise to overextend our capacity to provide the good services and relationships that we were now enjoying. We were already an eight Billion Dollar company and continuing to rise."

It was now late December, 1961, and we celebrated our first Christmas in our new home. Marilyn had gone all out in decorating the home and it was so very beautiful. I had gotten all of the children gifts--Jennifer got a new large doll and a teddy bear, Matthew was now ready for a bigger bike, the twins received a lot of new toys and clothing and Marilyn has a new van to carry this big crowd around when she travels with the children. I got a new watch for Christmas.

To me, it seemed scarry that things with the company were going so well, at this time, but, I was enjoying every minute with the company and its progress.

I was enjoying being able to go home, on most nights, to be with my family and enjoy the tender moments that I could spend with the children and Marilyn.

The twins were now crawling around, not able to walk yet, but exploring every thing that they observed. Marilyn was talking to them and they seemed to respond by making utterances that were still questionable to comprehend. But, they were the happiest kids that I had seen and I enjoyed every opportunity to spend time with them. Yes, I had become very good at changing those diapers, in order to give Marilyn a little relief, for which she seemed very thankful.

We took every opportunity to keep our wonderful sex life as active as we wanted. Actually, our sex life had become more, more pleasurable than ever. We had such a beautiful relationship that we were quick to enjoy it at every opportunity.

Things were heating up as we received permission to enter Louisiana and Texas with our Credit Union Division and Mr. Summers and Mr. Avery were quite busy. I told them that, "I would be available in the event they sought my assistance."

They assured me, "that all of my departments were responding to their needs, and they were progressing rapidly in securing Credit Unions and businesses to offer their employees the new services."

"Sales agents had been hired and licensed for our products, District Offices had been secured and staffed, and soon, the agents would begin scheduling visits to the businesses' employees," Larry confirmed.

I flew out with Mr. Summers and Mr. Avery, in addition to Product Specialists, in order to have breakfasts, lunchtime and dinners, to create morale and training in all of the District Offices. Texas had four District Offices and Louisiana had two, at this time. And, so, we were growing again. Bonuses were flying and our managers were so thankful for the added support for their families.

Marilyn had taken on the chores that I had been performing at home, but she understood and new that the family income was being enhanced by all of my time spent away from home. She knew that I would make it up to her when I did return home, in caring for the children and chores for the household. I would especially, take care of all pent up needs in the bedroom, to both of our pure and wonderful delights. We never let sex, for us, become dull, we were very cleaver in fulfilling our needs and joys in many and exciting new ways, we never tired of trying new positions as a way to increasing the thrills that we always shared.

Before I left, "I told her of my plans to make an offer on the Tract One of the original property, next to our twenty one acres, that we now live on."

"What a splendid idea, she said. That way, we will have protection from someone putting up a new home that might distract from the quality of ours." "If I can recall, that tract had nine acres and included a lovely lake."

"I believe you are correct." "They were asking one hundred twenty five thousand for it. 'I will offer one hundred ten for a cash sale."

"Sounds good to me," she said.

When I arrived at the office, I called the reality company and asked to speak with the manager, who I had dealt with when I made our original purchase.

He took my call immediately and asked, "what can I do for you, Mr. Knight?"

"I told him that I understood that they still had the tract next to my property for sale and I would like to make a cash offer of one hundred ten thousand for that property immediately."

He told me that, "yes the property is still advertised for one hundred twenty five thousand, but I will call the owner and relay your cash offer and get back to you. He continued, "what is your current phone number?"

I responded by giving him my number and thanked him for his efforts.

Fifteen minutes later, my administrative assistant, "announced that I had an incoming call from my realestate company."

I picked up immediately and was told that "the owner had accepted my cash offer of one hundred ten thousand for Tract One."

"Thank you for your quick response," I told him. "I will have my bank process a cashier check for that amount and my wife and I, along with my attorney will be in your office at 4:00PM, to complete the purchase."

"Is this satisfactory with your client"? I asked.

He assured me that, "he would make those arrangements and was looking forward to having us at four."

With the call to my bank completed, as I requested, I called Marilyn to see if she could be at the realestate office at four?

She assured me that, "she could make arrangements to have her friend come to our house and care for the children while we completed our transaction."

I thanked her and reminded her of the location and time to be there.

With all of that taken care of, I told my administrative assistant to "clear my schedule as of 3:30PM, today."

A call to my attorney resulted in a response that he would be at the realestate office to approve of the transaction.

I requested him, "to file the transaction with the Register of Deeds as soon as he possibly could in the morning."

He assured me that he would take care of that.

The rest of the morning, and early afternoon was taken up with all of those important functions that a corporate president, routinely carries out.

After stopping by the bank to pick up the cashiers check, I met Marilyn and my attorney at the realestate office and we were quickly sent in to meet the owner, the realestate agent, and their attorney, to complete the deed of new ownership.

I presented the cashiers check for the agreed amount, Marilyn and I signed the necessary papers, with my attorney's approval, the deed was printed, and we were out of there.

The attorney assured me that he would file the deed early tomorrow morning.

And, we were proud owners of nine more acres of what we considered prime real-estate. **This would be proven to be a real steal for Marilyn and me within two years in the future!**

Since I had cleared my schedule at the office, I was free to join Marilyn at home.

The children were glad to see me and we told them the good news, "that we had purchased another nine acres next to our property." Of course the twins were not old enough to understand any of this, but Jennifer and Matthew had seen the property, when we had first toured it, almost a year before. "I reminded them that it had another beautiful lake, that had lots of interesting wild life, as does our two lakes here, near our home.

Jennifer and Matthew asked "if they could see it now?"

I gave a quick glance at Marilyn, and she nodded her approval.

The twins were dressed appropriately and we took the carriage, which they could be pushed around with, as we toured the property. I drove the car to a good location that we could use as a starting point, we followed them, slowly, and closely on their bikes.

I knew that this would be a fun outing for all of the family, even the twins as I pushed them around in the twin carriage.

We had entered at the center of the acreage and there was very little vegetation making the stroller very easy to push. The sun was filtered by the clouds and was not too hot for the twins. They seemed to be very comfortable. It was very easy to locate the lake since it had a lot of vegetation with very little vegetation blocking our view.

Jennifer and Matthew were just flying around on their bikes and raced ahead to the lake, to scout it out before we arrived there.

They came back to tell us that, "there was no danger there, but it was loaded with white swans, blue herons and quite a lot of ducks, that we were going to enjoy seeing on our new property."

I wondered about whether the bald eagle couple were still nesting on the big lake, back behind the house. Surely their eaglets from last year had flown from the nest, but it was about time for the eagle couple to be looking over a new group of eggs. I certainly hope so, I thought.

Marilyn and I were thrilled at the beauty of it all, when we arrived there. There obviously had not been much traffic of humans there. The wildlife seemed to not be alarmed and take flight. We certainly had no objection to there being there and hoped that they would continue to make it their home, and give us the pleasure of visiting, on occasions, and enjoy watching them in this natural habitat.

I told the children that this lake, like the other two on our property, was off limits unless Marilyn or myself were along to watch out for their safety. I told them that it was always possible that an alligator might find it's way to the lakes. This is why we had to be present, when they visited the lakes. We had previously taken Jennifer and Matthew to an alligator farm, to point out how dangerous they can possibly be.

Later, Jennifer asked," if we were going to build a home on our new property?"

I answered, "no, darling, we are just protecting our interests in this area."

She questioned, "what does that mean?"

My answer was, "I suspect that in years to come, that property, and possibly, our property, where our home is located, may be of significantly more valuable, and could be sold for a lot more money than we have invested in it." "Of course we will always have a home for the family. If not here, it will be somewhere else that you would like."

This had been such a nice visit and we hated for the day to end, but it was getting late and we were looking forward to stopping by a Mac Donalds and getting a carry out dinner for us, the twins were still on baby food, which we had at home.

After the children were in bed and the twins properly diapered, Marilyn and I sat on the couch and toasted our successful day with a glass of wine and realized how wonderful our lives had been enriched. As we sat, a touch and a long kiss was all we needed as I carried her to bed.

As we lay there in anticipation of more to come, our breathing became more heightened and we both reached for the other, simultaneously and soon became one.

The magic, as usual, was there as we violently consumed each other with passion that was well spent until we slept, peacefully in each others' arms.

Fast forward to March 1962.

The building of the Louisiana and Texas operations had been completed and were going just as well as we had suspected. Dallas was the largest city selected, as well as three other cities throughout Texas for the District Offices.

New Orleans was the main location in Louisiana with several smaller locations, farther upstate.

The process of bringing in Credit Unions had been a success and businesses of all types had brought their employees into our visitation program.

A note about home--the eagles were back on the nest overlooking the big lake. The twins were growing rapidly and soon would be walking and talking, with their first birthday soon to approach.

Larry Summers has announced that "we will be moving into Tennessee by August. He has chosen Nashville and Memphis for District Offices and the new Commissioner of Insurance has approved our entry, there."

Mr. Summers expects to be in Kentucky by October and has selected Louisville and Lexington for District offices there. "The Kentucky Commissioner is debating some factors, prior to giving his permission in that state. But he thinks things will be resolved by the first of November."

Larry says that he is already making contacts with some potential businesses and Credit Unions in those areas in anticipation that the Commissioner comes through with a positive decision on our entry in that state.

He told me that "if he received a go ahead from the Kentucky Commissioner, we would definitely have Kentucky completed and in full operation prior to May, 1962."

Larry has speculated that by mid year, "we will descend on the state of Virginia and have that completed by late 1962."
I told him that "by that time, we would be content to solidify all states that we were operating in the South East." "Then we will have expanded all that we could expect to provide quality service, that we were expected to deliver to our clients."

The next meeting of the Board of Directors, held in June, 1962, gave me the opportunity to give a full recap of our progress, at that time. "I reported that we were now a fifteen billion dollar corporation, having installed our operations during 1962 in the states of Tennessee, Kentucky and, most recently, Virginia." I continued, "it is my opinion that we now solidify our position in the current states, that we now operate, and continue to provide quality service, that is expected from our company."
The Board Of Directors acknowledged by giving me a standing ovation and all agreed that we would follow this course at this time. They all knew that we had already expanded in just four short years from a company worth around two billion dollars to our present fifteen billion dollars. After all, we agreed to reexamine our decision at the beginning of 1963. All were content, at the present time, to cease expansion, at least for the present time.
One other item was settled during the meeting, My annual income was placed at three million dollars per year.

CHAPTER 35

TIME WAS PASSING very fast and very successfully for me and my wonderful family. I had been truly blessed by God in my work and the family that he had given to me to love and be loved in return.

Life with Marilyn was heaven on earth. Jennifer and Matthew, my adopted children, were so special and I loved them just as I loved the beautiful twins that had been born to Marilyn and me in May of 1961. It was hard to believe that they would soon be four year olds and be in preschool this year.

Jennifer is thirteen and a teenager, who thinks and looks as if she were sixteen.

William is now ten, and will be in the fourth grade this school year.

Marilyn has been a wonderful wife and helpmate to me. She is heavily involved with the Parent Teachers Association for all of the children and even finds time to volunteer at our church.

We all love our home and the beautiful thirty acres of Florida paradise that surround it.

My position as President Of Southern Medical and Life Services is unbelievable, and the benefits provided to me and my family are too good to be true.

I am surrounded by highly qualified and supportive associates, who always get the job right, the first time, and are well paid for their professionalism, and attention to detail.

I make sure that they are highly paid and able to support their families, well.

How could life possibly get any better?

You recall the thirty acres of property that I acquired and built a beautiful home there for my family, well, I have recently been approached by an entertainment organization, who is interested in acquiring my property and many other acres, from the family, who had sold Marilyn and me these thirty acres, that we love.

They have hinted at starting an entertainment resort that would be developed to entertain children and their families as well as individuals of all ages. It would have delightful animals that entertain, shows for all, rides that thrill riders of all ages, foods and exhibits of countries from all over the world.

My thoughts, which I shared with Marilyn, were that we were quite happy with our home and the life we shared here on our property, at least until they gave me an offer that they knew I could not refuse.

I was assured that the people of Florida and all over the world would greatly benefit from the establishment of this resort. They even mentioned Mickey would be a tremendous draw to people of all ages, and particularly children.

I told them, "to make an offer and I would have to consult with my wife and take it into consideration."

They smiled and said that, "they were prepared to offer me fifteen million dollars for my entire thirty acres, and this would include my home." "They continued that the entire resort would be completed by 1968, having required three years to complete. I and my family would have one complete year to relocate to a new property of our choice to acquire. I would be expected to have vacated the property by late, 1964."

I maintained my business face and took their information of contact, and would be in touch with them in several days. Thanked them for their offer and left to give Marilyn the news of the offer, that we had been given for our property.

She said, "Alvin Knight, you are gifted. We have had a wonderful life here on this thirty acres, but how could we possibly turn down an offer of fifteen million?"

I took her into my arms and kissed her so softly, and said, "Marilyn, you sure do have a good business sense, and I think you are right!" "I will call them tomorrow to tell them that we have enjoyed this property so very much for a few short years, but we understand that they will give the world an opportunity to enjoy it!"

"Very well, they replied. We have set up a temporary office in Orlando, in order to finalize purchase of all of the property, that we will require for this project at this time." "Can you and Mrs. Knight meet with us on Wednesday of this week to sign and finalize the contract of purchase as we described during our discussion, yesterday?"

We agreed upon 4;00PM and they gave me the address of their office. They accepted my request, to bring my attorney to go over the contract prior to our signing.

"By all means," they had said.

I immediately called Marilyn to ask "if she could be available for us to sign at 4:00PM tomorrow?"

"No problem, I will have my friend, who has been available many times, when I needed her to come and be with the children," she said.

I quickly called my attorney to make sure that he could attend and approve the contract prior to our signing it on Wednesday, and he readily agreed.

Wednesday came and Marilyn and me, along with my attorney, met with the buyer at their office.

They already had the contract prepared as to the agreement that I had accepted.

My attorney sat down and went over each detail and offered it to Marilyn and me to check the details. Marilyn whispered that, "they had been very fair to give us a whole year to vacate the property," and I nodded, and said that "this had been an item that I would have insisted upon."

My attorney quickly reviewed all of the documents and agreed that we were protected in every way and should sign to finalize the sale. A check for 15,000,000 dollars was presented to us and we proudly left, but a little sad that within one year we would have to vacate our beautiful home and have a new one built, which would fit our growing family needs.

On the way home, we picked up a bottle of our favorite red wine. You know what that can lead to, latter in the evening, after the children are in bed and asleep.

The days that followed led to a lot of decisions that we needed to make. The main one was what to do with our new found wealth of '15 Million.'

This was no problem, since we met with a noted Financial Planner. His name was Mr. C. Summers, no relation to my associate at Southern, Larry Summers. Mr. C. Summers reviewed our present financial program, including the 15 Million, that we had just received, and asked about our educational needs for the children.

We had not gone that far and told him so.

He asked for the ages of each child, which we readily gave him. Then he asked about current needs for our housing.

We told him that, "we would have to relocate, here in the Orlando area, and be in a new home of four thousand to five thousand square feet, completed and ready to move in, prior to one years time." And we continued that, "this may, possibly require a half million dollar investment."

Mr. Summers agreed with that estimate of cost, and said that, "he would call us for another meeting in a few days and present us with a plan, that we could accept or change, at that time." He continued that, "taxes would have to be taken into account for any program that he might recommend, for our final approval."

Marilyn and I thanked him for his time and would await his call for another meeting, at his convenience.

On the way home, we agreed that he seemed truly professional. If he would have come up with a quick plan, without taking time to consider all of the factors he had in the first meeting, we would have quickly questioned his real interest in our true financial situation, and left for another Financial Planner.

We spent quite a bit of time, over the next couple of weeks, looking at areas where we might consider buying property, to begin building a new home for our family. Of course, we had been spoiled by our present home on these fabulous thirty acres. Marilyn and I both agreed that the children loved the openness that they enjoyed, so we would have to take that into considerations.

We could not help, but wonder if there might be other locations that might be similar to what we had just given up. With that thought in mind, we started looking at advertisements for realestate within a ten mile area of where we now lived. We knew that Jennifer and Matthew were very happy with their present school, and it would be nice if we could find something in this school district.

In addition to advertisements, we spent a lot of time driving through and around this area. Since we had been assured that we had nearly a year to relocate, we had some time to spend on our search. Of course, when we were out driving on the weekends, we carried the children with us. They had been told about our need to find new quarters, to move to within a year. And we were including them in our search. Just a lot in a development was out of the question, we had to have space for them to ride and enjoy some openness, and possibly, another lake that they could enjoy, as they had enjoyed the lakes on our present property.

I was surprised when I received a call from Mr. Wesley; you will recall that he was the contractor of our present home. I told him that, "I was delighted to hear from him, and asked how things were going with his construction company?"

He said that, "they had really enjoyed building my present home, and had heard that we would have to move within the next year and may be looking for a similar home on some acreage."

I told him that, "yes, he was right on, that was just what we were looking for."

He asked, "if I could meet with him after work today?" "He had something to show me, that I might be interested in seeing."

"I can be in your office by 5:30PM," I told him.

I called Marilyn and told her that, "I was going to meet Mr. Wesley, our good contractor, and would be home in an hour or so."

"That sounds interesting," she said. "I hope you are on to something, that might be interesting, my love."

"We will see, Mr. Wesley sounded very encouraging."

At 5:20, I was in Mr. Wesley's office. And he showed me an outline of a new development within a mile of my present home. "The development, he explained, had plans for a total of about 92 acres and was presently designed into six plots of ten to twenty acres each." "The developer, he explained, was looking for six clients of quality, to build on each tract. There would be restrictions placed to require the buyer to build a quality home of a minimum of near forty hundred square feet."

"The owner really wanted to make the development a showcase and had specified that my company be the designated contractor for these six home sights."

"The minimum price, that he has made a restriction for, is for four hundred thousand dollars."

"You are the first one that I have approached about this development."
"Would you like to drive out, view, and have first choice of the available plots?"
"Yes," Mr. Wesley, "This may be just what I have been looking for, these last few weeks."
"Well, let's go have a look. My truck is the best method to tour the plots."
"Shall we go?"

We got into Mr. Wesley's truck and went south toward Kissimmee and turned on the road that leads to my home. As he reached the road where I turn left to my home, he turned right and went about a mile and a half and exited the road left. "This is plot one, he said, it is fifteen acres and has a one and one half acre lake in the back of the plot." "Would you like to drive back there, it is a little rough, but this truck can take it with ease."

We drove through the plot and back to the lake. It was just as beautiful as the lakes on my present homesite.

Mr. Wesley returned to the road and entered plot two. He remarked that "this plot included fifteen acres, without a lake," as he drove through it. Then, drove back to the road and entered plot three. "This tract is sixteen acres and has a lake toward the back of the tract" he said, as we drove back to and around the lake.

"I remarked to him that this was the most attractive plot that I had seen, so far."

Mr. Wesley did not comment and drove back to the road and entered plot four.

"This tract is thirteen acres and does not have a lake," he said.

Personally, I thought that it was a little blah, compared to the others I had seen.

He drove back to the road and entered plot five. "This plot has eighteen acres and two lakes in the back, they are a little difficult to get to, but wildlife is very abundant."

As for me, I was very impressed, but did not comment.

He drove through the last plot, six and said, "it contained fifteen acres and and no lakes It was wider, as far as frontage, but less depth," he said.

On the way back to his office, he asked, "if I was at all interested, and if so, which plot had interested me most"?

"I told him that if I had to make a decision today, I would be hard pressed to chose between plots one, three and five." "I liked them all equally, as well."

"And, asked, if I could bring Marilyn out this evening to make a decision?"

"Certainly," he said, "I will give you a few days to decide, prior to showing them to other prospects."

Before, I left Mr. Wesley's office, I called Marilyn and asked her, "to get the children together and we would drive through an area that I thought was a good prospect for building our new home."

Arriving home, we still had a couple of hours to tour the plots that I had just toured. It was cooler now and I felt the children would be reasonably comfortable.

We loaded up, and Marilyn had already told the children, Jennifer and Matthew, who were very excited and looking forward to seeing where we may live after this year.

Marilyn was quite pleased to find that the area was only about one and a half miles from where we now lived. She told the children that, "they would not have to change schools."

Jennifer and Matthew were glad to hear that..

To make the trip a little easier for all, I had already ruled out plots two, four, and six. I told them that, "there were six plots, but only three had lakes." I told them that, "I thought they could chose from those three."

I stopped at plot one and drove them close to the lake.

They all liked it, immediately.

Next came plot three and I drove back to the lake. Again they all liked it.

I drove back to the two lakes on plot five and they saw all of the wild life and fell in love with it immediately.

In unison, Marilyn, Jennifer and Matthew said, "we like this one," "can we have this one"?

"Of course you can have this one, it is the one that I had picked out to be the best," I told them.

We went back home after staying as long as Marilyn and the children wanted to stay.

At home, I called Mr. Wesley, and "told him to take plot five off of the market. At his request, Marilyn and I would come to his office and sign the contract to plot five and pay cash for the deed." I continued, that, "we would look forward to working with him to design our new home in the range of 500 thousand to 1,000,000 dollars. Thank you for presenting this opportunity to my family," I said.

Marilyn and I immediately began designing the home that we would build on plot 5. It would have most of the characteristics of our present home, except that it would now include around six thousand square foot. An extra bedroom was being added.

The additional bedroom was in anticipation that the twins would soon need the extra bedroom.

When we met Mr. Wesley, we presented our new plans for the new home to him and he agreed to a contract for 800 thousand, cash, to be delivered at the completion of our new home.

He said that, "a second floor may have to be designed into the home, and if so, sight appearance would be taken into consideration. He said that the master bed room may have to be moved upstairs."

We said, "that would not be a problem, and asked for an estimate of the date of completion."

"Six months is a realistic estimate," he assured us. And said that, "clearing would be started immediately in preparation for the new construction."

We received the deed to plot 5, after presenting him a check for three hundred fifty thousand dollars and we left happily that things were working out so well.

My attorney delivered the deed to the county Register of Deeds and our adventure continues.

It is now mid 1964, we are now in our new home and well pleased with the finished product. Daily we had visited the construction site and photoed the construction as it was progressing.

The children were always along and helping supervise the construction, as it progressed. Of course, this is the way they described it to their friends at school.

They said that, "when we moved into the new home, they wanted to throw a big party for their friends, down at the two lakes, which continued to attract such interesting wildlife." Thankfully, no alligators had ever found their way to the lakes. We did have all types of local birds, ducks, and heron. Yes, we did have bald eagles nesting.

The twins are now four and will be in preschool this year. Jennifer is fourteen and will enter high school this year and Matthew is eleven and in the fifth grade. Me, the President, is happy as I serve my company and all of our associated clients. Beautiful Marilyn, grows more beautiful and desirable, to me, as we age together as mates and exciting lovers, especially in our very large, upstairs master bedroom. We have had many visitors, who after touring our home, and when in our master bedroom, have raised an eyebrow and said, "I'll bet that there has been a lot of exciting things going on in this fabulous place."

Jennifer has enjoyed having some parties here with her age-group friends, and a few slumber parties with girl friends from school and church.

Matthew has been permitted to have his friends party, and take in the lakes out back. Of course Marilyn or myself always supervise any group trip to the lakes for safety sake.

The twins, Alvin, Jr., and Susan were honored on their fourth birthday, by friends, they have formed from the church and a group of Marilyn's many friends.

I even hung around, showing great, fatherly pride We have had several open house visits in honor of my associates from Southern. These were held to honor special achievements that had taken place in our company.

Marilyn and I were pleased that progress was being made in the development of the entertainment resort, which had purchased the thirty acres, just up the road.

It is said that the resort will eventually consist of hundreds of acres more by the time it opens in 1968. We have been following the progress of the development from the road that passed our former home. We are very pleased that they have retained our old house and altered it to include a visitor center for the purpose of promoting the resort, once it is finished. We were especially pleased that the three lakes that our property had held was being kept in it's natural setting to allow wild life to be a part of the resort.

We can visualize that the resort will be a tremendous drawing card and entertainment center for many millions of families, and especially children, with the attractions that are a part of the planning of this world wide attraction center.

CHAPTER 36

TIME MOVES ON and our wonderful and happy family has continued to be blessed in so many ways. The time is now April 1968.

The resort is now open and Marilyn applied for a position at the entertainment resort at the Visitor Center. The position is part-time and her position is to conduct tours of the visitor center and point out all of the highlights of benefits and services provided, here at the resort. Audio and visual presentations are made to allow for short tours, or any length of time the visitors plan to stay and enjoy the resort. The presentations are designed to show all of the wonderful assets of the resort from a view of the world cultures and artifacts, exotic animals (including the lakes and their wild life). Exotic rides (including auto racing simulation) and on and on, with seemingly no end to the world of entertainment.

With our financial status, Marilyn is not concerned with income from her job.

She simply does it for the joy of serving people and watching their thrill of the resort.

Jennifer has graduating from high school this year, with honors, and has been accepted at Stanford with a partial scholarship. She plans to major in design and is already planning to live in Paris, after graduation.

Matthew is fourteen and will enter high school this year. He has already set a goal of attending The University Of North Carolina at Chapel Hill, after completing high school. He has ambitions of being a journalist.

Alvin Jr., and Susan are now eight and will enter third grade in the fall.

As for me, I have continued to find ways as President of Southern Medical and Life Solutions to bring success and value to clients, associates, who we promote, and our most valuable employees of our company. Southern is now installed and serving clients in eleven states in the Southeastern, USA.

Southern is now a twenty billion dollar company and is traded on the stock exchange. The Board of Directors met this year and increased my annual salary to eight million dollars, which is quite an achievement for a farm boy from North Carolina, I believe!

Our family has remained a loving one with respect for each other's goals.

We have been a fun loving and closely knit family, having been able to receive great success and has remained very active in our spiritual life, with the church.

It has been said that if the church doors are open, there is at least one or two of the Knight family in attendance at some function of the church.

If you began reading this book from the beginning, you will remember the young sailer, who was continuous trying to find his place in life. You probable saw him as a womanizer, who really had no real direction in his life. He was really a nice young man, who fell in love with the wife of a Commander, serving in the far east on a Naval Destroyer. Alvin knew right from wrong and realized that his future was headed in the wrong direction, possibly Leavenworth, a destination for service men of lower rank, who were found guilty of defiling an officer's wife.

Loraine was the beautiful red-headed wife and mother, who was much older than Alvin and charmed him by giving him what she knew would make him incapable of turning down, her beautiful-seductive body, on many occasions.

You will recall that Alvin finally realized that his life was going nowhere if this affair was discovered by her husband. He would be headed to Leavenworth with little chance of getting out, anytime soon.

Alvin finally called the affair off, and began dating girls of his own age. But, was never satisfied with the womanizing life. There were a number of light affairs which really brought no satisfaction. Alvin continued to think of the beautiful Loraine, who he knew in his heart was obviously not right for him.

He had been in Hawaii for most of his tour in the US Navy and was due to be sent back to the states and Honorably Discharged.

On a trip to Wakiki Beach, north of Honolulu, while on shore leave, Alvin had met a beautiful blond-headed woman that he thought looked just like Marilyn Monroe. They talked and she asked if he would like some dinner and Alvin accepted. Marilyn admitted that, "she does get lonely with her husband, David, serving as a naval pilot off of Asia, and was not interested in cheap sex with me or any other man." She told Alvin "she loved David and respected him too much for that to happen."

He went to dinner and had such a wonderful time in the visit. She introduced him to her two delightful children, a girl and a boy. After dinner, they talked and he told her that she had made a very special impression on him. He confided in her that he admired her love and respect for her husband, which he was not accustomed to seeing with some of the wives that he had met.

She reminded him that, "this was just for laughs and may see him again on that basis."

He agreed, but had to tell her that "he was awaiting orders to be shipped back to the states for discharge, very soon"

He was surprised when she asked him, "what he was going to do with his life after discharge?"

He reminded her that, "he had been a star baseball pitcher and would probably go to college and hope for a scholarship by pitching, while he prepared for his future in the business world."

Marilyn said, "why don't you go to acting school in Hollywood? You do have the good looks for that."

He told her that, "she was being too complimentary." And was surprised when "she asked for his address, back in North Carolina."

He did give her his address, and "told her that she had made a very pleasant impression on him." "He felt that he had finally met a very nice woman, he respected very highly and would now set his goals for someone just like her in his future."

She laughed, and "wished him a very happy and successful life in his future."

As he was leaving, she stuck out her hand as if to shake good by, but changed her mind and gave him a light hug and quickly stepped back, shocked with what she had done, and then wished him a good night.

Later, as he thought about their parting, he felt, "now that was a real woman, if only she was not already married." David was one lucky guy, to have Marilyn waiting for him, when he arrived home from the war, off Asia."

His orders came the next day and Alvin was able to call Marilyn and gave his sorrow that he would not be able to see her before sailing back to San Diego.

He had boarded the aircraft carrier and sailed back to San Diego, California, and received his discharge in a few days. Remembering what Marilyn had said about going to Hollywood, but he headed for home instead.

After four days on a Greyhound Bus, he arrived home with his parents and began looking for work. Finally he became very successful in the medical insurance field and met a very nice girl, Michel. They had quite a few dates and liked each other a lot. She and her friends were even talking marriage.

He was not too sure if that would be the right thing for them to do. He still remembered Loraine, and thought often of Marilyn.

His life changed immediately when he received the letter from Marilyn. He had been home over a year

"David had been transferred to Pensacola, Florida and was flying off of the Florida Keys. He crashed at sea and did not survive."

Marilyn said that, "she was so lost and did not know what to do." She continued, that, "she was being quite presumptive, but would he like to see her?"

You know the rest! He quite the job that had trained him well, and gave them a notice and received a very good recommendation, that he took to the Orlando, Florida area, and began the fantastic future that he had with a leading firm in medical and life insurance. Bringing the author up to date, his word follows:

When Alvin became successful there, he married the beautiful and loving Marilyn, within a one years' time. Marilyn and Alvin were living in Pensacola at her home, both craving each other sexually, before we were married, but he "told her that he now respected her too much for that to happen prior to marriage."

Her goodness and faithfulness to David had made a transformation in him that he now wanted to make it right--'No sex for us until marriage.' He quickly admitted, "since our marriage we both have had heaven on earth, we are perfect for one another, both lovingly and sexually." We made a pact to "never say no to one another in our lovemaking," "no headaches or, I am tired."

That pact has been kept to this day and has made our love for each other so strong that we both feel that we are living heaven on earth and is forever binding.

I quickly adopted Marilyn's children, Jennifer and Matthew within a year and a half after we were married. Within a year of perfect married bliss, we gave each other wonderful, perfect and loving twins, Alvin, Jr. and Susan, who are now ten years of age. Matthew is fifteen and Jennifer is now at Stanford University and will be going to Paris, France after graduation. She plans to have a degree in fashion design.

As President of one of the largest insurance companies in the South Eastern United States, my Board Of Directors gave me a pay raise to ten million dollars this year. Marilyn is working part time in a large entertainment resort, just west of Kissimmee, Florida. She works because she enjoys it, we really do not need the money, since we are well off after we sold our first home on thirty acres, to the resort, that now is a destination of families from all over the world. We now live in our new, larger home that we built after selling our other dream home and property, to the entertainment resort for that 15 million dollars.

"I now attribute my success and happiness in life to the wonderful Marilyn Monroe look alike, my beloved Marilyn Knight."

Yes! I married well!!

THE END

Loyd E. Hill

CPSIA information can be obtained
at www.ICGtesting.com
Printed in the USA
LVOW07s0426281016
510599LV00001B/21/P